GARDEN OF THE GODS

by

Nancy Arant Williams

ISBN: 1-933582-06-5

Credits
Cover Artist: Carolyn and Edward Aish
The cover photo is used with permission of the photographer

POR: PawPrintsPOD

Printed in the United States of America

Dedication

This book is dedicated to the memory of my dear
friend and sister in the Lord, Susan Bradley, who let the
Lord shine through her even in her darkest night.
Nancy Arant Williams

Chapter One

I had no idea when I shoved the last box of cereal into the cupboard, that in only moments, my life would change forever.

As I folded the last grocery sack, the phone rang, and I picked up to hear an unfamiliar female voice.

"Is this Jolie Stevenson?"

"Yes…"

"You don't know me, but I am the woman who gave you up for adoption when you were born fifty years ago. My name is Jeanette Kelly." She didn't give me a chance to respond before she said without warmth, "I need to see you as soon as possible."

"Okay," I stammered, unable to think straight.

After giving me her address, she said she would expect to see me on Saturday, three days hence, at her home, at two p.m.

I didn't know what to think, as I stood staring at the phone, without realizing it, until it finally set up a wail that slammed me back into the moment.

Why would my mother be calling after fifty years of silence?

My hand shook as I unplugged the curling iron and stuffed the snaking cord into the crock on the bathroom counter. I frowned at my reflection, wishing I had made time to get my hair trimmed and colored. At this age, it takes real effort to look good.

I stuck my toothbrush in my mouth and brushed with one hand, buttoning my shirt with the other. Hurriedly, I slid into low-heeled black pumps and ran down the stairs. I couldn't afford to be late.

Brian stood, smiling in amusement, at the bottom of the stairs, and before I could ask, he said, "Nervous?"

"I am. Terrified. What if she's disappointed in me? What if we're nothing alike? What if she isn't interested in having a relationship?"

He gently rubbed my tense shoulders and then wrapped his arms around me, holding me close.

"Listen. One thing at a time. You just need to go easy here. Just remember, she's been looking for you, not the other way around. And if that's the case, she has to be at least a *little* interested in getting to know you. Right?"

I turned, pulled on his collar, bringing his face down to mine, where I planted a kiss on his lips. "Thanks, honey, for the pep talk. I feel pretty shaky right now."

"You know, I'm hoping this will change the way you see yourself."

"What do you mean?"

"That you'll see you weren't given away as a baby because you were unwanted, unloved."

"Oh, well, I'm not getting my hopes up." But how could I not?

He held the car door for me and I slipped in, unable to recall ever feeling so frightened.

This little journey would change my life, for better or worse, for all time. After wondering about my birthmother my whole life, I had only recently begun to entertain the idea of searching for her, but had decided the risk was just too great. How did anyone ever cope with the rejection if a reunion went bad?

The sun was making a meager attempt to warm the earth as we drove through our small city of Dunlap, situated not quite an hour and a half south of Kansas City. For some reason, spring seemed to be taking its sweet time getting here this year, and a damp chill I despised permeated everything, including me. *Come on, sun, get busy and shine.*

Once we were on the road, Brian reached over, took my hand and squeezed it. "You doin' okay, babe?" After a glance at me, he said, "Relax, honey. You're stressing out over nothing. You know that, right?"

"That's the thing. I have no idea what to expect."

"I thought you said she sounded anxious to meet you."

"She did, but not in the way you'd expect. And I can't help but wonder why—if I was so unimportant that she gave me up. And why wait until now to get in touch?"

With a wry smile, Brian said, "Jolie, there are all sorts of reasons why mothers give up their babies. And many have nothing to do with rejection. I just wish you could understand that."

I shook my head and uttered an audible sigh. "I know. You've said it in a thousand different ways, but somehow, the fact that she gave me up at all speaks louder than a million words to the contrary."

He tilted his head. "You mean you won't be able to entertain a single positive word from anyone else until you know she didn't reject you?"

After a pause while I realized how stupid it sounded, I frowned. "I hate to admit that I've given anyone so much power, but that's how it feels to me."

I felt ambivalent about the seemingly endless trip. On one hand, I wanted it to hurry up and be over, yet wished at the same time that it would never happen at all. I couldn't have felt worse had I stepped off a cliff; I could practically see myself crashing to the earth.

Lost in my own thoughts, I was surprised when Brian finally stopped the car and said, "Honey, we're here. Are you ready?"

With a shake of my head, I sighed. "I don't think I'll ever be ready for this. Honestly, I'm a wreck."

He gave me an enigmatic smile. "Well, my lovely wreck, let's get it over with, shall we?"

Holding the door for me, he took my hand, searching my face for a smile at his witticism. But I could barely breathe, let alone smile.

I glanced at the house and took in the surrounding neighborhood. Tidy forty-year old brick ranches, hovered over by mammoth shady oaks and ashes, lined the street. Most boasted window boxes with soon to bloom, tulips, crocuses and what would later be petunia patches, cheerfully meandering the length of curving cement sidewalks.

My mother's house—the words seemed strange to my own mind—was beautifully landscaped, displaying a colorful array of plantings and bushes, with white-painted wrought iron benches encircling the trunks of two huge red maples on either side of the walk. Her expansive blonde brick home, topped by a white roof, sported cheerful colonial green shutters and a matching front door, on which she'd displayed the most beautiful silk floral wreath I had ever seen.

The door opened suddenly, and I stopped in my tracks, nervously pulling against Brian's arm. I shuddered in anxiety and let him pull me close as he whispered, "It's going to be all right."

I've always thought of myself as a 'together' woman, at least until now. I've known since I was four, that I was adopted by the people I called Mom and Dad. The fact that my parents hadn't given birth to me had never really bothered me that much. Or if it had, I'd ignored the feelings. But their deaths within three months of each other, ten years earlier, had left me feeling orphaned and surprisingly insecure, at age forty.

I have one sister, Elly, three years older than I, who is also adopted. Somehow, though, unlike me, she always seems sure of everything. Annoyingly sure.

The woman standing in the doorway looked exactly the way I had pictured myself at seventy years of age. She had the same big hazel eyes, fair complexion and smile, but that was where the resemblance ended. Her eyes, unlike mine, held little warmth. *Oh, God—why did I come?*

The woman was more slender than I, and wore a shimmering white silk blouse over perfectly creased gray flannel trousers. Her gray low-heeled sandals displayed toenails painted to match glossy red, manicured fingernails.

She held out her hand as I walked through the door. I shook hers, wishing she had reached out to hug the stuffing out of me. But how could she know that? Her hand felt cold in mine before she finally pulled away.

"You must be Jolie. You're exactly as I always pictured you."

"Oh, well, thank you," I stammered uncertainly, unsure whether it was a compliment or not.

She gestured toward a tastefully decorated living room, done in muted shades of teal, gray and mauve. The semiformal room looked like no one ever sat in it. The gray carpet still bore the tracks of a vacuum cleaner and the scent of lavender potpourri filled the air, making me want to sneeze. I'm allergic to lavender.

The sofa and loveseat were covered with stunning cream, burgundy and teal flame stitch upholstery in a pattern I had never seen.

My mother stood before us and said, "You must introduce me to your husband."

"Oh—of course. This is my husband, Brian."

"I thought so. Hello, Brian. May I offer the two of you something to drink?"

"Oh, I'm fine," I said, brushing her off, feeling awkward.

To Brian, she said, "Coffee, iced tea or perhaps apple juice?"

"Apple juice sounds good," he agreed.

"Please, have a seat," she said before disappearing out the door.

When we were alone, Brian reached for my hand as we settled on the sofa. "You okay?" he asked softly.

"I don't think she likes me," I whispered, feeling shaky and uncertain.

He shook his head, a sad frown in his eyes. "Now, you haven't spoken ten words to her. Try not to jump to conclusions yet. All right?"

"I'll try."

Glancing around the room, I took in a framed print of a calla lily that looked so real, I wanted to get up and touch it, but I sat utterly still, barely able to breathe in my anxiety.

My mother returned, a moment later, with a fancy white wicker tray. It looked as if everything in her life was chosen with great deliberation. Why hadn't she chosen me the same way?

She set down the tray and handed a glass to me. "I brought you apple juice, too. Hope that's all right."

"Oh, yes, thank you," I said as I felt my mouth go dry. I sipped my drink, nervously waiting for her to speak.

She sank into a teal, flame-stitched, overstuffed chair and sat back, crossed one leg over the other and carefully smoothed her slacks. I observed her features. She had the same slightly rounded face as mine, but hers was more chiseled. And she was quite pale; only her cheeks were rosy with blush. Her graying ash blonde hair was done in the current slightly messy style that barely brushed her shoulders, and I thought it suited her.

Her eyes were alert and savvy, but not warm. I wondered what was going through her mind. If she felt no warmth toward me, why had she called?

After sipping her iced tea, she set it on a coaster beside her and folded her hands in her lap, as if trying to still nervous movement. Perhaps she was as uncomfortable as I.

Trying to overcome my anxiety, I said, "I really love your home."

"Oh," she said, glancing around. "Thank you."

She turned again to face me. "You're probably wondering why I have suddenly shown up in your life after all these years. Isn't that right?"

Chapter Two

"Well, I…"

"Listen, I'm going to make this easy. I'm sixty-seven years old, which is neither young nor old, but I have a problem. Now, I don't expect you to suddenly become all emotional over me at this late date, but let me say now that I simply had no other choice but to contact you."

I didn't know what to say.

She continued, "I've recently been diagnosed with leukemia, for which there is no cure. The doctors tell me I have only a couple of months to live without treatment. Maybe less." She took a deep breath, closely examining her cuticles before she looked up and added, "They say I have a nearly 100% chance of recovery with a bone marrow transplant, which is where you come in—if you choose to."

Her head tilted slightly as she studied my face. "Listen, maybe this wasn't such a good idea after all."

"Oh, dear. Please don't say that," I said, feeling shaken. I hadn't even gotten to know her and she was dying. Compassion filled my heart as I stood and walked toward her. I knelt in front of her and pulled her gently into my arms. "Bless your heart. Of course I'll give you my bone marrow. How could I say no to my own mother?"

I could feel her shuddering as she tried to stifle sobs. I held her, but her hold on me was tentative, uncertain. When she pulled away a second later, she had apparently swallowed her tears, carefully composing herself. Oddly, I noticed that even her eyes were dry.

I blinked, unable to understand what was happening as I returned to my seat.

She said, "I don't want you to donate under any false assumptions. I have no wish to have you in my life, but I do need your bone marrow. So if you can donate to me with that understood, we can go from there."

I had to swallow to keep from choking on my own saliva. What had she just said?

A glance at Brian told me he was as confused about the situation as I.

She said, "Let me give you my number. You can think about it and get back to me. I'm sure this is all very awkward for you, and I can't say I blame you."

When I finally found my voice, I said, "Jeanette, maybe you could just tell me why you feel the way you do."

Tersely she answered, "I'd rather not go into it, but if I must, to get your cooperation, I suppose I have no other choice."

I bit my lip, waiting for her to continue and yet not sure I wanted to know.

She moved restlessly in her chair before she finally began. "I was sixteen when I met your father. He was from a wealthy family, and I was quite taken with him. He led me to believe we had something very special, but I would never give into pressure to—well..."

She took a deep breath and added, "Finally after we had been dating for about eight months, he decided he could simply take what he wanted, and he raped me. At that point, I knew that we had could never have any kind of relationship. Unfortunately, I ended up pregnant.

"I didn't care for the idea of abortion, even though I could have afforded it. So I was sent to St. Louis to stay with my aunt, where I gave birth to you. I still feel nothing but regret as I recall the horror of it all."

An audible sigh escaped her lips as she gave an involuntary shrug. "You probably think me quite cold and calculating, speaking like this. But please understand, I was brought up to be very proper, and none of what happened fit in with my plans for my life."

Her gaze returned to her hands, which again fidgeted in her lap. "I'm sure you've turned out to be a lovely woman. I can see you're warm and gentle, but that has little to do with me. I am neither warm nor gentle, and I have little use for a daughter in my life at this late date. Except for my husband, whom I told only yesterday, I have never told a soul about your existence, and if you don't mind, I would prefer to keep it that way."

I felt wobbly inside, as though I would fall when I finally stood. When I could speak, I said casually, "Well, I'll get back to you by the end of the week. All right?"

Brian shook her hand and took a firm hold on my arm as he ushered me toward the car. My mother spoke not another word as she closed the door behind us.

If she wanted to conduct this as a simple business arrangement, then that was perfectly all right with me. I mentioned as much in a low voice.

If Brian hadn't had a tight grasp on me, I would've turned into a puddle on the sidewalk beside the car.

As we pulled away, he said, "Are you all right?"

"Oh," I said lightly, "I'm fine. She simply needs my bone marrow."

He gave me a doubtful look. "You know…."

I waved my hand in the air in a dismissive gesture. "I'm fine. Fine. Just take me home."

I squared my shoulders and held my emotions in check until we arrived home. I noticed Brian, every so often, looking at me with a worried frown.

Once home, I walked slowly up the stairs, feeling shaky and hurt. In my closet, I slipped out of my clothes and donned jeans and a soft cotton shirt. After hanging up my clothes, I slid to the closet floor and burst into silent, heaving sobs. Brian pulled me up a minute later and held me tightly. "Don't give the woman another thought, okay? So now you know she's a jerk. Come here."

I nodded, still unable to stop crying.

He sat down on the bed and pulled me onto his lap, making himself comfortable against the headboard. Pushing the hair from my eyes, he said softly. "Can you let this go?"

"Oh, Brian, I guess I was hoping you were right. That she wouldn't have called if she didn't want a relationship. I never imagined it would turn out this way."

He frowned and pressed my head to lean against his shoulder. I could smell his cologne and feel the roughness of his nubby linen shirt against my cheek.

He sighed. "No one could've imagined it would turn out like this."

"I just can't believe I am the product of rape. No wonder she hates me."

Meeting my gaze, he said softly, "You are not a *product* of anything, and she doesn't really hate you. She just hates what happened to her."

I wiped tears from my swollen eyes. "Well, she certainly didn't beat about the bush, did she? She told me in no uncertain terms that she has no use, but a medical one, for me."

I took a deep breath and added, "I wish I could just leave my organ donation at the hospital and never see her again. It would be easier that way."

"You know, I have no idea how a bone marrow donation works."

Thoughtfully, I said, "I think I have to go through a screening process to see if I match, and then endure more tests, before they finally agree to take my marrow."

"Does it hurt? This procedure?"

"Oh, some, I think, but the pain is nothing compared to its potential for restoring health."

He held me away from him and met my gaze. "So you're planning to go through with this?"

"Of course. Whether she has any use for me or

not, how can I say no when it will save her life?"

"Well, I think that's very unselfish of you, considering she just shattered your heart with her words."

"Never mind. I'm fine now. I need to go figure out what to fix for supper."

I moved restlessly toward the edge of the bed.

"Wait. I want to know how you can do this when she treated you so badly. Can you explain it to me?"

Softly, I said, "I can't. If I do, I'll drown, pulling you under with me. Can't you understand?"

He shook his head, looking confused. "I guess not." With a frown, he said, "Whatever."

After going downstairs, I headed toward the kitchen, where I pulled out ingredients for chili. The early April day had turned, during the last hour, from sunshiny to blustery and overcast, perfectly matching my mood.

I could hear the television turn on. CNN blared loudly before he finally muted it and sank into his creaky caramel leather chair. I knew he would put his stocking-clad feet on the buttery soft hassock, close his eyes, intending to rest them, only to fall asleep. When I heard no sound coming from the den, I tiptoed down the hall and peeked around the corner.

I smiled as I took in his still, sleeping form.

Our sons, Seth and Cade, are grown, married and moved away, Seth, to Arizona and the Cade to Florida. They come home twice a year, usually for Thanksgiving and Easter, simply because the two dates are spaced evenly on the calendar. They call about once a month, and I keep waiting for the phone call that will tell me I'll soon be a grandma, but so far, it hasn't happened.

Both of our sons have legal careers, following in their father's footsteps. In fact, indirectly, the law brought us together. My first job as a legal secretary, at twenty years of age, turned into what I saw then as a dream love affair, when the boss, Brian Stevenson, pursued me, with increasing fervor, until I finally agreed to marry him. As a third year student in elementary education, I had taken the secretary's job to pay for my last two years at the university.

Back in the kitchen, I finished browning the meat before starting a pot of coffee. A short time later, I stuck a Mozart CD in the player and sank into a chair. I'd struggled with self-image over the years, not realizing until recently that its roots grew out of insecurity over my adoption.

Pulling the phone toward me, I picked it up and automatically began dialing. I heard it ring several times in my ear before it finally hit me that my mother hadn't answered at that phone number in ten years. Abruptly slamming down the phone, I put my head in my hands and wept.

Who am I, Lord?

When I picked up my Bible, it fell open, as usual, to the Psalms of David. He and I had much in common. Confusion, depression and insecurity, under what looked like a solid veneer.

Oh, I knew the scriptures well. I knew it said that God had created me and loved me enough to redeem me from the clutches of sin and death. I had heard a thousand times that He had made me a new creature, set me on a rock and cared about my deepest needs. But for some reason, I could never feel in my heart what I knew in my head. *Why is that, Lord?*

Psalm 73:23 echoed my hope.

"Nevertheless I am continually with Thee. Thou hast taken hold of my right hand. With Thy counsel Thou wilt guide me, and afterward receive me to glory. Whom have I in heaven but Thee? And besides Thee, I desire nothing on earth. My flesh and my heart may fail; but God is the strength of my heart and my portion forever. But as for me, the nearness of God is my good; I have made the Lord God my refuge, that I may tell of all Thy works."

Silent tears streaked down my cheeks at the words. Even if I never figured out who I was, He promised He wouldn't abandon me.

Drying my face with the backs of my hands, I poured my coffee, added creamer and a no calorie sweetener, then turned my attention to the laundry.

Not long after, I glanced at the list on the counter. I'm a compulsive list maker, but at my age, it's strictly a safeguard against my unpredictable menopausal brain that sometimes refuses to retain the most elementary of facts. Scary.

I turned the flame down under the meat, to let it finish cooking and flipped on the timer. Had someone once said, "Diamonds are a girl's best friend?" From my point of view, it's not diamonds, but *timers* that are a girl's best friend. At least at this age.

Crossing off items as I completed them, I sighed as I realized I had about thirty papers to grade. Thirty second-grade papers entitled "If I had one wish…"

If *I* had one wish, it would be that thirty second-grade papers would grade themselves. Digging into my soft leather satchel, I unearthed the papers, pulled out my red pencil and sank down at the table, fortifying myself with a stiff swallow of coffee.

Lindsay Shepherd's masterpiece was on top. Lindsay, a dark haired, brown-eyed pixie of a girl, had a reputation for being more clever than her years, so I wasn't surprised to read—"If I had one wish, it would be to teach second grade at this school when I grow up and be just like Mrs. Stevenson. I hope I'm as beautiful as she is, too."

Kid knew how to brown nose with the best of them, and at age seven, no less.

Sifting through the papers, I pulled out the tough
 ones first, saving the easy ones till last. I only gave Lindsay a C. It was not her best work.

I had to laugh when I read Mac Gentry's paper. It said, "If I had one wish, I would grow up to own General Motors, Dell Computers and AT&T." Knowing he sold candy bars he bought for twenty-five cents apiece for seventy-five in the cafeteria—on the sly, I could imagine his wish coming true in spades. His paper continued, "To achieve my goal, I have already begun to buy stock in small amounts with the money my grandpa gives me for Christmas and birthdays."

I gave his paper an A. At least he was working toward a goal, which was more than I could say for most people. I had to stop and sigh.

"You're talking about second graders here," I lectured myself. "They don't need goals yet. They just need to be kids. Give them a break, will you?

"Okay, okay," I retorted in annoyance.

A minute later, Brian walked into the kitchen, poured himself coffee and sat down beside me. "Who were you talking to?"

"Oh," I said, shaking my head. "Sorry if I woke you. I was just talking to myself."

He laughed. "The question is—did you answer back?"

"Um…Actually, yes."

He gave me a wide, mischievous grin. "Oh-oh. That's no good."

I rolled my eyes. "You're right. I'll try to reform."

He laughed and raised his eyebrow. "You're funny. You know that?"

"I just wanted her to love me. That's all I've ever wanted. If she could just love me, everything would be all right."

He shook his head, looking doubtful. "That's ridiculous. You've got everything going for you, honey. You have beauty, brains, a great job and tons of people who love you, with me at the top of the list. You've done miracles with the kids you teach. I mean, come on, what more could you want?"

"I don't know. I really don't, so don't ask me, okay?"

"It's crazy that the opinion of one woman should make you so nuts. Am I right?"

I shrugged, swallowing hard.

"Listen," he said seriously, raising my chin to meet his gaze, "I think you need to get some help. Why don't we find someone for you to talk to?"

"What? A shrink? No way, Jose'."

I shook my head, adamant. My parents had tried that when I was younger, but the psychiatrists were always stranger than I.

"I'm fine, Bry. I just need some time to get used to the idea of my mother coming back into my life, even briefly and even because she needs a body part."

He looked at me with tenderness for a long moment. "Jolie, who made you believe you didn't measure up? Your dad? It was your dad, wasn't it?"

I made a face. "How many times do we have to have this conversation, Brian? I don't remember anyone demanding that I be perfect."

"Of course you don't. They wouldn't have said it quite that way. They infer things like that, making it clear, sometimes without a single word."

"Well, I really don't want to discuss it right now. I have to make chili and finish grading papers."

He grabbed my hand as I walked past him, bringing me up short beside him.

Pulling away, I said, "Please, Bry, I told you I have things to do."

"You always duck out when we start examining your issues."

I laughed and softly slugged his arm. "Since when did you hang out your shingle?"

"Since you need to get past this stuff. There's nothing more pathetic than a grown woman as classy as you, who sees herself as less than nothing."

I frowned, fishing a wooden spoon from the crock on the counter. "Who said I did?"

He pointed at his chest. "Me. I say you do. You show it in everything you do and much of what you say."

"Well, I have one suggestion. Stop listening to me. I haven't got much to say that's balanced these days anyway."

He put up his index finger. "See? That's exactly what I mean. That's a derogatory statement, lady, and I want you to knock it off. Understand?" By now, he stood beside me, pulling me into his arms. He took the wooden spoon from my hand, laid it on the counter and kissed me.

"Come on, honey. The chili can wait. You and I have some serious necking to do."

"Not now. Don't you see I have a list of things a mile long to get done before bedtime tonight? I can't stop now."

"Yes, you can. You and those crazy lists. Why do you make them anyway? You let them run your life. Well, not this time, sister."

Brian, at two hundred and sixty pounds and six feet-five and a half, swooped down, scooped up my five foot-two inch frame, and swung me over his shoulder in a fireman's carry.

My mouth fell open in shock. "Brian! Put me down this instant. I am not a toy doll for you to haul around by the hair."

"The hair? Oh, is that how it's done? Well, let me see what I can do."

He set me down on our bed and slipped in beside me. "You know I care about you, don't you?"

"Of course I do…." I stopped myself just before adding that I didn't know why, but I was glad he did. Those words would only add fuel to the fire.

I gave him an enigmatic smile. "Brian, it's the middle of the day. What's gotten into you?"

"Shut up, woman, and kiss me, will you?"

I laughed. "You're a crazy man. Do you know that?"

"So I've heard, but I really like hearing it from those sweet lips of yours."

My husband, the romantic. If only I could see what he sees in me…

Chapter Three

As we snuggled in each other's arms a while later, he nuzzled my cheek. "So are you really planning to donate bone marrow for your mother? I guess I'm surprised, as nervous as you are about medical procedures."

"Don't call her that, please. She's simply Jeanette to me."

He propped his head on his elbow, surveying my face. "Okay, then, Jeanette. So what's your answer?"

"My answer is the same as it was before. Yes, I'm planning to donate. I can't *not* do it when I know this may give her the time God needs to capture her heart."

"I should've known you'd feel that way. Well, that's big of you, but I guess I still don't understand why. Can you explain it to me?"

"I don't know, so how can I tell you?" I said, as I slid out of bed, tied on my robe and strode toward the shower.

"Now wait. You can't walk out in the middle of a discussion."

"Yes, I can. I need to shower. Then I have work to do."

"Then I'm coming in the shower with you."

"Suit yourself, big guy, but remember how crowded it gets when there are two of us in there?"

He laughed. "I call it cozy. And that's not such a bad thing when a man loves a woman."

"Well, listen, I need to wash my hair, so why don't you just give me five minutes and then come in?"

"Okay, you win."

By the time five minutes were up, I was stepping out of the shower, already squeaky clean. He grabbed my hand as I passed him, wrapping a thick terrycloth towel around my middle.

"Hey, you were supposed to wait for me in there. What is this?"

Sliding from his grasp, I said, "What can I say? I'm a quick study. I've got papers to grade and chili to fix. Come find me when you're finished, and I'll feed you. Okay?"

"Shucks, woman, that's not exactly what I had in mind."

I laughed, rolling my eyes. "I know exactly what you had in mind. That's why I'm doing this. With you at home, I can never get anything done."

"Okay, I'll expect some of that chili when I get out."

"I'm on it."

I went down to the kitchen and added spices, beans and Prego to the meat and turned the flame to simmer. After turning on the timer, I sat down and picked up my red pencil, scanning the next paper.

Frannie Grigg was thinking big when she made her wish. "If I had one wish, I'd be queen of the univers even more impartant than the good witch in the Wizard of Oz." Frannie got a C, mostly for her poor spelling and sloppy penmanship.

Dicky Vale, a husky brunette with a foul mouth, wrote, "If I had one wish, I'd forget this school forever." Dicky got a D for his rotten attitude.

Meryl Jardine, a small redheaded imp, had penned her latest tome with her usual precise penmanship. "If I had one wish, it would be to give my little brother, Robbie, a new kidney. He has to be on a machine three times a week, and he's getting sicker and sicker. If I was a good enough match, I'd give him one of mine."

I scratched an A plus and a happy face on the top of her paper as I blinked moisture from my eyes.

It occurred to me suddenly, that I didn't

know if Jeanette was married or had a family or a job. Then I recalled that she'd mentioned a husband. Other than that, the woman had volunteered exactly zero information about herself. Nor had she wanted to know anything about me, except my husband's name. I frowned when it hit me—she hadn't even thanked us for coming. What a warm and delightful creature. Not. *Maybe I should rethink my marrow donation.*

It took about three seconds to realize that it didn't matter at all what the woman was like or whether she loved me or not. She still needed what I had to give.

The buzzer went off at the same instant Brian entered the kitchen. "So, is my chili ready?"

"Yup. Just let me whip up a salad and some garlic bread."

"Stay put, woman. I can do those things while you read me your papers."

I made a face. "You're kidding, right?" That wasn't usually his style.

"Nope, I want to know what the kids have to say these days."

"Well, I told them to write at least a half page on "If I had one wish…""

"Hey," he grinned, "I could get into that assignment myself."

I laughed. "Nobody asked you. Now are you going to listen or not?"

"Yup. Hey, before you get started reading, tell me where you've hidden the garlic powder, will you?"

I pointed to the cupboard to the left of the stove and turned back to the paper in my hand.

"Okay, here's one from Ricky Kennedy. 'If I had one wish, it would be to have a pet monkey. My dad says they stink and get fleas, and my mom says she'd end up feeding it and cleaning up after it, so I guess I'll never have a monkey.'"

When I turned to look at Brian, his shoulders were shaking with laughter as he offered, "I guess all kids must have that dream, huh?"

I cringed, just thinking about it. "Not me. I hung around my Uncle Jake's high school biology lab, where they actually kept live monkeys, and it was no picnic."

"So what did you have to do when you went there?"

"Oh, he always cleaned the cages. At least he never made me do that, but I had to cut fruit until I was blue in the face. They loved apples, lettuce, oranges and, of course, bananas."

He slathered butter on both halves of the giant crusty loaf. "I'm sure. Okay, what else are you learning from these budding geniuses?"

"Here's one from Kerrigan Manley. She says, "If I had one wish, it would be to go to heaven to be with my grandma Lucy, who died last week. I miss her a lot because she loved me like no one else."

"Wow. I guess not all of these are silly little kid wishes, huh?"

"Nope. I have another little girl, who wishes she was a donor match for her little brother, who needs a new kidney."

He stuck the garlic bread under the broiler, turned on the timer and pulled the salad ingredients from the fridge. Less than a minute later, the buzzer sounded, and he pulled the crunchy golden bread from the oven; its fragrance made my mouth water and set my stomach to growling.

He finished the salad, added his specialty homemade ranch dressing, which was actually Hidden Valley Ranch that he never admitted to, and sat down beside me.

"You never think of little guys that age having to deal with such huge problems, do you?"

"Oh, lots of them carry adult baggage. Several have parents who are divorcing right now."

"Man," he said, running his long fingers through his thick thatch of graying hair. "That's tough."

Sifting through the pages, I found the one I sought. "It is. Listen to this. This is from Micki Freed, who says, "If I had one wish, it's for my mom and dad to stop yelling at each other and move back into the same house. I miss my daddy so much, I feel sick all the time."

He tapped his finger in the middle of the paper. "Well, I hate to break up this party, but I'm starved. How about you? Ready to eat?"

"Sure. Thanks."

I cleared the table of papers and took the plates and silverware he handed me.

"Here. Make yourself useful, why don't you?" he asked in a teasing voice.

While he brought steaming bowls of chili to the table, I cut the garlic bread and arranged it in a napkin-lined basket. I set the bread on the table and watched as he headed back to fill our glasses.

"Hey, listen, I was thinking. What if I make reservations for a cruise over spring break?"

I made a face. "Honey, you always forget— spring break is all of three days long, including Friday, Saturday and Sunday. They don't give a week anymore at the elementary level. They'd rather get out of school in May than June."

"Bummer," he said, slipping his long legs under the table as he sank into his chair. "I'm dying to get you out of here. Go somewhere where we can kick up our heels for a change."

"Maybe after school is out. How about that?"

He shook his head in consternation. "I'm thinking now, today, not two months from now."

"Now? But that's crazy. We can't just drop everything and go."

"Why not? Surely they have substitute teachers just for that very purpose."

"Honey…." I said before I blew on a steamy spoonful of chili.

I watched him crumple a handful of crackers into his soup and send crumbs flying. He flushed in embarrassment. "Sorry. I'll clean it up after we eat."

"Oh, sure," I said with a laugh and a dubious shake of my head. "You say that every time and then conveniently forget after we finish eating. Leaving me to clean it up."

"Well—" he said tentatively, "want me to stop now and do it before I forget?"

"No, honey, never mind. You eat. I'll take care of the mess later. Just don't do it again, all right?"

He gave me a bad boy smile. "Now I know why I'm so crazy about you."

I laughed. "Why? Because I let you get away with murder?"

"That's about it."

"Glad we got that straight. Now eat, before your chili gets cold."

The phone rang twenty minutes later while we were drinking our after dinner coffee, and Brian handed the phone to me, looking puzzled.

"Who is it?" I asked in a whisper.

He put his hand over the receiver and said, "I don't know. Some guy."

I took the phone from him, and a voice I didn't recognize said, "Is this Jolie Stevenson?"

"Yes, it is."

"I'm Steven Kelly. Jeanette is my wife."

"Oh, yes. How are you?"

"Not so good. I'm afraid my wife has taken a turn for the worse. I know she only met you today, but I'm afraid things have reached a crisis, and she needs you to donate as soon as possible—that is, if you've decided to go along with this."

"Oh, of course. What hospital is she in?"

"St. Gregory's in the city."

"We'll be there as soon as we can."

"Don't eat or drink anything, please, before you come."

"Oh, dear. I just finished dinner."

"Well, that's my fault. I should've phoned sooner."

"What floor is she on?"

"Third. The medical floor. Before long, they'll have to admit her to five. That's the oncology floor."

I frowned in confusion. "Well, okay. I guess I need to ask, where do we go when we get to the hospital?"

"Just go to the information desk and tell them who you are. They'll know just where to direct you."

I hung up a minute later and saw Brian clearing the table. He said, "You get your things together. I'm on top of the cleanup. I'll be ready in five, okay?"

At the kitchen door, I turned. "You know, I have no idea how this works. Do I pack an overnight bag or what?"

"I'm not sure, but I think that would be wise, just to be on the safe side, don't you?"

"I suppose so." I was thoughtful as I made my way up the stairs, unsure what I was getting into.

It took an hour and a half to arrive at the hospital, and by the time we pulled into the parking lot, I had worked myself into a state of near panic.

Brian turned to me after setting the handbrake. "Ready?"

"I'm scared, honey. I've never been fond of needles, and if I recall, they use a really long one for this kind of procedure."

"Well, if they do that, I'm sure they numb it with something first. They won't hurt you."

I looked at him hopefully. "Think so?"

"Sure thing. Okay, I'll get your bag. Come on. Let's get this over with."

"Thanks for coming with me. I don't think I could handle it alone."

He lifted his left eyebrow, in a look of impatience. "You keep saying that, but you know what? You'd manage just fine..." After taking a breath, he teased, "In fact, if you want, I could leave right now."

He hustled me through the door, and we soon found the information desk. Brian gave my name, and the congenial white-haired woman, who wore a pink smock, picked up the phone. Not a moment later a dark-haired young man came toward us with a wheelchair. After getting me situated, he smiled. "Okay, onward and upward. You coming, too?" he asked Brian.

"Of course. Lead the way, my man."

It was 8:15 before I finished answering questions and letting them draw blood for matching purposes. An hour later, a doctor came into the waiting room and called my name. He looked at me and said, "You're a very close match to your mother, and we are ready to take your marrow as soon as possible."

Brian interrupted. "She had dinner a short time ago. Is that a problem?"

"Well, if at all possible, we ask that donors not eat or drink, but since she won't be under a general anesthetic, it's not that big a deal." He turned to me. "Ready?"

I wanted to run away, but instead I nodded.

He smiled. "Good. Want to kiss your husband goodbye?"

I flinched at his words. They somehow sounded awfully final.

Chapter Four

Brian leaned down and said, "Listen, you're going to be fine, honey, so just relax. I'll be right here when you're finished, okay?"

I knew he read the look of panic in my eyes, because he pulled me into an unscheduled hug. "Chin up now, okay? You can do this. You can."

"I know," I agreed, a little uncertainly.

When we got to the surgical suite, I changed into a gown and when they had started my IV and situated me prone on the rather hard metal table, I asked, "How is Jeanette? Do you know?"

The nurse attached my arm to a metal board extending from the table.

The doctor, who wore green scrubs and a co-ordinating cap and mask, said, "She's bleeding, which is why we called you to come so abruptly.

We're doing all we can, but if this doesn't work in short order, she'll be in a world of trouble."

After a brief pause, he said, "Okay, Jolie, I want you to close your eyes. Now, even after I deaden it, you'll feel some pressure in the pelvic area. But just relax, take slow deep breaths, and above all, do not move or flinch. All right?"

I nodded, but felt shaky and afraid as I saw the long needle he held in his hand.

Someone wiped something wet over my right lower back, and it felt cold, making me shiver.

He turned away and said softly, "Ten milligrams of Valium, please, Vicki."

After that, I slept through the entire procedure.

Chapter Five

It was after seven the next morning when Brian took my arm and helped me into the house.

He settled me onto the sofa, tucked a quilt over me and headed toward the kitchen, where he clanked pots as he put together and let simmer— a crock of vegetable soup, his answer to every complaint. Though it was common knowledge that he used a commercially prepared soup starter, he always took credit for the resulting 'homemade' concoction. But it never failed to fill the air with a wonderful fragrance.

I slept for a time while he worked on a legal case. Finally he came to stand beside me. "Hungry?" A glance at my watch told me it was noon.

"Not very."

"Don't go back to sleep. I want you to try some of my delicious homemade vegetable soup."

"I'm not hungry right now, honey."

He shook his index finger at me, scolding. "Oh now, none of that. You have to eat."

I shrugged, knowing he'd get soup down my throat if he had to feed it to me one spoonful at a time.

He had to wake me again when he brought the soup. He set the tray on my lap and roughly tucked a napkin in my neckline. "Come on now—you can do this."

I shrugged, not wanting to argue with him.

"Look, this soup will fix you right up, I guarantee it."

I smiled. "Thank you, Mr. S. I appreciate it."

He sat beside me, watching as I spooned his delicious soup into my mouth. I felt full after about four bites, but he seemed to sense me slowing down and said, "Oh, no, you don't. Get busy. I only gave you a half bowl and even you can manage that."

Without warning, I felt too tired to care about food. "Honey, I'm too tired to finish it. Please. I need to lie down."

"Whatever," he conceded with an attitude, taking the tray. "You should be in bed." By that time, I was half asleep and didn't answer. I felt him lift me, carrying me upstairs, where he tucked me into our bed. I roused slightly when he said, "Sleep now. You'll feel better after a good nap."

Interestingly enough, I slept, and only woke

the next morning to the blare of the Weather Channel. I felt confused, wondering what day it was. I processed the thought and realized it was Saturday morning, and I had slept past nine. I could count on one hand the days I had slept past seven, and they were all during illnesses.

I crept gingerly out of bed toward the bathroom, with my lower back nagging like a toothache. As I washed my face and brushed my teeth, Brian stood outside the door.

"Need any help in there?"

"I'm fine," I called with my mouth full of toothpaste.

"What?"

"I'm fine," I yelled, louder this time.

"Well, you don't have to yell. I'm not deaf, you know."

I smiled, shaking my head. He's slightly deaf in one ear, and things are either inaudible or, oddly enough, deafening. And at the rate we're going, our golden years may leave a little something to be desired.

He had disappeared when I exited the bathroom, heading to the closet to dig out a pair of soft knit shorts and a t-shirt. My whole body felt hypersensitive to pain. I gasped as the shorts slid past the place where they had removed the marrow.

Brian appeared as if by magic.

"You all right?" he asked, looking concerned.

"I'm fine, really."

"Then what's all the groaning about?"

"I'm old, that's all."

He laughed and ruffled my messy hair. "You are not. Quit saying that. Feeling better this morning?"

"You might want to think of another question to ask for a few days. Okay?"

"That bad, huh?"

"Just tender, that's all. Sort of like a bad toothache. But I think I'll probably live to tell about it."

He gave a low chuckle. "Glad to hear it."

"Listen, could you bring me a glass of water and some Tylenol? I want to take something for pain."

"Sure. Be right back."

By the time he returned, I had laid my head on the pillow to rest a minute and had fallen asleep. I barely felt it when he lifted my legs and scooted me into a more comfortable position before pulling the covers over me. I murmured a soft thank you as I drifted deeper into sleep.

I woke some time later with a terrible ache in my back and got up to take some pain medication and use the bathroom before crawling back into bed.

Several times, I heard Brian go in and out of the room and even felt his cool hand on my cheek, but I was simply too worn out to waken.

Finally, he woke me and insisted that I needed

to eat and drink, so I let him help me downstairs, where I had another helping of his soup.

Over our meal, Brian said, "Jeanette called while you were sleeping. She sounded a bit weak, but said she's looking forward to being a new woman by the time this thing is over. She just wanted to say thanks. I told her...."

I frowned at him.

"No. Now I didn't volunteer anything until she asked, then I told her honestly that you weren't quite up to par yet. She seemed properly concerned, almost like a real mother." After a brief pause, he frowned and shook his head, "No, I guess I wouldn't go quite that far. But she said to tell you she's grateful and that she'll be thinking of you, hoping you feel better soon."

"That's nice," I said, noncommittally.

He frowned in concern. "Jolie, is there something you're not telling me?"

"No. I'm okay. Just a little tired."

"What's up?"

"Maybe I could take one of those super duper vitamins you bought me a while back? You know, the ones you're always trying to force on me?"

"Man, you must really feel awful if you're asking for vitamins."

I laughed. "You're a funny guy, Bry, do you know that?"

He grimaced. "Well, that's the last thing I'm

trying for right now."

"Good soup, honey," I remarked, licking my lips.

"Don't you be changing the subject, girlie. I'll be right back with your vitamins, all right?"

"I'll be here," I chirped in my most cheerful voice.

I sighed. I had never felt less like being cheerful in my life. I had to teach tomorrow, and I hadn't finished grading papers, nor had I done lesson plans for the upcoming week. How could I keep up with thirty second-graders when I could barely negotiate a flat surface?

Brian handed me a handful of pills. I frowned. "What is all this? I only asked for one."

"Never mind, just take them like a good girl. I've studied this stuff. Maybe I should've gone into medicine. This is really great stuff, honey. Down the hatch. That's it."

I frowned and clamped my lips shut. "Brian, come on. I'm not a little kid. Tell me what these are, will you, please?"

"Just vitamins and herbs, and I'm not going to go into detail right now, so just trust me on this, will you, please?" His voice held a note of irritation.

I swallowed the pills, chasing them with water, and shrugged. "Listen, will you bring my leather satchel from the kitchen? I still have papers to grade before I go back to school, and I'll be in a world of trouble if I don't get my lesson plans done. Mr. Hested comes around to collect them every week so he can look them over—I guess he wants to reassure himself that we aren't shirking our duties."

He was incredulous. "Are you serious? You've been teaching for twenty-five years, and they still can't trust you with planning lessons?"

"I guess not. Anyway, I'd appreciate it if you could just get the satchel for me, okay?"

"I will, but I don't think you're in any shape to worry about this stuff right now."

"I have no choice, so help me out here, will you?"

After I took the proffered satchel, he wandered off, and I could hear him dictating notes into a small voice-activated recorder, so Genevieve Harmon, his sixty-two year old secretary, could transcribe them.

After moving to the living room, where I put my feet up, I was down to the last ten pages of essays when my eyes closed involuntarily, and I nodded off.

A short time later, Brian took the papers from my hands and moved me to rest on the pillow. As he covered me, he whispered, "You're not going anywhere but your bed in this kind of shape, my love."

In my sleep, I heard him speaking in low

tones over the phone, but I was too far gone to grasp what was said.

The sun's rays were just petering out in a blaze of glory when I woke again. I felt grubby and longed for a shower, but I couldn't recall whether or not I had the doctor's permission to take one.

Brian's office door was closed when I dug in my handbag for the pink dismissal sheet, unearthing it, all wadded up from beneath my wallet. It said *activities as tolerated*. I assumed that meant whatever I felt like doing. Which was basically very little.

I frowned. I had heard that there was almost no recovery time from giving bone marrow, but I felt like I had just emerged after a major procedure—brain surgery for instance.

Slowly making my way upstairs, I had to sit on the bed to rest. Once again, some time later, I woke, realizing I had fallen asleep. *What on earth is the matter with me?*

Peeling off my clothes, I stepped into the shower and made fast work of cleaning up. Standing, for any length of time, took everything out of me. Maybe I was just too old to be a bone marrow donor.

That evening, I found Brian had called in for me and requested a week off from teaching, and for that, I was grateful.

Two days later, I finally began to feel my energy returning. I walked around the house, and started a load of white laundry. I put Swiss steak in the slow cooker and a pan of scalloped potatoes in the oven.

I could at least see the glimmer of light through the long dark tunnel.

After pulling the potatoes from the oven and sliding the pan into the fridge, I curled up on the sofa and finished grading papers.

The phone shattered my reverie a short time later, and I answered to hear the voice of my pushy sister, Elly. She was named after Eleanor Roosevelt and unfortunately, shares many of that woman's most dominant characteristics.

She said loudly, "Hey, Buzzy, what's up?"

"Oh, not much. And don't call me Buzzy."

"I've always called you Buzzy, and it's a little late to teach an old dog new tricks, don't you think?"

"Say, why do you call me that anyway? I can't recall you mentioning it."

"When you were a baby, you made this funny little buzzing sound with your mouth, blowing bubbles, and I've called you Buzzy ever since."

"Well, listen, Ell, I don't do that anymore, so can't you just call me Jolie or Sis, anything but Buzzy?"

Succinctly, she said, "Nope. Sorry. Old habits die hard."

I frowned. "Did you call about anything in particular? Or just to annoy me?"

"Oh, just had to check in. But I wanted your advice about something. Tell me what you think."

"About what?"

"I have a chance to buy a pet grooming van, equipped with everything I need to become a dog groomer. I could get it for a song. Do you think I should do it?"

After a slight hesitation, I said, "Well, I suppose it might work—if you could actually stand getting within ten feet of an animal."

She flew into a conniption fit. "How dare you? I should've known you'd pour ice water on my one chance at immortality."

I laughed. "Immortality? What's that about?"

"You know, fame and fortune."

I was incredulous. "How on earth is buying a pet grooming van going to earn you fame and fortune?"

"Never mind. You just don't get it, do you?"

"I guess not."

She huffed, "Well, then, I guess we have nothing more to discuss, do we?"

"Beats me," I murmured with a frustrated sigh. Most of our conversations ended in a similar fashion. No win.

Chapter Six

I hung up the phone, shaking my head. I might not know who I am, but I could be certain of one thing: Elly is no blood kin of mine. *May God be praised.*

Elly is three years older than I, with a wild head of Cruela DeVil hair, but in silver and tawny-blonde instead of black and white. She stands about five feet nine skinny inches high, to my five feet two, and she's notable for being married and divorced three times.

We have absolutely nothing in common, and I always cringe when I hear her voice on the phone, because it usually means she's got nothing better to do than make me nuts. The word *obtuse* was invented expressly to describe Elly.

She only shops at Dillard's and Sak's Fifth

Avenue. She has, as you may have guessed, accumulated a tidy sum in alimony from each of her ex mates, making her the best-dressed divorcee this side of the Mississippi.

She has one twenty-year old son, Denver, who is attempting, without success, to become a rock sensation in Albuquerque, of all places. He is her current fixation. Better him than me, I always say.

Feeling hungry, I fixed myself a peanut butter and banana sandwich. A childhood favorite, it always makes me feel good. Brian scoffs at stuff like this, but I always tell him he just doesn't know what he's missing.

Brian's parents and his brother, Ken, live in Seattle, I guess because they hate sunshine, but they get back once a year, usually in early May, and I knew that we were due for a phone call from them any day, to make plans for their annual visit. *Whoopee. I couldn't wait.* In case you can't tell, I'm being facetious.

As much as I try to love them, Arnie and Juliette are probably, no make that, undoubtedly, the most uppity, superior people I have ever met. She, too, buys from only at the most exclusive shops, and avails herself of commuter flights to California for the sole purpose of shopping on Rodeo Drive.

My own love affair with clothes, other than

my necessary dressy-casual school wardrobe, is limited to anything soft and slightly threadbare, so you can imagine how she regards her only daughter-in-law.

Brian's brother, Ken, at age fifty-nine, is divorced, with two grown children, and he only accompanies his parents on their annual trip because they insist on paying for it. He could spring for the entire airline if he wanted to, but Ken rarely parts with a farthing he doesn't have to, and even though he makes at least triple what Brian does, he down-dresses for effect—hoping for a handout, is my guess. His job as a headhunter for a large Seattle firm seems about as secure as any these days. I decided I would think about their visit when I was in better shape.

Pulling a writing tablet from the shelf, I jotted a list. Laundry, loads one, two and three were at the top. Somehow as I get older, I can never remember to finish laundry unless it's on my list.

Searching my mind for something I was forgetting, I realized my sister's birthday was in three days, so I pulled a card from the drawer. I keep a stash on hand for just such occasions.

For forty-eight years I prided myself on remembering everything and staying on top of my game, but it had deteriorated badly from then on, and now I have a well-deserved reputation for forgetting. I even joked to Brian that I needed to tie a string around my *neck* to keep from forgetting things. He always laughed and said it was a bad idea since it would cut off what little oxygen still reached my brain. Then he would always tell me to give myself a break—reassuring me that I didn't have to be perfect. *Didn't I?*

It occurred to me that I felt inadequate for lots of reasons, and my way of compensating was to work harder to excel where I could.

I read the card. It had an open-mouthed bald infant grinning from ear to ear. It said, "I'm tickled pink…cause it's your birthday instead of mine." The rest of the page was covered by Xs and Os, which I would have omitted, if it were up to me.

I addressed the envelope, stuck in the card and sealed it, adding a stamp before realizing I hadn't signed the card. *Man, am I losing it.*

Carefully I slit the side of the pale pink envelope, removed the card, signed it and taped the edge, sealing it inside.

I jotted it down and crossed it off the list, heading for the laundry room, where I opened the dryer door and added the wet clothes.

With a glance at my watch, I realized Brian would be home shortly, so I made a three-bean salad and a chocolate cheesecake. He enjoys having the occasional dessert and suffers from a worse chocolate addiction than I.

Twenty minutes later, he walked in the door,

wide-eyed. "So, it looks like you're perking right along. Feeling better today?"

"Yes. How was your day?"

"Well," he said, looking pleased as he pulled me into his arms. "You're looking at the newest senior partner at Lester, Hamlin and Pardee."

"Oh, honey, congratulations. I'm so proud of you."

"Thanks." His eyes lit up in a proud grin. "So how would you like to go out to dinner to celebrate?"

"Oh, I'd love to, but I have dinner all ready."

"Well, let's not let a little thing like that stop us. Just put it in the fridge for another day, all right?"

"Really? Well, okay. I suppose I could."

"Come on, honey, loosen up. It's not a big deal to change gears on the spur of the moment."

"For you, maybe. For me, it's a bit harder. You know that."

"I know. I know." His tone held an edge of irritation.

He helped me stow everything in the fridge before I said, "Okay, I'm ready. Where are we going?"

"Somewhere nice, so go change, will you?"

I repeated, "Really? Well, okay." I frowned, wishing we could go to an ordinary restaurant so I could wear jeans.

Twenty minutes later I was dressed in a pale

blue silk pantsuit he had given me. I had just finished applying makeup and sprayed my hair when he called out, "Honey, are you ready? I made reservations, and we're going to be late if you don't get the lead out. What do you say?"

"I'm coming."

With a slow grin spreading across his face, he said, "Hey now. You never dress up that way for me. Maybe we should stay home and just pretend we went out for a romantic dinner. I could take it from there…."

I laughed. "Oh, no you don't. We just put my lovely dinner in the refrigerator, if you recall, and I'm starving, so you're not getting off that easy, Bub."

As he pulled out of the driveway, he said, "So what did you do with your day today?"

"Well, Elly called."

"Oh, yeah? What did she want?"

"It's the funniest thing. After she hung up, I realized her birthday is in three days. I have this feeling she was angling for a gift."

He had just stopped for a traffic light when he said, "Well, what did she have to say?"

"She wanted to know if I thought she should buy a mobile pet grooming van so she can make her mark on the world."

He laughed. "Oh, yeah? And what did you say to that? To the woman who climbs walls when she sees a kitten?"

"I said I thought she might want to reconsider for that very reason."

He shook his head, obviously confused. "What reason?"

"You know—she can't stand getting within spitting distance of a gerbil."

His eyebrows danced upward. "Seriously? You said that?"

"Um...not exactly, but close."

"And what did she say?"

I rolled my eyes. "You don't want to know. She was fried, as a matter of fact."

"Oh, yeah?"

"I gently mentioned what I thought, and she got mad and hung up."

"I'll just bet she did. Well, I'll say one thing for you, you've got guts, lady."

I changed the subject. "Honey, you never said how your promotion came about."

He smiled. "Oh, well, Dutch said because I had proved my value to the firm on the Jeffrey case, they are making me a full partner as of the first of the month. So what do you think of them apples?"

I gave him a wide smile, laying my head against his arm. "I know how hard you've worked for this, and I'm very proud of you."

"Thanks. It looks like I'll have my plate full. They're giving me Ted Pardee's cases. It was horrible the way he died, but I guess they figure life must go on, right?"

I frowned in puzzlement. "Wait. What happened to Ted? I mean—how did he die? Did you tell me about this and I just forgot or what?" I had a nodding acquaintance with the members of the firm, and was shocked to learn the quiet middle-aged gent had died.

"He died in a light plane crash over Denver about six weeks ago. I told you, didn't I?"

"I don't remember hearing this."

"Oh, man. I'll bet I was deep in the middle of the Jeffrey case at that point in time. You know—against the tobacco industry. Maybe I forgot to mention the accident."

Annoyed, I quipped, "Listen, you—you ornery cuss, if I can't trust you to keep me informed, who can I trust?"

He shrugged and explained, "He was out in Denver on company business when it happened, so the company made a nice settlement on his wife and family. I mean, not that that could ever take Ted's place, but...."

"Well, that's good."

The restaurant, called The King's Table, served the best prime rib in the city. Brian, like most men, favored steak as his entrée of choice.

The place was filling up fast, and we were not

close to the front of the line. But from the way the blonde hostess looked at Brian when he caught her eye, it was clear that the attractive woman knew him. With a wide smile, she offered to seat us immediately. I glanced, with a frown, at Brian, who said softly, "The partners come here. They keep a company table reserved, so don't look at me like that." We followed her to a table where tall plants framed a wide picture window that looked out over a spotlighted sunken garden.

After she left, I raised my eyebrow and whispered, "I didn't look at you *like that*. But she certainly gave you the eye."

"Don't be ridiculous," he said with a shake of his head. I would never get used to the way women threw themselves at my good-looking husband.

The building had been remodeled since our last visit, and now sported sea foam green walls and mauve accents, with miniature crystal chandeliers hanging over each seating area. The walls were hung with Monet and Degas framed prints, and each table was set with a pristine mauve tablecloth and burgundy linen napkins. Its patrons dripped satin and diamonds, making me feel very uncomfortable in my simple silk.

Over our fork-tender steaks a short time later, he smiled, laid his hand on mine and said, "Honey, I really want to get you out of town. Let's leave tomorrow and go somewhere nice.

What do you say? Just for a few days?"

"Why do you want to leave? I'd be happy just hanging around the house if you could take a few days off."

"I just think it would be nice to have a change of scenery, don't you?"

I eyed him skeptically. "Does this have anything to do with my mother's appearance in my life?"

He shrugged. "Listen, I admit it. I really think this has been hard on you. Why won't you agree to come away with me?"

"I just don't enjoy traveling that much. You know that."

"We won't go far. Listen, honey, just humor me, will you?"

I blew out a breath of air, knowing I wasn't going to win this argument.

"I suppose," I agreed reluctantly. "But only for a few days."

"Good. Then I'll book our reservations."

Happily, he turned back to his food.

Not long after, Brian excused himself, saying he had to make a phone call and was gone for a couple of minutes. When he returned, he was grinning like the proverbial Cheshire cat.

I raised my eyebrows, lowering my chin to study his face. "What's going on?"

"Oh, nothing," he said evasively.

Not a minute later, the orchestra, which wouldn't ordinarily be playing until an hour from now, did a few practice chords, then began to play our song. "Stardust."

I smiled at my cagey husband, and he smiled back, humming along.

I couldn't resist teasing him. "Okay, how much did you pay them?"

"None of your business, nosey," he said, with a chuckle.

Resting his chin on his palm, he regarded me with interest. "You know, I can't wait to have you all to myself. We never have any time together anymore."

"And whose fault is that?"

He grimaced. "Okay, okay. I take full responsibility. And I have a feeling that becoming a partner will only complicate our lives further. That's why I want time alone with you now, while we can still pull it off."

"You're still the hopeless romantic I married, aren't you, honey?"

"Guilty as charged, kid," he conceded, letting his left eyebrow dance upward in amusement.

"Well, listen," I added. "Never change, all right?"

He smiled, tilting his head. "I thought I drove you nuts with this stuff…"

"Oh, you do, but I've sort of gotten used to it after thirty years."

He laughed and said smoothly, "Well, well, the lady finally admits it. Maybe she even likes it a tad."

"Yes, maybe she does," I said, unable to squelch the smile that tickled the edges of my lips.

"Hey—how about some of that yummy fudge almond pie you like so much?"

Pointing to my still half full plate, I murmured, "Oh, dear. I'm already stuffed. I couldn't eat another bite."

"Well, I'm ordering a slice, and we'll share it, all right? I'll even feed it to you off my fork. What do you say?"

I shook my head, unable to resist his wheedling. "You talked me into it. Just a bite, though."

"Good." He waved down a waiter and asked for pie with two cups of decaf. At our age, we can't do regular coffee after seven without paying for it all night.

A minute later, he was feeding me, tempting me with his scrumptious fudgy pie.

I nearly swooned it was so rich. He grinned at me. "Makes you mellow, doesn't it?"

"What?" I asked before nibbling a second creamy bite off the end of his fork.

"Chocolate fudge makes you mellow."

I grimaced, shaking my head. "Where do you

get this stuff?"

He raised his left eyebrow as a mischievous grin lit his eyes. "Listen, girlie, I've lived with you for thirty years, so if anyone should know what makes you mellow, it's me."

"That's ridiculous."

"No, it's not. It's true. In fact, I think they say there's a chemical in chocolate that does that, particularly to women."

"So you're drugging me. Is that it? For some ulterior purpose?"

He frowned. "Not really."

"I see."

"Come on, honey," he said, taking a last sip of coffee. "Let's go home, okay?"

A half hour later, we walked in the front door, shocked to see, first the living room, and then each succeeding room, in total disarray.

Chapter Seven

Unable to help myself, I burst into tears. "Brian, who would do something like this?"

"I don't know. I thought I turned on the alarm. Guess I must've forgotten."

The alarm was deactivated, and neither of us could recall arming it, which meant it had been left unsecured and perhaps even unlocked.

Brian, looking glum, phoned the local authorities and hung up to say, "Listen, babe, don't touch anything, all right? We need to let them finish checking things out before we clean or rearrange anything."

I had sat down hard in the corner of the sofa and laid my handbag in my lap. Gazing around, I felt violated and wondered if I would ever feel safe in our home again.

Brian searched the house for signs of the intruder, but thankfully, found the space abandoned. I breathed a sigh of relief, unable to imagine how I'd handle seeing the vandal face to face.

The phone rang just then, and Brian's brother, Ken, said, "So how's my favorite sister-in-law?"

"Not so good right now. And I'm your only sister-in-law, in case you've forgotten."

"So what do you mean, not so good? What's going on?"

"We just got home from dinner out to find the house has been ransacked. It's very unnerving."

"Don't you guys have a security system?"

"Yes, but...."

"But what?"

"Never mind. Do you want to talk to Brian?"

"Oh, I won't bother him now. I just wanted to find out if Mom and Dad have made arrangements to come down next week for our annual visit."

"Next week? Next week? Is that what you said?"

"Yes. What's the matter?"

"Oh, never mind. I'll...."

"Hey, maybe I should call back when you're better able to think straight."

I argued, "I'm thinking straight. Just a little flustered by the whole thing. And no, your mother hasn't called me to arrange anything yet."

"Oh, I thought she said she'd call you this past weekend. Maybe I misunderstood."

"Well, if you talk to her, please tell her next week won't be very convenient. Perhaps you could make it the following week."

"I'll tell her, but she isn't going to like it," he said in a singsong voice I hated. His mother was definitely used to calling the shots and expecting those around her to dance to her minuet. I was a very reluctant dancer.

"Whatever. I'll tell Brian you phoned, okay?"

By the time I hung up, the police had converged, including several uniformed officers, followed by a fingerprint team and a detective. I wondered how we rated. Maybe they were having a slow night?

Then I saw my husband slap the detective on the back, and I knew as surely as I knew my name, that Brian was calling in favors. I sighed as he ushered the detective over to introduce us.

The man standing beside my husband was in his mid forties, just under six feet tall, with a bushy head of blonde hair and a tan that made me wonder if he coached tennis on the side. He had brown eyes, a dazzling grin and very white, perfectly capped teeth. He wore a navy pinstriped suit with a burgundy and navy tie, looking more like an attorney than a detective. Maybe he'd read Malloy's "Dressing for Success" or whatever it was called.

"Honey, this is Max Case, a detective with our local sheriff's department."

I nodded in response to the man's wide-eyed smile and warm handshake.

"I didn't know the sheriff's office had detectives."

He pulled a pen from his pocket and began clicking it absentmindedly. "Ever since the Nodding Hill addition came into being, burgeoning the county coffers, they've been adding staff to protect the esteemed citizens in the area. And others, like you, are the blessed recipients of their largesse."

I laughed in spite of myself. "Do all detectives talk like you?"

"Hopefully not. I'm a police commissioner wannabe, so I do all the right things, hoping my number will come up someday."

"Rather frank, aren't you?" I offered, to the shocked look of my husband.

Max laughed. "Guess so. Sorry about that."

I flushed, chagrined at my behavior. *What has gotten in to me?* "Oh, dear. No, I'm the one who should be sorry."

Max Case said, "I need you to make a list of anything that's missing. Can you do that?"

Brian looked at me. "Don't worry, honey. I'll take care of it."

One of the officers pulled the detective aside,

and they commiserated before he turned back toward us. "Sounds like they picked up a good print off the garage door knob."

With a smile I said, "Listen. It's nice to have met you, Detective. Now if you two will excuse me, I think I'll go upstairs now, if it's okay."

Max nodded. "They're all through upstairs."

It seemed, suddenly, as though all the struggles of the day hit me at once, and I sagged on my feet as I walked toward the stairs.

Catching up to me, Brian asked, "You okay, honey?"

"I'm okay. Just tired. Did they mess up the upstairs?"

"Some, but not as bad as down here."

"Can you tell if anything is missing?"

He shook his head. "I don't think so, but things are such a mess, it's really hard to be sure."

With a glance at my watch, I said, "Well, listen, if you don't need me, I'm going to bed."

"Okay, I'll be up in a few minutes."

The room was worse than I had anticipated. The covers were stripped from the bed and the clean linens had been pulled from the bathroom closet. The vanity drawers had all been pillaged and dumped, resulting in myriad bottles, jars and miscellaneous debris scattered across the wide ceramic bathroom floor.

My dresser drawers had been plundered and

overturned, and for some reason, all the shoes had been tossed out of the closet and into the middle of the bedroom floor. The framed prints on the walls hung askew, and it was all I could do not to burst into tears at first glance at the mess. It would take hours to clean it all up, and I was simply too tired just then.

Gathering up the sheets, I remade the bed and donned my gown. After scooting the bathroom mess toward the wall with my foot, I found my toothbrush still in the bottom of the drawer, dug the toothpaste from the pile on the floor and brushed my teeth. After washing my face, I applied moisturizer and slipped, with a sigh, into bed.

Some time later, I heard Brian straightening up and could only hope he understood my neglect of things.

I woke in the night, with Brian beside me, unable to decide what woke me. A vague scraping sound outside made me get up and look out the window, but I could see nothing unusual.

As thirsty as I was, I knew I would never sleep until I could get a drink.

Making my way down to the kitchen, I tripped over something and barely caught myself, just before tumbling down the last few stairs. It took several hours before I was able to go back to sleep. I knew the break-in was making me feel insecure.

Brian was gone when I woke in the morning. He had put most of the house back in order, and I had heard absolutely nothing.

Still feeling insecure, I opened my Bible to Psalm twenty-seven, where I read, *The Lord is my light and my salvation; whom shall I fear? The Lord is the defense of my life; who shall I dread? Though a host would encamp against me, my heart will not fear; though war arise against me, in spite of this I shall be confident.*

The last verse ministered to my spirit as though meant just for me. *For my father and mother have forsaken me, but the Lord will take me up.*

After making my way into the kitchen, I found a note from that said, "Honey, I had to go to the office, but I'll be back shortly. Our plane leaves at 2:10, so be packed."

The kitchen had been tidied, but the few dishes in the sink needed washing if we were leaving town, so I did them up, then swept the kitchen floor, which was still peppered with cracker crumbs.

The library was strewn with Brian's many newspapers, slippers stuffed with dirty socks, empty coffee cups and crumbs from his nightly cookie and popcorn forays. I shook my head. No matter how many newspapers stacked up, if the rest of the space was tidy—it was clean as far as Brian was concerned. It must be a guy thing, huh?

I surveyed the mess for a minute, then sighed and began to straighten it, unable to imagine leaving town with the house in such disarray. But in the end, I left the papers for him to deal with. With a shrug of my shoulders, I headed toward the stairway.

In our room again, I pulled down the dreaded suitcases. I couldn't help frowning, wondering where we were going that required luggage in the first place. I much preferred day trips, where I could be home in my own bed by nightfall. For years, Brian had felt the same way, but the pull of the partners, who traveled whenever the muse struck, had been like a siren song he couldn't resist, and he was dragging me along all too often these days.

Tahiti, for instance. For my birthday two years ago, he'd surprised me with a trip, knowing I wasn't comfortable hobnobbing with the beautiful people on St. Croix or St. Thomas, which I knew he would've preferred. Tahiti wasn't much better, but he had distracted me with shopping and visiting the local tourist attractions, most of which at least had some historical value.

He could tell, after three days, that I yearned to get home, and I knew from his frequent phone calls home, that he wasn't faring much better. So he cancelled the rest of the trip and whisked me toward the home fires, for which I will be eternally grateful.

What I wish now is that he would just admit to his co-workers that we, as in he and I, have little desire to traipse all over kingdom come when we can enjoy all the comforts of home *at home*. I'm giving him six months to get it out of his system, at which time, I will turn my luggage into patio planters or garden fertilizer. Bury 'em deep—is my motto.

When the phone rang a short time later, I picked up to hear the less than agreeable voice of my boss, Principal Leo Hested. At age sixty-four, Leo is simply waiting out his days until retirement, all the while, attempting to hold onto what little remains of his hair.

In a crisp, business-like tone, he said, "Listen, we've had a small emergency, and we need you back tomorrow. See you then…"

"Now wait a minute. I can't do that. We're leaving town this afternoon."

"You can't do that!" he exploded.

I couldn't stifle an annoyed frown. "Leo, why on earth are you so upset?"

"Marigold Bliss, who, as you know, is no spring chicken, had a fall the other day, on some peas that were inadvertently spilled on the cafeteria floor. She's in traction in St. Bart's, and we can find no one to take over her sex education class."

My mouth dropped open and I blinked. "Oh, man, no way. I wouldn't touch that one with a ten foot pole, Leo."

I grimaced. It was unthinkable to call our fearless leader by his first name, even by accident. I waited, but he said nothing, no doubt hoping my slip of the tongue would force me to reconsider my decision.

Finally, he said, "It would only be for two weeks. She should, hopefully, be back by then."

"No way, *Leo*. Who on God's green earth decided second graders needed sex education in the first place? I absolutely refuse to teach it, because I object to it being taught at all to such young children."

"But you can't do that."

"I most certainly can. So there."

He was yelling now. "And I can fire your kiester, young lady."

I burst out laughing at the *young lady* comment. "You cannot. I have tenure."

"I'll figure out something. You just watch me."

I felt my eyes narrow in anger. "Give it your best shot, Bub."

He snorted, right before he said, "I'll expect you here at seven thirty a.m. on the dot."

"Leo, I already told you. I'm not coming," I said with exaggerated sarcasm.

With a loud click, the phone went dead and a dial tone took its place.

I was shocked at myself. I never talked to my elders that way. But I had taken about all I could handle of Leo's high-handed coercion. He had a reputation for sneaking around and nailing his teachers for the most insignificant and unreasonable of infractions. Like having the classroom windows open when it was a thousand degrees inside during the sweltering heat of late August.

Suddenly I felt a little sick at the idea of losing my job, but hey, after twenty-five years, maybe I needed a break. Maybe I would take advantage of time off and let my husband support me while I tackled my version of the Great American Novel.

When the phone rang again, less than a minute later, I felt my heart pounding in staccato, thinking it would be Leo again.

When I picked up, Brian said, "So, are you ready to roll?"

"Oh, no. Not yet. I was just getting ready to pack, when I was rudely interrupted."

"Well, get a move on, kid. I'll be home in twenty minutes. We'll have to hurry to be there for the in-depth security checks they do these days. See you shortly."

With that, he was gone, and I hung up, shaking my head. What was my life coming to?

Fifteen minutes later, he walked in the door as I closed and locked my bags.

Smiling, he said, "Here. Let me get those for you."

In a pleading tone, I said, "You know, I really wouldn't mind staying home. What do you say?"

"Too late. I already paid for the tickets."

"Where are we going, by the way? You never said."

"Orlando. I'm taking you to Disney World. You always said you wanted to go."

I frowned at him. "When did I say that? I never said that."

"Don't you want to go? Everyone wants to see Mickey Mouse, don't they? Don't you?"

I sighed. "Not particularly. Hey, I know. Let's don't and say we did, okay? Really. Couldn't we just wait and do this some other time? Besides, you promised we wouldn't go far."

He rolled his eyes. "Listen, honey. I know you. If I let you chicken out on this, we'll never get to Disney World or anywhere else, for that matter. You are such a party pooper these days. What's going to happen when you have to attend functions for my work?"

I stammered, "Well, uh—I'll cross that bridge when I come to it, I suppose."

Impatiently, he said, "Let's just go ahead with our trip, all right?"

I sighed, realizing he wouldn't be taking no for an answer.

He grinned, knowing he had won, then said, "So what can I do to get this show on the road?"

I grumbled, "Just give me five minutes to get ready. And while I'm doing that, you can go pick up the piles of newspapers off the library floor."

"Now? Why?"

"Because I'm not leaving our home looking like a toxic dumpsite while I go off gallivanting with you."

He laughed. "All right. All right. I'll take care of it."

After he disappeared, I made my way to the bathroom, touched up my makeup and did my hair.

A minute later, he peeked around the corner of the bathroom door. "Mission accomplished. So are you ready?"

"As ready as I'll ever be."

"You look good enough to eat."

"Flattery will get you nowhere, Bub," I said, raising one eyebrow at him.

"Okay, well, let's just go then, all right?"

The drive to the airport was silent as I resisted the idea of leaving my home. Someone had just broken in, for heaven's sake. I frowned. "Honey, did you remember to arm the security system?"

"You can relax. I took care of it."

"Good," I murmured as I laid my head against the seat and closed my eyes.

He pulled me over to sit beside him and leaned my head on his shoulder. He couldn't help but notice me stiffen at his touch.

"You okay?"

"Don't ask."

"Now, listen. I'm doing this for you, so I'd like to suggest you adjust your attitude and at least try to be a little cooperative."

I sighed, knowing he was right. *Help me, Lord.*

After checking our luggage, we handed our carry-on bags to the security guards, who rummaged through them thoroughly, before handing them back. Because of the short line, we had time to spare before taking off.

Brian smiled at our good fortune, looking pleased. "Listen, how about something to eat? I'll bet you're hungry."

"Whatever—you want," I mumbled, as he hoisted a carry-on over each shoulder and herded me toward a lounge area in the middle of a food court.

"So what would you like to eat?"

When I didn't answer, he said, "Never mind. I'll order for both of us."

He settled me at a table and went to the counter, returning a minute later with two miniature pizzas, two side salads and two sodas.

Setting mine in front of me, he patted my shoulder. "You'll feel better if you eat something."

Still wishing I were at home, I took a deep breath and tried to adjust my attitude to accommodate him.

"I got you pepperoni. So eat now."

"Mm-hmm, good," I said, after nibbling off a small bite.

He laughed. "I can't wait to be on our way. Just the two of us. I'm going to love it."

I said nothing, but concentrated on pouring the low-fat ranch dressing on my salad. After stirring it around, I took a bite and looked up to see him still smiling at me.

Covering my full mouth with my hand, I asked, "What? What are you laughing at?"

"Nothing. I'm not laughing. Just anticipating how it will be, just the two of us, away from the phone and the demands of our work. I can't wait."

I watched as he bit off a long bite of pizza, its stringy mozzarella cheese stretching between his fingers and his lips.

"Been spending too much time with the trave-holics in the office again, haven't you?"

An instant, fleeting frown flitted through his eyes. "Why would you say a thing like that?"

"You never used to like to travel. What changed your mind?"

"Honey," he said, laying down his fork. "Everyone needs to get away and have fun once in a while."

"I agree it's good to get away from the routine, but I can't understand this sudden yearning to see the world. I mean, you used to be satisfied going to Joplin to shop for antiques with me."

He said nothing, just stared awkwardly at his food.

I took a sip of my drink and turned to watch the people walking by. They came in all sizes and styles of dress. Kids with purple spiked hair and stacked heels wearing torn low-rider jeans passed oblivious elderly white males, wearing Walkmans, walking for the sake of their cardio systems.

Women in groups of two or three, congregated, talking, during their business lunches, while others were dressed up, shopping till they dropped. It was a slice of Middle America if ever there was one.

My cell phone rang just then, and I had to swallow a hurried bite before answering.

Chapter Eight

"Where are you?" asked a very annoyed Leo Hested.

"At the airport, waiting for our flight."

"Who is that?" asked Brian, looking confused.

"My boss, Mr. Hested," I whispered, covering the phone.

"Well, what does he want?"

"I'll explain later, okay?"

Leo, by now, was working his way from conniption to stroke, fueled by my lack of response.

"What is the meaning of this?" he bellowed. "I told you we needed you today, and here I find that you simply didn't show up. I can fire you for no notice. You realize that, don't you?"

"Leo," I said succinctly. "I told you yesterday that we were leaving town. We'll be gone—"

Turning to look at Brian, I waited.

"A week."

"A week?" I stammered. He hadn't told me that.

Leo stumbled on in his locomotive style. "But you can't do that. Okay, that's it. You're fired."

"*Leo*, you can't do that. You know I'm on sick leave right now."

Instant quiet ensued, as I waited for Leo to cross the line I had drawn in the sand.

Instead, he said, "I'll see you when you get back." With that he was gone, and I closed my phone, breathing hard, with my heart thumping wildly in my chest.

Frowning, Brian said, "What was that all about?"

"Well, I forgot to tell you, but Leo called yesterday and said they needed me to substitute for our sex educator, one Marigold Bliss, who slipped on peas in the cafeteria and ended up in traction. In fact," I said thoughtfully, "I'll bet she's suing their socks off."

Now shaking his head, Brian said, "Whoa, honey, I haven't got a clue what on God's green earth you're talking about."

I laughed. "I'll bet that did sound a little fragmented."

"Right. So start again—this time from the beginning."

They called our flight at that moment, and he dumped the lunch debris in the trashcan, before picking up our bags and taking my arm. As we walked toward our boarding area, I explained the previous day's conversation with Leo.

Brian's tone was annoyed when he said, "You've given the best years of your life to that school system, and this is how they repay you? Well, we don't need the money you bring in, so why don't you just quit?"

"I'll give it some thought. I mean, it would mean a lot less stress. But I'd miss those kids as much as I miss my own."

He handed our boarding passes to the flight attendant, who gestured us on, cheerfully offering her encouragement that we have a pleasant flight. The only pleasant flights, however, were headed *home.*

Brian found our seats, stowed our bags in the overhead compartments and settled me in the window seat. Bad move. My heart fluttered as I thought of being so far off the ground. Flying has never been my favorite pastime, so it was with trepidation that I sank deeper into the seat, snapped the seatbelt around me and leaned back, closing my eyes. *Help me, Lord. I really hate this stuff.*

Sensing my discomfort, Brian took my hand and squeezed it. "Listen, get a grip, will you? Honestly, we're going to have a great time, you'll see."

"I know. I just…"

"Just what?"

"I like having my feet planted firmly on the ground."

"I'd forgotten about your fear of flying."

"I'm not afraid of it, as much as I'm just not crazy about it."

"Same thing."

"No, it's not. I mean, I'm not hyperventilating or anything. Listen, give me some credit, will you?"

He smiled. "Of course. You just need to change your attitude. Learn to relax and let your hair down. You have to admit it's pretty hard to enjoy life if you refuse to fly."

"So that's what we're down to? Suddenly we can't enjoy the simple things? Just because your coworkers think you aren't living if you aren't seen in Mazátlan or St. Croix? Well, I beg to differ."

I lowered my voice at the stifling motion of his hand. "I've lived perfectly well, doing short day trips in the car, and I don't see why that can't be good enough for the rest of our lives as well."

"Jolie, please. Could we have this conversation later, when we can be alone?"

Smartly, I asked, "Oh, do people argue in Never-never land?"

His chin dropped and his brows lifted as he looked at me. "Say, what's gotten into you?"

"I don't know. Never mind. I just—never

mind." Once again, I leaned my head back and closed my eyes.

We'd been in flight for about a half hour when I suddenly sat up and opened my eyes. "Honey, do you smell something burning?"

He turned his head and sniffed. "Oh, man. What's going on?"

Instantly he was on his feet, making his way toward the flight attendant. Taking her aside, he spoke quietly to her then returned to his seat. He whispered, "Come on, honey, we need to move up to coach, where there are a couple of empty seats."

I whispered, "But what about the other passengers?"

"The flight attendant will take care of everything. Come on now, girl, move."

In minutes, we had stashed our bags in the overheads and settled into our new seats.

I asked, "What's going to happen now?"

"I think they're going to have to make an unscheduled landing. Buckle up, honey, just in case, all right?"

I shuddered at the memory of the in-flight fires and other emergencies I'd seen portrayed in the *Airport* series of movies of the 1970's. The thought did nothing to calm my already fretful mind.

It wasn't long before the captain's matter-of-fact voice said, "May I have your attention, please. Due to technical difficulties, we will shortly be making an unscheduled landing in Nashville. Your flight attendants will be asking you to adjust your seating arrangements in certain areas of the aircraft, and we'll appreciate your cooperation in this effort. We're sorry for the inconvenience, folks, and will do everything in our power to reroute you to your destination in a timely manner. So please bear with us, and as soon as possible, secure your seatbelts and prepare for landing."

I could overhear several coach passengers quietly discussing the possible causes for such a change in venue. Less than a minute later, someone behind us said, "There's a fire in first class!"

Our blond male flight attendant put up his hands and said evenly, "Now, please. Everyone stay calm. Everything is under control." I thought he was assuming a lot since he hadn't yet been back to first class to check things out.

As he disappeared behind us, Brian took off his seatbelt and stood. "Listen, I need to see if there's anything I can do. So stay put, okay?"

"Oh, honey…."

"I know you're frightened. But that's the reason I want to see what I can do. I'll be right back." I frowned in puzzlement. *He's leaving me because I'm frightened?*

He turned and headed toward the back as I began to pray in the spirit. Only the Lord could comfort the feelings of panic that threatened to undo me.

I looked up as people started pushing past my row of seats. A frail-looking elderly man slid into Brian's seat as I watched dumbfounded.

"Is everything all right?" I asked him.

"There's a fire back there. They're using extinguishers, but it's in the electrical system, so all they can do is try to keep it under control until we land. Sure hope it's soon."

"Oh, dear."

"You can say that again," he murmured, with a nervous shake of his head.

The plane banked sharply, and I could see the landing lights of the runway through my window.

With a rush of relief, I looked around and saw Brian as the attendant hurriedly crowded extra passengers into each row of seats. Finally he motioned the elderly man to make room for Brian, who squeezed in beside me.

The man next to me said, "The fumes are toxic back there."

A slender female flight attendant smiled, as if to calm my fears.

"Don't worry. He's incorrect. The fumes are not toxic, and we should be landing any second now." With that she took wet cloths from another attendant and handed them out, telling us to cover our faces with them. Her words were of little comfort. It didn't take a genius to know that all smoke is toxic to one degree or another.

Coughing at the irritating smoke as its foggy tendrils meandered into the space, I was relieved when the landing finally went without a hitch, and soon we were evacuated in an orderly fashion. Not a moment too soon for my frayed nerves.

Brian took my arm and steered me across the tarmac toward the terminal.

I looked at him and said earnestly, "Couldn't we just rent a car and drive the rest of the way to Orlando? Or better yet, couldn't we drive home?"

"Don't you realize we already paid for this trip? We're going, and that's the end of it, okay? Besides, it would take us nearly a whole day to drive it. Why would you want to do that anyway?"

"I told you, honey. I like having my feet planted firmly on the ground."

"I know, but it's simply not practical. Just take a few deep breaths. You can do this. You can."

"I know, but I don't want to. Please, Brian. Please rent a car. I'll even drive part of the way to Orlando, as long as you tell me which way to go."

"Oh, yeah," he said sarcastically. "I can see it all now. The woman who gets lost in parking lots wants to drive from Nashville to Orlando. We'd be lucky if we didn't end up in Moscow."

I laughed in spite of my annoyance. "Now that's ridiculous. In case you've forgotten your third grade geography, it's absolutely impossible to drive from here to Moscow."

"I know—" he said, grinning. "That's why I said it. To get you to lighten up. So lighten up, Teach."

He reached over, tweaking my chin, as I rolled my eyes.

In the terminal a minute later, we joined the throngs in line, trying to make connections to their destinations. Finally, realizing we were in for the long haul, Brian parked me in a chair and resumed his place at the end of the long line.

After an endless hour wait, he came to find me and said they were putting us up in the Holiday Inn, since there were no other planes available until the early hours of the morning.

"How early?"

"Six."

"Oh, dear."

"Come on, honey, they're bussing us a couple of miles from here. Then tomorrow a bus will pick us up at four a.m., so let's go get settled."

I shook my head. "I knew I didn't want to do this."

"Now, listen, it will be okay. In fact, depending on the way we look at it, this can be our first romantic night alone together in ages. A whole new adventure, you might say."

"It could be if I wasn't dead on my feet."

He looked at me. "I wondered about that. Why didn't you sleep on the plane?"

"How could I sleep when I worried we might either die from smoke inhalation or crash land? Huh?"

"Oh, now, honey," he said, leading me toward the charter bus. "There was never any real danger."

"Oh, yeah? Do you know how many *Airport* movies beg to differ? I mean, I've seen them all, and they aren't that far from reality. You know that, and I know that. So there."

He seated me and sank into the seat beside me as I stared out into the now dusky sky. He shook his head, "Well, it's clear that I can't force you to enjoy it, but I'm going to do everything in my power, during this trip, to change your mind about flying."

"You and what army?"

He chuckled, rolling his eyes. "Okay, okay. Now take a powder, girl, and relax, will you? Please?"

I leaned my head back and yawned, feeling overcome by fatigue.

"Oh, no, you don't. This is supposed to be a romantic evening. So the first thing we're going to do, after we claim our rooms, is rent a car and find a nice place to have a quiet dinner."

I frowned. "What time is it anyway?"

He glanced at his watch. "It's 8:30. Why do you ask?"

"By the time we get settled, it will be nine or later. I'm not used to eating so late. Neither are you, for that matter. Maybe we could just split a sandwich at the hotel restaurant. You know you don't sleep well on a full stomach."

He made a face. "Man, you are such a wet blanket."

"I'm sorry. Really, but I'm tired. It feels like I've been up since yesterday noon."

"Well, it's all in your head, honey, because you slept like a baby last night."

"And how would you know that?"

"Because I couldn't sleep, and I lay there, envying how easily you drop off these days."

"Well, don't bother to envy me. I'm not thrilled at being tired enough to sleep at the drop of a hat. Besides, I was awake for several hours last night, and you were the one sawing logs."

Studying my face, he said, "You weren't serious about splitting a sandwich, were you?"

"Yes. What? You were planning a ten course meal at midnight?"

"Well, I'd say that's a bit of an exaggeration, but I was hoping for a steak."

"Now, I don't think that's...."

"Listen, don't think, honey. Just relax and let me handle everything. You're just along for the ride. Okay?"

In a singsong voice, I said, "Please, just get me a bed. Any bed. Anywhere—and I'll do whatever you want—tomorrow."

He sighed in annoyance. "You're just not going to make this easy for me, are you?"

"I'm not doing it on purpose. I'm just tired."

"No, now we're going to have a nice meal, and you're going to enjoy it. Come on," he said in a low tone, helping me off the bus.

A half hour later, I glanced at my watch and shook my head. It would be at least nine thirty before we were ready to go eat.

As I sank onto the bed in our room, Brian hung up our hanging clothes, stowing our luggage in the closet. He snapped his fingers in my face. "Okay, I'm ready. Let's go eat."

My eyelids were heavy, and I sighed as he pulled me to my feet. I murmured, "I'm coming. I'm coming."

By the time a cab pulled to the hotel's front door, it was ten, and I was, by that time, pretty far gone.

Brian saw me struggling to stay awake as he motioned me to follow. "Come on. The cab is waiting."

I sighed, stifling a yawn.

"Stop this now. You can't possibly be that tired. All you've done today is sit."

I shrugged. "It's the change of routine and time that's so exhausting. Please, honey, can't we just go to bed and start doing the tourist thing tomorrow?"

"No, we can't, because I'm hungry."

"Well, the hotel restaurant is right over there."

"I want a nice meal."

Knowing I would not win this argument, I caved in. "Whatever."

He nearly dragged me toward the cab in his hurry. "Brian, slow down. I'm coming."

"Come on. I'd really like to eat before midnight."

He let go of my hand and gave the cabby directions as I slid inside.

I studied Brian's face in the dim light of the cab as we pulled away from the hotel. "You're really enjoying this, aren't you?"

Glancing at me in surprise, he said, "Yes, aren't you?"

"No. I'm sorry, but I told the truth when I said I'm tired."

"Okay, honey. We'll eat and then go right back to the hotel."

"You mean you'll eat."

"What? You're not going to eat with me?"

"I can't eat at eleven o'clock at night. It's too late."

"Then just have a salad."

I said nothing more as we pulled up in front of a steakhouse. *What in the world kind of steakhouse feeds people at midnight anyway*, I wondered.

Chapter Nine

We arrived at Buckingham's Steak and Seafood Palace at ten thirty. After being seated, our waiter informed us that they would be closing at eleven, so my husband, in tried and true take-charge fashion, held out his hand and said, "Well, then, don't go away, young man. I'm ordering for both of us right now." With a single glance at the menu, he said in one breath, "Two steaks, a ten-ounce T-bone for me, and a filet for my wife. We'll have side salads with low-fat Italian dressing and baked potatoes with butter and sour cream. Make the steaks medium, please, with A1 steak sauce on the side. Also bring us two unsweetened ice teas."

Taken aback, the sandy-haired young man jotted the order as fast as he could then simply nodded, before disappearing in the direction of the kitchen.

I said, "I told you I'm not excited about eating at this time of night. Why didn't you just order me a side salad and leave it at that?"

He didn't answer or even look in my direction.

Trying to cool my rising ire, I glanced around, studying the Palace décor. Amazingly, it resembled a medieval castle, with lances and swords adorning the terra cotta walls, and a full suit of weathered armor standing at attention against each vertical surface. Fortunately, they hadn't gone for period stone floors. The carpet was a muted rust and white with trellises of vines and flowers running through it.

The tables were glass and pewter-colored metal. The chair upholstery repeated the carpet design exactly. The lighting was indirect, breaking from medieval style, but tendrils of vine-y greenery crawled up the walls from large terra cotta pots and traced its way across the high ceiling, meeting other vines in the center of the room, as if we sat under a living bridal arbor. Tiny twinkling white lights peeked out from between the leafy vines, lending an air of romance to an otherwise rather large and austere space.

"Brian, what on earth has gotten into you? You never used to act like this."

After a brief pause, he admitted, "My coworkers say I need to be more assertive, so that's what I'm doing."

"With your wife?"

"Yes."

I said nothing, just waited for our meal to be delivered. I would've preferred a cup of yogurt and a piece of fruit.

Brian eyed me suspiciously. "You are going to eat, aren't you?"

"The salad."

At his look, I added, "Listen, could we talk about something else?"

"Sure—how do you feel about quitting your job to stay home and take care of me?"

"Take care of you? Since when? I mean, you're not exactly helpless."

He moved restlessly in his seat. "But it looks better for a partner in the firm to have a stay at home wife who dotes on her husband, not someone who teaches second graders."

I was incredulous. "Are you listening to yourself?"

"Of course. I'm just wondering how you'd feel about it."

"Well, I've given some thought to staying home, but I'd like to do it so I can write a novel."

"I can live with that, as long as you do it quietly.

I don't think the firm would approve of a partner whose wife is an artsy writer type."

I laughed. "You are kidding, aren't you?"

"No, my dear. I'm not. This is a very conservative firm, with definite ideas about what wives should do with their time, and I can say with confidence, that they will not be excited about a partner's wife, writing the Great American Novel."

"Well then, you can tell them to go jump in the lake, because I don't care what they think."

"Shh…you'd better, my girl. Because from now on, we dance to their tune or else."

"Or else what?"

His voice was low. "Never mind. Here comes our food."

At that point, I couldn't have shoved a morsel of food past the massive lump in my throat.

After cutting a bite of steak and dipping it in his steak sauce, Brian chewed thoughtfully, before turning to fix his level gaze on me. "Why aren't you eating?"

"I can't, so please, don't scold me."

He ate silently for a time before he finally said, "You know, I'm sort of interested to see how this partner thing will go. And I suppose I should explain why I've spoken the way I have tonight. The partners called me in the day I received the promotion and made it clear, in no uncertain terms, that they had in mind only a certain type of attorney to fill Ted Pardee's position."

He stopped long enough to sip his tea and dab at his lips with his linen napkin.

"In fact, they didn't come right out and say, "So will you change to fit the job description, but that's exactly what they inferred…."

With a grimace and a sigh, he said, "And I wanted that position so much, I couldn't say yes fast enough."

"Well," I said, morosely, "that explains a lot."

"It does, doesn't it?"

When I said nothing more, just sipped my iced tea, he frowned. "Well, aren't you going to say anything?"

"What can I say? It sounds like you've already dumped us into the ship of fools."

"How can you say that?" he asked in a low voice, looking stunned.

"Because, more than anything, I've always admired integrity and strength of character, and that's not what you're going for here, sweetheart. You're going for approval. And, if you'll pardon me for being frank, I see it as a sellout, pure and simple."

His fork, poised in midair at that moment, came to such an abrupt halt that the bite of steak it held ended up hanging from it for a brief second before he returned it to his plate.

He stared at me with a furrowed brow. "Is that what you think?"

"Yes. I mean, when they say jump, what's to prevent you from asking 'how high', simply for the sake of holding onto the job?"

With a look of consternation, his lips flattened into a thin grim line. "Now, listen, I haven't decided to compromise my integrity, and I am hurt that you would even suggest such a thing." In spite of his words, his eyes glanced around uncomfortably, as if even he knew his words were a lie.

I swallowed, trying to think of how to rephrase my statement. "I'm sorry if I've misunderstood you, but you just told me that I can't be me and express my artistic self in writing without offending the partners."

I took a deep breath, and continued thoughtfully," If I may be so bold—if you and I have to change who we are intrinsically—well, that, my fine, feathered friend, is a sellout, whether you admit it to yourself or not. And besides that, you said they aren't crazy about second grade teachers…

"Well, I've taught my whole adult life, and if I weren't burned out and ready to quit already, I can tell you right now that I'd probably keep my job just to watch them squirm—the stuffed shirts. That mindset, as far as I'm concerned, is a nasty form of elitism, not far from the country club scene."

I was picking up steam now. "You and I have never aspired to that sort of thing, and for good reason, I might add." After a pause, I added, "And if that's what you signed me up for, you can keep it, because I hate that stuff and so does God."

His food sat untouched as he studied my face. "What is this? You've never been this vocal over anything in your entire life. Why now? Huh?"

"I never had to, because we always agreed on everything, but if this is a harbinger of what's to come, I believe we've come to a parting of the ways."

I gave an audible sigh, unable to help myself. "I guess it boils down to one thing—You're saying I have to conform to someone else's idea of what—" I gestured, making quotation marks with my fingers, "*a good partner's wife* should be."

He said nothing as he pushed his plate away and stood, tugging his wallet from his pocket. I followed, saying nothing, but prayed silently. I wasn't sure I could stuff this particular genie back in his dinky bottle. But a larger question begged an answer. Did I want to?

The trip back to the hotel was silent, and I could tell Brian was stewing over my words. I hadn't meant to insult him, but I simply refused to roll over and play dead for the sake of the firm.

It was nearly one o'clock when I finally crawled under the covers and let my head drop onto the pillow. This vacation would definitely be memorable, but not for the usual reasons.

For the first time in our married life, Brian did not draw me into his arms and tell me he loved me, nor did he even lean over to kiss my cheek. Instead, he faced the wall away from me and simply went to sleep.

My last fleeting thoughts were fearful. What had I done in speaking my mind? Could I live with the consequences?

The wake-up call came all too soon, and brought reality crashing in with it. I could see, by the look on his face, even in the dim light, that Brian was still smarting from our discussion.

Ignoring his tiff, I gave him a wide grin and said, "Hi there, handsome. Care for a back rub?"

Instead of smiling, he slid from beneath the covers, wearing a scowl, and headed for the shower.

"Oh, good," I muttered under my breath. "The start of another really great day."

Ten minutes later, he emerged, unsmiling, from the bathroom and said, "We need to be out of here in fifteen minutes, so you'd better get moving."

"I'm on it," I murmured, pulling the hairbrush and makeup case from my bag.

Neither of us said another word as we made our way downstairs toward the front desk. The sky was like a huge black void outside the wall-to-wall lobby windows. When Brian gave the thin male clerk our room number, he punched it up on the computer and said, "Oh, yes sir. The bus should be here momentarily. I trust you had a pleasant night. Please help yourself to the complimentary breakfast being served in the alcove to your right."

Brian motioned me to follow him and I did, wishing I were at home in my own bed. The alcove was actually a huge room, about eighty feet by fifty feet. Never fond of crowds, I sighed, seeing the throngs of people milling around the hot tables of food. Three white-uniformed servers were hurriedly filling plates with scrambled eggs, bacon, sausage, toast, sweet rolls and bagels. A fourth young man was pouring drinks, coffee, juice or milk.

I asked for eggs, bacon and toast, with juice and coffee. A fifth server kindly accompanied me to an empty seat and set my coffee in front of me. I nodded my thanks and sank down to an anxiety-filled, silent meal, where I knew Brian would stew over his breakfast.

In the next fifteen minutes, I ate a couple bites of bacon and egg and sat pushing the rest of the food around on my plate.

"Honey," said Brian, with a look of irritation, "we're in a hurry. Why aren't you eating? You ate exactly nothing last night, and now this. What's going on?"

"Never mind," I said softly as I set down my fork and sipped my coffee.

Knowing I had said all I would say on the subject, he turned his attention to his food.

I watched as he ate a huge breakfast, studying his food as if it were a career-breaking legal brief.

Our ride appeared shortly afterward, and Brian seemed miffed that he wouldn't have time to finish his meal. These days, he seemed annoyed at anything that was beyond his control, including me. At the final call for boarding one of three buses, he grabbed a last bite of sweet roll, chasing it with a hurried sip of coffee and stood and motioned me to follow.

As we found places on the bus, he said, "You're not going to spend the entire trip moping, are you?"

I frowned. Softly, I said, "Me? You're the one acting like a bear, rudely awakened from sleep."

"Excuse me?" he said, and I could feel the tension congealing in the air around us.

I casually rotated my head on my neck and sighed, trying to ease the stress headache that nipped at my forehead. "Never mind. It's going to be great. We're going to have a lovely vacation."

I found myself nervously chattering to fill the uncomfortable silence, before I finally stared out the window to keep from meeting Brian's perturbed gaze. *Please, Lord, help me.*

We were boarded directly from the bus to the plane, this time a Boeing 747, even bigger than the DC-10 we had flown on the previous night. Just thinking of how they kept that big bird in the air made me hesitate at the door.

"Honey," said Brian, pressing on the small of my back, "You're holding up traffic. What's going on?"

"Nothing. Nothing," I said as I forced myself to smile at the upbeat flight attendant, who immediately read fear in my eyes.

With an even wider smile, she took my hand and whispered, "You'll be fine. Just take a few deep breaths, all right?"

I nodded, saying nothing, as Brian edged me toward our assigned seats.

He looked at me after I had fastened my seatbelt around me.

"Nervous?"

"A little."

"Oh, come now. You can admit it. You hate this. Every minute of it."

"Well, now that you brought it up, you're right." Wistfully, I added, "I just wish I were back in my own bed in my own home."

Resolute, he said, "It will be fine. Just like you said. We're going to have a wonderful time, meeting Mickey Mouse and Donald Duck."

"Oh, yeah. Something I've looked forward to for years."

He burst out laughing, and it made me relax a bit as he took my hand and squeezed it. I guessed the tiff was over. After an uneventful takeoff, we removed our seatbelts and got comfortable.

When we'd been airborne for about ten minutes, we were nearly hurled from our seats by unexpected turbulence. The captain came on after the fact, suggesting we might want to buckle up.

I had grabbed Brian's hand in my terror and held it tight enough to leave bruises.

"Honey, it's okay," he said, readjusting my hold on his hand and patting it. "Just take a slow deep breath. There's nothing to worry about. It's just an occasional air pocket bumping us up and down."

"How can you tell?"

"You forget. I've experienced turbulence before."

"Oh."

He frowned as my gaze darted out the window and then back at him.

"Listen, honey, why don't you lean back and close your eyes. I'm going to talk, so just fix your mind on my words, okay?"

I nodded, tightly closing my eyes.

"I wanted to tell you this anyway and just forgot. Did you know that Ginger Snipes just had her sixty-fourth birthday?"

Ginger was the firm's classy front office secretary/ receptionist.

My eyes jerked open. "Ginger? You're kidding. She doesn't look a day over fifty-five."

"That's what she was hoping the partners would think. She falsified her paperwork when she was hired ten years ago."

"What? Why?"

"Well, her husband, Dan, had a seasonal construction job, and she was worried that she would be put out to pasture, leaving them in financial straits, so she put on her records that she was forty-five instead of fifty-four."

I frowned in confusion. "How did they find out?"

"Well, some auditors came in to check the books not long ago, and they came across the discrepancy."

"What discrepancy was that?"

"According to government records, she had been paying into Social Security ten years longer than she should have."

"What did they do about it?"

"Well, that's the funny thing. You knew her husband died of a stroke last year, right?"

"Yes, I think you mentioned it…."

"Well, while the auditors were there, she and this guy, Larry, one of the auditing crew, got—well—close, and the partners noticed it. They usually discourage office romances, but they had little control over these outside guys, doing temporary contract work. Anyway, it all came to a head when the guy Ginger fell for, turned her in for falsifying her age. I guess his job came before his romance with her."

"Oh, dear. Poor woman. What happened?"

"Well, she had evidently bought him some Speedo trunks, and when she found out what he had done, she walked right up to him and pulled these electric blue trunks right down over his ears. In front of the whole office." He acted it out for me in pantomime.

He looked pleased, just then, and I realized, as I laughed, that his story had completely distracted me from my fear.

"Thanks, honey," I murmured, squeezing his hand.

"Don't mention it," he said, kissing mine.

Suddenly, I made a face. Brian had never been one to gossip before.

By the time his story ended, the turbulence had also ceased. But because I was worn out by the constant stress of the past week, I leaned back and dozed off.

I woke to the sound of the captain's low voice, requesting that we buckle up, in preparation for landing.

With my hand in Brian's, we walked out of the terminal into sweltering summer heat and overheard conversations referring to this spring being the hottest on record. "Oh, good," I said to Brian. "We left a beautiful spring at home to come down here to fry with Mickey and Donald."

"No, now don't think like that. This will be fun. You'll see."

The shuttle bus took us to the nearby Le-Grand Hotel Suites, a new and stunning but homey apartment suite, recommended by the firm. As much as I hated the firm running our lives, I had to admit, the place felt comfortable even to me—the world's most reluctant traveler.

When we were settled, I sank onto the bed and tugged off my shoes, before curling up to nap.

At the sound of my name, I sat up and blinked. Shortly Brian appeared at the door and frowned. "You're not thinking of sleeping at a time like this, are you?"

"What do you mean?"

"Listen, woman, we have places to go and things to do."

"After only three hours of sleep last night? You've got to be kidding."

"No, I'm not—now find some comfortable shoes. We're going to do the tourist thing."

"Honey, please, I'm not trying to be difficult, but since the bone marrow transplant, I struggle to put one foot in front of the other, just like I am right now. I can't seem to manage on so little sleep, unlike *some* people." The inflection in my voice made it abundantly clear that I wasn't going to be bullied.

He stood in the doorway, contemplating his next move as I once again curled up with my pillow and let my eyes close involuntarily. If he said anything else, I never heard it.

When I woke, the room was stuffy and hot, and I was drenched in perspiration. I rose and found a note on the glass-top table saying that Brian had gone to play a round of golf with another hotel guest. Even though the air conditioning was turned to its highest setting, nothing but stale, tepid air filtered wanly out as I held my hand in front of the vent.

I phoned the front desk and spoke to an apologetic manager, who said they would send a repairman within fifteen minutes. After waiting nearly forty minutes, I could no longer wait to shower and get into dry clothes. I would wait in the lobby until the repairs were completed.

No repairman materialized as I hurriedly dressed. My clothes were damp with sweat within seconds in the sultry room air. Feeling frustrated, I picked up the phone and listened to a busy signal.

Gathering my handbag and key card, I exited the room and made my way toward the elevator.

Two people in front of me waited for the harried manager to notice them. As I overheard him talking on the phone, it sounded like the building had numerous malfunctioning air conditioning units and dysfunctional computerized key cards, among other problems.

Even the sumptuous first floor lobby was oppressive with heat and humidity. As it turned out, the two people in front of me were checking out, and expressed their displeasure in no uncertain terms to the now-frazzled middle-aged manager, who apologized profusely and offered them each a certificate for a free weekend stay. Both waved away his offer, and after demanding refunds, each one picked up his luggage and stomped angrily toward the door.

My overheated heart went out to the man when he gazed at me, as though waiting for the other shoe to drop.

I said, "Listen, I don't mean to make your day any more difficult, but I need to ask—how soon will the air conditioning be repaired?"

"I have no idea what's going on. Each unit is separate, so it's highly unlikely, no—make that—impossible—for every unit to malfunction simultaneously." He shook his head. "I have never, in my life, seen anything like this."

"Well, have you checked to see whether the rest of the city is experiencing similar problems?"

"Oh," he said, distractedly rubbing the side of his face. "I hadn't even thought to do that. Thanks for thinking of it."

I nodded as he picked up the phone and dialed. Within seconds, he turned back to me. "It sounds like the entire city is struggling with a brown out, so perhaps people will be more understanding when they know it's not simply *my* problem."

A bead of sweat trickled down the back of my shirt and another hit my left eye, as I suddenly felt ill and breathless from the dense, sultry heat.

The manager looked at me, squinted and asked, "Are you all right, ma'am?" But I heard nothing further as I sank to the floor in a heap.

Chapter Ten

Brian was beside me as I lay on a gurney in the emergency room of an unfamiliar hospital.

"What happened?"

"You're dehydrated and went down with heat exhaustion."

For the first time, I noticed an IV line trailing from my hand to a clear bag on a stand beside the bed.

"I feel yucky. And it's not even cool in here."

"I know. The entire city is feeling the pinch of a brown out."

I shook my head. "I just want to go home, Brian."

"But what about our vacation?"

"I don't care about our vacation. I just want my own home and my own bed and my own fans and air conditioning. In fact," a thought had just occurred to me. "How did you manage to play golf in this awful heat?"

"Well, we played a couple of holes before packing it in. Even in the shade, it was sweltering."

"That's too bad. I know how much you love golfing."

"Yes, I made a new friend, an attorney from Ft. Lauderdale, who brought his family to see Mickey and Donald."

For some reason, I couldn't get my breath in the overheated room. With a worried look, Brian said, "Honey, what's wrong?"

"I don't know. I just can't breathe."

"I'll get the doctor. Hold on."

Shortly, an exhausted-looking young doctor came in and listened to my lungs. His white coat was smudged and wrinkled. He said, "Where do you folks live?"

"Not far from Kansas City."

"Well, if you know what's good for her, you'll get her home to her air conditioning. Her asthma isn't thrilled with our brown out conditions."

"Asthma?" I wheezed.

"Yes, ma'am. In fact, I'm prescribing a nebulizer treatment right now, and I want you to use your inhaler when you start wheezing. How long have you had asthma?"

"I don't have asthma."

"Oh, yes. You do now."

Within minutes, I had been set up with a thirty something, blond male respiratory therapist and was breathing medicated moist air from a tiny tube, leading from a nebulizer. After reading my chart, he remarked, "Listen, folks, I hate to put a damper on your vacation, but I agree with your doctor. You need to get home—I know, I know, you haven't had a chance to meet Mickey Mouse yet. Well, maybe next year."

To Brian, he said, "If I were you, I'd book reservations now, if you still can. I'll bet the entire population of tourists beats a hasty retreat elsewhere in this heat wave."

Brian pulled his cell phone from his pocket, and I heard him talking in low tones, before he finally closed it and said, "We're booked to fly out at 5:30 this afternoon."

I nodded, with the tube still in my mouth. I could feel myself breathing easier, but I felt exhausted from the effort and finally laid my head back and closed my eyes.

Just after the respiratory therapist left, Brian said, "Well, are you satisfied?"

"Satisfied—with what?"

Studying my face, he shrugged. "We're going home. I just wondered if you were satisfied."

Softly, I answered with another question. "What? You're acting like this brown out is my fault."

After returning to our steamy hotel room, we had four hours to kill before boarding our flight, and for some reason, Brian decided the only place we would be cool was a shopping center.

I said, "Honey, nowhere is cool right now, except maybe in water."

Irrationally, he argued, "Oh, the malls are always on top of everything. And besides, you can buy yourself something nice while we're there. You'd like that, wouldn't you?"

I grimaced, realizing I was finding it harder all the time to win an argument with my husband. *Why is that?*

When I didn't answer, he said, "Well, what do you say?"

"I really don't need anything, and I guess I feel like resting more than walking a mall."

"Oh, come on. Let's go shopping."

I frowned at him. "I don't get this. You hate shopping. So why are you so insistent?"

He tilted his head, wide-eyed. "Well, now that I'm a partner, I think we can afford for you to dress nicer. You know, get some really classy shorts outfits for summer, dynamite evening dresses—that sort of thing?"

"Evening dresses? Why would I want evening dresses when we despise the cocktail scene?" Looking intently at his face, I sighed. "Oh, I get it. Now that I'm a partner's wife, you want me to look the part. Is that it?"

Chagrined, he shrugged. "Well, sort of."

"Okay, so are you saying you don't like the way I dress?"

"I suppose if you're cleaning or doing something casual, it's all right, but please, for my sake, try to dress well the rest of the time, will you? Especially when you leave the house."

"Even to go garage saling and antiquing?"

"Well...."

"Well, what?" I asked, feeling a gnawing pain grip the back of my head.

"I was thinking maybe you could just go *buy* what you want from now on. I mean, why would you want to go and buy other people's junk when you can purchase whatever you want right off the store shelves?"

I made a face. "Honey, you know me. I like second hand shopping, and I've never been thrilled with mall shopping."

"Well," he paused, working his mouth into a pucker, "maybe I should put it another way. I don't want you shopping for junk anymore. Is that clear enough?"

"I don't buy junk. I only buy beautiful things other people have finished with." After a slight pause, I asked, "Are you forbidding me to go garage saling with Chrissy Dailey?"

"As a matter of fact, I am."

"But Chrissy and I have been junking for nearly thirty years. How can you ask me to give it up now?"

"You don't need to pinch pennies anymore, honey, and you don't need friends of Irish descent, like Chrissy Donovan Dailey. Don't you understand?"

I was angry now. "Oh, I understand perfectly. The firm is calling the shots, and you can't have a wife who likes being an ordinary guy, junk shopping, cherishing her friends and writing a Christian novel. Oh, I understand all right." Crossing my arms in front of me, I turned away from him. "Just take me home."

Silently, he pulled work from his briefcase and set it on the desktop. I turned over, wishing I could cool off, and finally dropped off to sleep.

Brian woke me by tapping my shoulder. "Honey, you need to get up. We have to get to the terminal."

I got up, washed my damp face, tidied my wilting hairdo and added last minute items to my bags, then did one last sweep of the room to make sure we hadn't left anything.

Brian held the door, while carrying our heavy bags and his carry-on, while I heaved my soft leather duffel over my shoulder.

Down at the desk, he signed us out, paid our bill and asked for a shuttle to ferry us to the terminal. His face grew grim, when the chagrined desk clerk informed him that the last shuttle had just left and the next one wouldn't leave for an hour.

"Then call me a cab, will you?" he asked brusquely. For the first time I could remember, he had neglected to say *please*.

"Of course, sir. Right away, sir."

Brian's sour look seemed permanently affixed to his handsome face.

I frowned, unable to believe the changes I was seeing in my husband. After thirty years, he was turning into a social climbing despot, and I felt sick at the thought.

The heat seemed even more oppressive as we exited the hotel and made our way toward the Yellow Cab, waiting at the curb. The inside of the vehicle felt like heaven, and the Middle Eastern cabbie, who looked at me in the rear view mirror, seemed inordinately pleased with himself as he said, "You like cool? I turn colder for you if you want."

"It's fine," said Brian, off-handedly.

I said, "It feels wonderful, thank you."

The cabbie turned onto the main thoroughfare, evidently in a chatty mood. "Everyone very hot, but I make cab cool. Like a dream."

I smiled, mentally predicting his success in marketing his cab-driving skills. He would, no doubt, find people in this city, who would take longer drives just to keep cool, adding to the jingle in his pockets.

A stifling crush of bodies met us as we entered the terminal doors. The torrid air reeked of old perfume and unwashed bodies as tired, cranky people of every description, made even more testy by the relentless heat, fruitlessly angled, trying to coax a ticket out of the harried counter clerks or from the lucky few travelers who actually held them in their hot little hands.

Like a scene out of a movie, an older red-headed woman ran up to Brian and said, "Listen, where are you headed? Wherever it is, I'll pay you three times what your tickets cost if you're willing to sell."

He gave her a stern look. "How do you know I even have tickets?"

"Just a lucky guess. But I'm right, aren't I?"

"Excuse me," said my irate husband, pushing past the woman to get to our boarding area.

"No, listen," the hapless woman begged, before Brian waved her off with a decisive and angry move of his hand, just as he grabbed mine and began pulling me away.

Under his breath, he murmured, "This is nuts. Remind me how much I hate this if I ever suggest it again."

I almost laughed, but instead said, "You say that now, but.…"

"Yeah, I know—don't say it. You told me so."

"Did I say anything?" I asked, innocently over the clamor of the crowd. It occurred to me that now might be a really good time for the Orlando police to practice their riot control measures.

The wait seemed interminable before we finally boarded the flight for home. The plane's air conditioning didn't seem to be faring much better than anyone else's, and I couldn't help but wonder why. Brian, now nearing the end of his rope, pushed me into my seat and seemed surprised at my unreceptive glare. I watched, frowning, as he removed his suit coat and carefully folded it before handing it to me.

"Put this down by your feet, will you?"

I pushed it into the skinny space between my feet and the thin gray wall.

Trying not to start anything I couldn't finish, I sighed, silently praying in the spirit as I closed my eyes and leaned my head back, hoping to sleep.

The pilot's cultured voice sounded over the PA system. "Because of the brown-out, ladies and gentlemen, I'm afraid the air traffic control system is also experiencing difficulties. In other words, folks, we're in a holding pattern, awaiting our turn to take off." After a pause, he added, "I know it's not very cool in here, but we seem to be experiencing some difficulty with our own air conditioning system. Hopefully, before we leave the ground, that problem will be remedied. The flight attendants will be taking orders for complimentary soft drinks, and I would like to suggest you just lean back and relax. Thanks for your cooperation."

Brian bristled at the captain's words. "I've never seen such a fiasco. Why does everything have to be such an ordeal?"

"Never mind. We aren't in any hurry."

With a perturbed grimace, he said, "How can you say that? You, who've done nothing but complain, since we left home?"

"I...."

"Never mind. Just go to sleep, why don't you?"

I turned away from him, swallowing a rush of tears that bubbled up in the back of my throat. I closed my heart as well as my eyes to the hurt, and I slept.

I didn't waken until Brian's hand touched my cheek.

"Honey, wake up. We're getting ready to land, and you need to buckle up."

When I sat up and reached for my seatbelt, he tipped my chin up to meet his gaze. "Ready to land?"

"I'm fine," I said in a wobbly whisper.

Within a half hour, we were deplaning to a dazzling, crisp sixty-eight degree day.

With a sigh and a glance around the parking lot, Brian said, "Home sweet home, huh?"

"I couldn't agree more. Now where did we park the car?"

He searched the area with his gaze and finally turned to me. "Can you recall where we parked?"

"Look at the ticket, why don't you?" As he dug in his pockets, trying to find it, I said, "Let's see. It wasn't far from the building. I think area B. Let's try there."

We located our car after a short search and headed home. I couldn't wait to be back in familiar territory and knew I was smiling like an idiot as we finally pulled into our garage.

"What's with you?" asked Brian, with raised brows.

"Can I help it if I'm happy to be home?"

"I guess not."

After setting down my bag inside the kitchen door, I pushed the button on the answering machine and heard the croak of my boss, Leo Hested. His authoritative voice boomed at me.

"Clean out your locker, Jolie. You're through teaching in this school system. And don't bother the union about it, because they are siding with me. You were supposed to give a written thirty-day notice to quit, and since you didn't, you're out of here. And that means no severance or references, and no right to appeal."

I sighed. The man had gone over the edge, and the sooner I could be rid of that job and him, the better.

There was a second message from my sister, Elly.

"Listen, Buzzy, my pet grooming business is up and running, and I was still wondering if you'd like to invest. You could make a pile of money, you know. And besides, it would be fun working together. Let me know, okay?"

Pushing the rewind button, I shook my head. "Not in this lifetime, sister dear."

Chapter Eleven

The next morning dawned cool and exquisitely beautiful, with the smell of spring in the air. As I opened the window, I could feel the breeze on my skin and smell the scent of the earth, beginning to swell with new life. I watched a fat mama robin red breast tilt her head, listening to subterranean sounds, and shortly pull a fat, juicy worm from the ground. Somehow, I never failed to be awed each time I saw signs of spring.

After showering and dressing, I went downstairs to find Brian reading the Sentinel at the kitchen table. He glanced up and smiled. "So you're finally awake. Get enough sleep?"

"I think so. What time is it?"

"Seven."

"Do you have to go to the office today?"

"No. I'm not going to let anyone know I'm

back in town yet. I mean, we still have several days before I have to be back at work."

"So what's on the schedule?"

"How about taking a walk?"

I couldn't stifle a grin. "Really? Haven't known you to do anything that prosaic in a long time."

"I still enjoy the simple things, you know. In fact, I think I enjoy them even more than I used to, now that life has gotten so complicated."

"Well, listen, I need to run over to the school and clean out my locker."

"Just like that? Why?"

"Leo fired me for no written notice." I sighed. "I feel sick that I might've lost my pension."

"Don't worry about it. I'm perfectly capable of taking care of you, you know."

"I know. It's just that—well, you know…."

"Well, listen, maybe I can threaten to sue the school system. You've put in your thirty years. You should be able to collect on that no matter why they let you go."

"That would be nice."

"Okay, well, we'll take our walk when you get back. All right?"

It was several hours later when I returned home with two boxes of personal possessions. Brian helped me haul them inside and then asked if I still wanted to go for that walk.

"In a minute, okay? Just let me get my sweat-shirt." I was feeling overwhelmed with a sense of melancholy, having just said goodbye to the people I had grown to love.

He picked up his coffee cup. "Give me a minute to finish my coffee and put on my shoes."

As we slowly strolled the neighborhood, he held my hand, swinging it the way he had when we were young. At length, he smiled. "This is fun. How long has it been since we did this?"

"I can't remember. A while."

"I guess. So tell me, how do you feel about being a partner's wife?"

My head bobbed as I said, "Well, I was trying to figure out how to break it to you gently."

"What?"

"To be honest, I'm not that wild about the idea."

"And why is that?" I couldn't believe he could ask the question, when I had already been so explicit on the subject.

"For the same reason we've done nothing but argue for the past four days."

"But we were just out of sorts from the heat."

I pulled my hand away and turned to face him. "Brian, you know very well that wasn't the real issue."

His eyes narrowed in a fit of pique. "Listen, I believe this promotion is a gift from God, a dream come true, and I'd really appreciate it if you could try to think of it that way, too."

I protested, "But I don't want to have to change for anyone. I told you that. And if changing is a prerequisite for this partnership, I would rather you turn it down. I mean, we aren't exactly hurting for money, are we?"

He reached out and grabbed me by the shoulders, giving me a slight shake. "What are you talking about? Can't you see this is the dream of a lifetime?"

I pushed out his grasp and glared at him. "That's not the way I see it at all. I see it as a trap. They've hung out the bait of 'success' like a brass ring, but to get it, you first have to crawl into the mold and let them remake you to your very core."

"Okay, tell me—in what way are they remaking me?" he demanded.

"Well, for one thing, you have to dress your wife like a Barbie Doll when that's not who she is. For another, you have to be seen at all the fashionable restaurants and resorts, and we have to travel when we would prefer to enjoy our home and each other.

"Not only that, but teaching second grade is out and garage saling with my best friend is out, to say nothing of my dream of writing. I mean, what's left that they won't have tampered with if you don't put your foot down right now?"

Standing ramrod straight, he shook his right index finger at me. "You're being ridiculous. I don't know what happened when you gave that bone marrow to your—Jeanette, but you've changed somehow. Can you explain to me what happened?"

"Nothing. And it has nothing to do with Jeanette. It's just that through that whole thing, I started seeing what was really important, and you know what? Remember that old quote by Shakespeare, 'To thine own self be true?' As I see it," I said slowly and with emphasis, "that's the-only-really-important thing here, as well as being true to our faith in God."

After stopping for a breath, I said, "Listen, honey, I am not saying any of this to hurt your feelings, but I want you to know that as far as I'm concerned, the changes required for this partnership are too great a price to pay. I'd rather we both took lower paying jobs, even moved into a smaller home, than resign ourselves to being what we really aren't—and even more important, what we really hate. Do you get what I'm trying to say here?"

"I just think you're not seeing the whole picture, Jolie," he insisted with a furrowed brow.

"The picture is crystal clear. The question is—what are you going to do about it?"

He shook his head, with fury in his eyes. "Oh, I get it now. You want me to choose between you and the partnership—is that it?"

"Well, I suppose since you put it like that, then yes. I've just realized I did the 'submerge your identity routine' when I was a kid, because I was adopted, and my parents subtly insisted I perform so they would love me. That's why I still struggle so—because it took me years to take off my mask and relax, comfortable just being myself. And let me tell you right now, I can't go back to that kind of existence. I just can't."

"You mean you won't."

At that moment, I happened to look around and saw several people, sitting on their wraparound porches, with ringside seats to our squabble.

"Honey," I said softly, "let's go home and talk about this. People are watching us."

Coloring as he noticed our audience, he hissed, "Fine thing, a partner, airing his dirty linen in public." With that, he turned and stomped back toward home.

He flung the door shut behind me and turned to face me. "So you're saying you won't cooperate with me—Can't you see that this is the opportunity of a lifetime—one, I might add, that most women would kill for?"

"Not me. I've been there and done that, and it's lousy. I will not change who I am to be a partner's wife."

He turned and stalked off toward his office and left me shaking my head. How were we ever going to get past this?

The phone rang just then and our son Cade said, "Hi, Mom. I've been trying to get in touch for several days. Where have you guys been?" Without waiting for an answer, he said, "I was worried about you. Because you never leave home, I wondered if something had happened."

"Oh, honey, we're all right. Your father just made partner, and he insisted we needed a vacation to get away from it all."

"He made partner? Well, tell him congratulations from me." After a slight hesitation, he said, "You took a vacation? *You* who hates to go more than a hundred miles from home?"

"Well," I laughed at his exaggeration, "I'm not quite that bad, but yes, he booked a flight to Orlando. We just got back, in fact."

"So how was it?"

I rolled my eyes involuntarily. "Don't ask."

"So you're saying you didn't have a good time?"

"That's exactly what I'm saying."

"What happened?"

"For the first time in years, they're experiencing

a record-breaking early spring heat wave that's taxed their resources beyond all limits. They had a brown out while we were there, and no one's air conditioning worked very well. That wouldn't have been so bad but it was about one hundred twelve degrees in the shade with terrible humidity."

"Bummer. So what happened?"

"Your father finally took some good advice and booked an early flight home."

"Well, glad to hear you're all right. Oh, I almost forgot to tell you our news. Beth is pregnant, due around Thanksgiving."

"Oh, sweetheart, I'm so happy for you. Congratulations. Give Beth our congratulations and our love, too, will you?"

"I will, Mom. You guys behave yourselves now."

When I'd hung up the phone, I found Brian in his closet, ripping clothes from hangers and stuffing them in a garbage bag.

"What are you doing?"

"I can't wear crummy stuff like this now that I'm a partner."

"You never wear crummy stuff."

"You know what I mean."

"What will you wear then?"

"I need to go shopping and get some high quality stuff. Armani—you know the drill. Top of the line designer."

Not long after, he drove off, without a word. When he came home several hours later, he was heavily laden with boxes and bags, but he wasn't smiling.

Brian didn't leave his office until I called him for supper, barbecued chicken, baked potatoes and salad. For dessert, I had made his favorite, a cherry cheesecake.

He sat down, surveyed the meal and bowed his head, and automatically said the blessing. After that, he simply rolled up the sleeves on his pale blue dress shirt and picked up his fork. Palpable tension hung in the air as he ate in silence.

Finally, I asked, "So how is the food?"

Without speaking, he simply nodded.

My fork held a bite of chicken, which I laid on my plate. "Are you going to pout like this through the whole meal? Through our whole lives?"

Still he said nothing. Only seconds later, I rose abruptly and left the table without eating a single bite.

He was locked in his office by the time I went downstairs to clean up the kitchen. I reheated my plate of food, took it out to the deck and ate to the accompaniment of twittering birds. They were better company than my mate.

When the phone rang, I had just put my plate in the dishwasher. I picked up to hear my mother-in-law say in a catty tone of voice, "For heaven's sake. Where have you been? We thought you and Brian had dropped off the face of the earth."

"Oh, I'm sorry, Juliette. We were out of town for a few days."

"And you never let us know?"

"It was a rather sudden decision on Brian's part."

She was quiet for a time before she said, "Well, you know, it's time for our annual visit. We booked a flight for the day after tomorrow. Just wanted you to know, this year we'll be spending two weeks instead of one."

"Oh, really? And why is that?"

"The spring in your part of the country is so lovely. I just thought we'd take advantage of it."

"So you're coming the day after tomorrow?"

"Yes. Is there some problem?"

"Well, yes, actually. This isn't a very good time for a visit."

"And why is that?"

"I'd rather not go into it right now."

In a snide tone, she said, "Well then, it can't be that much of a problem, can it? So we'll expect you to be there to meet our flight." She gave me the flight number and the time of arrival, clearly unwilling to believe their visit might be an inconvenience.

I sighed as I hung up and left a note on the kitchen table for Brian. Two could play this little game.

Upstairs, I pulled a mystery from my stash of books, opened it and began to read, but it wasn't long before my eyes refused to focus. Finally admitting defeat, I changed into my nightgown and went to bed.

If Brian came to bed, I never heard him, but I was alone when my eyes opened to another exquisite spring morning. After dressing, I went downstairs, and after noticing his closed office door, I poured a cup of coffee, then went to sit on the deck. The earth smelled damp, and when I walked around the yard to inspect my plants and flowers, the grass was dewy with moisture. My Nikes were drenched in minutes, but I didn't care.

Inside, I finished my coffee just in time to hear the phone ring. Jeanette Kelly spoke in her cultured tone. "I'm calling to see if you've recovered from your ordeal."

Unable to help myself, I laughed. "To which ordeal are you referring?"

"You mean you've had more than one?"

"Oh, yes. Several, in fact."

"Well, it sounds like you're in good spirits. So you are feeling better?"

"Oh, yes. I'm fine now. What about you?"

"My oncologist says I'm well, only stops

short of using the word 'cured'."

I couldn't help but smile. "Well, I'm glad for you. Really."

"Thanks for that. In fact, thanks for everything. If it hadn't been for you, I probably wouldn't be here now."

I didn't know what to say.

She continued, "Well—I was just checking up on you. Glad to hear you're feeling better."

"Thanks… Jeanette, is there something else you wanted to say?"

"Well, I—uh…." Something was up with this lady, who never stuttered, stammered or otherwise lost control.

"It's okay, Jeanette. I'm listening," I coaxed.

"Well, I was wondering if perhaps you'd like to meet for lunch some day soon. I mean, you don't have to, if you'd rather not, but—well…."

"Of course. I'd enjoy that." I had almost said 'I'd love to', but stifled the words, knowing effusive 'gushing' would make her uncomfortable.

"Oh, that's fine," she said, sounding pleased. "Shall we pin it down on the calendar?"

"Well, I'd love to, but I'm afraid my husband's family is coming for a two-week visit."

After a pregnant pause, she said, "Of course—family. Well, you can't be running off while you have guests."

"Oh, no. Listen, these are Brian's parents,

and to be honest, I'm not their favorite person, so—well—let me just say, I'm sure I'll be glad for a break, if you don't mind me phoning some morning to schedule something. Would that work for you?"

"That would be fine. Well, okay. That's settled."

She seemed relieved, and I wondered if she struggled through all her social relationships. Perhaps closeness was scary for her. I was feeling a bit shaky myself.

Chapter Twelve

Brian came out of the office after I'd hung up the phone. He stood in the doorway, holding his coffee cup, as if trying to decide whether or not to speak to me. Finally he said, "Who was that?"

I warmed my coffee and sank into a chair. "Jeanette. She wants to meet for lunch."

"Your mother? Why?"

I shrugged. "I don't know. I guess she's decided she wants us to get acquainted."

"You're not going, are you?"

I frowned, feeling confused. "Yes, why?"

"I don't think it's a good idea."

"But honey, you were the one who encouraged me to go meet her."

"Yes, but that was before I was named a partner."

"What does that have to do with anything?" I

asked in annoyance.

"Though they didn't say as much, it was very clear that the firm wants partners to maintain certain social and economic positions—to hold certain values. They like the idea of solid family values, not broken families. Not flimsy bonds, not adoptions or diluted bloodlines."

I blinked, trying to get this straight.

He demanded, "Well, aren't you going to say anything?"

"To be honest, I don't think I'd better, or we'll be in the middle of an argument faster than you can say *Jack be Nimble.*"

He filled his coffee cup, added his creamer and sweetener and turned, leaning against the counter. His left brow danced upward as he waited, knowing I was building a head of steam.

Finally, I said, "No diluted bloodlines, huh?"

He nodded.

"How did the subject even come up?"

"It didn't actually, but all that stuff was inferred as beneath the firm."

"Then *I* am beneath the firm. Isn't that what you're saying?"

He put up both hands in protest. "Now, I didn't say that, but I am saying this. I think in this case, it's best just to let sleeping dogs lie."

"What, may I ask, does that mean?"

He took a long, slow sip of his coffee before

answering. "I didn't tell them about your adoption or the rape. I mean, it's not like they have to know, but you know, people talk, and if you and Jeanette are seen together and there are questions… Well—I just think it's better not to even open this particular can of worms."

"So you think I should just let the only mother I have left—well—jump in the lake, for lack of a better term?"

"Just let her go, honey. Don't do anything to rock the boat. I mean, I've got to prove myself here. Have to uphold the firm's values."

I gritted my teeth before I took a deep breath and said evenly, "You mean the party line. Honestly, Brian. I can't believe you're saying these things. I don't know who you are anymore, and I don't think we want the same things. I *will* be seeing my mother, and there's nothing you can say that will change my mind.

"In fact, the reason I gave her my bone marrow in the first place, if you recall, is so she might have more time in which to maybe come to know the Lord. So what if I refuse to spend time with her? Who's going to be Jesus to her then?"

"Now you aren't the only one He can use to soften her heart."

"That's true, but what if He's chosen me for the job?"

Frowning, he set his cup down hard, making

a brown puddle on the table as it spilled over the top. Clearly angry now, he clamped his hands to his hips. "Hey, what's with you? Where's the woman who said, "If she wants this to be a business relationship, that's okay with me? Why are you changing your mind all of a sudden?"

I shook my head, knowing he was purposely choosing to misunderstand.

"I was hurt and angry when she rejected me again. If anyone should be able to understand that, you should. You watched the whole thing. But now, she wants a relationship. What kind of person would I be if I held her previous attitude against her?"

"Just admit it. You're being obtuse because you don't want me to be a partner. Well, I *am* a partner, so get over it. And you'll skip this touchy-feely stuff with Jeanette if you know what's good for you."

After an uncomfortably long pause, I finally said, "You mean what's good for *you*, don't you?"

"Okay, good for me. What's so wrong with that? I've worked hard for this partnership, worked for years, with my eyes on this goal, and now that I've got it, you're doing everything you can to undermine it."

I shook my head. It was like talking to a lamppost. "I'm sorry, Brian. If this is what it's come to, then I just have one thing to say. You'll have to do what you have to do, and I will do what I must. It's not the way I want it, but I will not live the way the firm dictates." I stopped for a breath before adding, "In fact, have you noticed that whatever topic I bring up, you counter with the opinion of the firm on the subject?"

"That's because you don't know the ropes yet. But you will."

"I already do, and I don't like what I'm seeing. As I said before, I will not change who I am simply to please them."

He frowned, pursing his lips. "You know, don't you, that disobeying your husband is sin?"

"How dare you throw that in my face?"

His voice was unwavering. "Think about it. You know I'm right."

With that, he stalked back to his office and closed the door harder than necessary, as if to prove a point.

Because I felt stifled in the house, as if I couldn't breathe, I went out on the deck and sank into a cushy chair, tucking my feet under me.

"Is he right, Lord? Am I supposed to comply when what he wants is wrong? I'm really confused here. Please, show me the way."

The birds flitted around me, but their songs seemed oddly out of tune, as though they, too, felt the confusion in the air. Shortly I went back in the kitchen, pulled my Bible across the table and let it fall open.

Psalm 16:4 said, *Their sorrows shall be multiplied that hasten after another god; their drink offerings…will I not offer, nor take up their names into my lips. The Lord is the portion of mine inheritance and of my cup; He maintains my lot. I have set the Lord always before me; because He is at my right hand, I shall not be moved. Therefore my heart is glad and my glory rejoices; my flesh also shall rest in hope.*

I talked to the Lord, asking Him what to do. Was I to do it Brian's way or argue my point at every turn? It didn't take a genius to see the bumpy road ahead if I argued. I felt the Lord whisper to my heart that He would take care of everything if I chose to rest, waiting on Him for answers.

I said, "Okay, Lord, for the time being, I'm going to cooperate when I can, but I still believe you want me to spend time with Jeanette."

I knocked on Brian's office door and heard him mumble a grumpy, "Come in."

Once inside, I studied his stern gaze, before looking away.

"Listen, Brian, I've been thinking about what you said, and I am honestly not trying to be difficult, and I will try to cooperate when I can, but I want you to know—I will be spending time with Jeanette." Again meeting my gaze, he sighed, set down the pen in his hand and said, "Well, if that's what you've decided, what can I say?"

"I just wanted you to know."

"Okay, now I know. So what do you want me to say?"

"Nothing." I closed the door softly and felt anxious butterflies fluttering in my chest.

When I'm nervous, I usually throw myself into projects at school, but since I no longer worked there, I put on a sweatband and pulled out my cleaning supplies. If nothing else, I would have the cleanest house this side of the Bermuda Triangle.

I started with the kitchen, hauling a six-foot wood ladder from the pantry. I cleaned cupboards, scrubbing the grime from the display area on top, where I have silk flowers and baskets, a few standout antiques and lots of dust bunnies collecting as well.

The kitchen floor shined by the time I dripped sweat all over it, punctuating the success of my efforts.

In the living room, I dusted, moved furniture, picked up newly vacuumed rugs and cleaned under them. I removed cobwebs from corners and finally surveyed my handiwork. Still not satisfied, I rearranged furniture until even the look was fresh and new.

In the library, I repeated the process until everything shone and glistened. The library windows were gray with dirt, so I cleaned them inside and out with Windex, and ended up scrubbing outlet covers and woodwork and sweeping the ashes from the fireplace.

After washing my hands and face to remove grime and sweat, I cleaned the two main floor guest rooms.

I had just shoved the antique brass bed toward the wall with a resounding thump before I noticed Brian at the door.

"What," he demanded, "on God's green earth are you doing, making such a racket?"

"Just cleaning. It's needed it for some time. Never had the time to do it while I was working. Now I do. It's that simple." I knew I was chattering nervously, but I just couldn't seem to stop.

"Well, keep it down, will you? And watch banging furniture into the walls."

"I will. Sorry," I murmured, feeling suddenly deflated. He hadn't said a word about how nice it looked.

I swallowed hot tears that threatened as I laid the rugs back in their places.

I realized he was obsessed with the partnership, and I was fully convinced it would take the Spirit of God to show him what I already knew.

By afternoon, I had run out of things to do, but not out of nervous energy. Before I knew it, I was on a ladder, scrubbing the siding and shutters and polishing the rest of the windows.

Brian appeared at the bottom of my ladder. "You know, you don't need to work like a char-woman anymore. Just look at you, all smudgy and dirty. What if someone should see you looking like this? Come down now. We can hire this stuff done. You know that, don't you?"

I licked my lips and sighed, trying to think how to put this.

"Honey, I clean when I'm anxious, and the amount and depth of cleaning depends on how upset I am."

In a low voice, he said, "So you're trying to tell me you're extremely upset. Is that it?"

I nodded, hoping it would give him pause.

His eyes widened as he gave an exaggerated sigh. "Okay, okay. I get it. But I want you to in-terview cleaning ladies as soon as possible."

"What will I do with my time if I can't clean my own home?"

"You'll join a garden club, or if you'd rather, a book review club. You can volunteer at the hospi-tal or a nursing home. Of the two, a hospital would, of course, be preferable."

"Could I come and work for you at the office?"

"Oh. No. I don't think that's such a good idea anymore."

"Why not?" He had been asking me to con-sider it for years.

"The firm doesn't approve of the partners' wives working for pay. And they aren't fond of having wives underfoot, involved in office politics either."

My mouth dropped open in shock. "Underfoot? You think I'd be underfoot?"

"Maybe I didn't put that quite right." He tilted his head, met my gaze and raised his brows. "You're purposely misunderstanding what I said, aren't you?"

"No, I'm not. Okay, well, I suppose I'll just have to find other things to do with my time, won't I?" I was thinking about the book I wanted to write.

He motioned me off the ladder and held me briefly, if loosely, in his arms, as if tossing a bone to a dog. Then, noticing my grimy shirt, he let go of me. "I'm sure you'll do just fine."

I, however, was not so sure.

"Listen," he added, turning my chin up to meet his gaze. "Are you sure I can't talk you out of this little get-together with your mother?"

"Um, nope. That's one thing that's not negotiable."

"Well, see that you keep it under your hat, then, all right?"

I sighed, frustrated. "I suppose."

"Good. I'm hungry. What do we have to eat?"

A few minutes later, I got busy and fixed one of his favorites, sloppy joes with salad and fruit. He made a face as I set his plate in front of him.

Feeling confused, I asked, "What's the matter?"

He shoved the plate away. "I can't eat junk like this anymore."

"What?" I swallowed, trying to hide my hurt.

"Ground beef is no longer the meat of choice. From now on, you no longer buy ground meat. You buy steak and cut it up. Do stir-fry or stroganoff, if you want, but no more hamburgers or sloppy joe's. No more spaghetti and meatballs. No more chili. Got it? No more ground meat."

"Honey," I said, "what is going on? These are foods you've loved for thirty years. I don't get this."

"Partners don't eat like that. They eat food meant for the gods."

"The gods. I see." But I didn't. This was getting ridiculous. Trying not to let my emotions run off with me, I stifled my thoughts, submitting them to God. As Brian watched, I simply took the plate away and started cooking again. Now I knew what I would be doing with my spare time.

Chapter Thirteen

He cleared his throat. "You know, honey, we could hire a woman to cook."

"It's okay. I'm cooking," I insisted evenly.

He picked up his newspaper and hid behind it as I boiled water for rice, chopped vegetables, and cut sirloin into small cubes.

I had just pulled spices from the cupboard when he looked at me over the top of his tiny bifocal glasses and newspaper. "Oh, and no more garlic. It's too ethnic. Use cilantro and onion instead."

"No more garlic? But you love garlic."

"Not anymore."

"But I hate cilantro. You know that. In fact, you hate it, too. You've told me so a thousand times."

"Well, we'll just have to get used to it. It's the *in* thing to use these days."

Frowning, I stirred the veggies into the meat. "Okay. I'll season your food with it, and make a separate dish for me without it. I hate that stuff."

"Whatever."

Ten minutes later, he began to eat. "Is this instant rice?"

"It's Minute Rice. The same kind of rice I've always used."

"No more instant anything."

"It's the only instant thing I use. But you like it."

"Not anymore," he repeated.

I blew out a frustrated puff of air. "Okay. No more Minute Rice," I said, starting a list.

"Here," he said, handing me his plate. "Dump off the rice, please."

My mouth fell open. "Are you serious?"

"Yes. Very. Now please, just do it."

After swiping the rice off his plate and onto mine, I said, "That's the only rice I have."

"Then I'll get along without the rice tonight. Just be sure to buy another kind tomorrow. Partners eat a lot of rice." I made a face. I loved Minute Rice, and no one would change my mind about that.

I needed to be alone to think. Excusing myself, I escaped to the covered deck, hugging the post, looking into the sky, where clouds had obscured the sun, and the wind was beginning to blow in earnest.

I watched as a huge gust of wind blew rain in my face that mixed with my tears, but still I could not go inside.

Finally, drenched to the skin, I stepped inside and took off my shoes, planning to take a shower.

Looking stern, he demanded, "What on earth has gotten into you? You're drenched. Go change. Now."

Suddenly, I turned back to him and said resolutely, "Oh, I forgot to tell you. Your parents and brother will be here for their annual visit, starting tomorrow. Only this time, they're staying two weeks instead of just one."

"What? Why didn't you tell me this before?"

"I left you a note, but you must not have seen it."

He hurried to stand beside me and took hold of my upper arm. "You've got to call them back. Tell them it won't work, not for another month at least. I've got no room for them in my life right now."

"Then you call them."

My frustrated tears mixed with the shower water that reddened my skin and beat on my head. "I can't do this, Lord. I really can't. You've just got to help me."

A short time later, I dressed and walked downstairs to find Brian, dragging furniture toward the garage.

"What are you doing?" I stood, obstructing his path.

"Dumping our old furniture."

"But why? I love that furniture. It's exactly what I would want at any price."

He frowned. "Most of this stuff you got second hand, though, didn't you?"

"You know I did. I got it nearly new and in perfect condition. It was a godsend."

"Partners don't live with used furniture."

"But *I* do. It's mine. Please, Brian, don't do this. There's absolutely nothing wrong with this furniture."

"I'm calling the junk dealer to come and haul it off tomorrow. Then we're going shopping for new."

"I don't want new. I want that furniture. Could we at least put it downstairs? Please, Brian?"

"No, it's going."

I had reached the end of my rope and couldn't help it. I burst into angry tears and shouted at him. "Who are you? I don't know you anymore, and I like you even less. You don't care one iota how much you're hurting me. You're crushing the life from me an inch at a time!"

With a grimace and a wave of his hand, he brushed me off and returned to the living room for another piece of my beautiful chintz-covered furniture.

As I followed him, I said, "If you get rid of my furniture, you are saying goodbye to me, because I will not let you do this. I go where my furniture goes."

He turned with raised brows and tilted his head in disdain. "You're bluffing. Where would you go? You can't live without me."

"I'll figure it out." My voice rose as I said, "You've already told me to change my personality, dictated what I wear and eat, decided what I must do with my time, who I can be friends with and now you tell me I can't keep the furniture I love. Well, just forget it, because I can't do this. I can't!"

I was screaming now, feeling like I could jump out of my skin. Suddenly Brian grabbed me and pulled me into a bear hug, pinning my arms to my sides.

"Stop it. You're hysterical. You keep this up, and I'll have you committed, Jolie. I'm not kidding."

I fought against him until finally he let go and pushed me away from him. He scowled at me. "Just go, why don't you? Here I am, trying to give you everything you could ever dream of, and you're acting like a crazy woman, completely out of control. Just go."

"Okay, I will. But you will leave my furniture in the garage. You will not get rid of it."

"Fine. Do what you want with it, but I want it out of here by this time tomorrow. Is that understood?"

I nodded as my chin quivered with stifled hurt. After brushing past him, I hurried toward the stairs, before stopping abruptly in my tracks.

Confidently I turned, met his gaze and glared at him. Softly, I said, "No. Now wait a minute. This is *my* home. It's you who are going to leave. You pack your bags or I will call your boss and tell him what's been going on."

He laughed. "You think he'd side with you?"

"Won't he? I could share our disagreement. Or even better—what will he think when I tell him you've threatened to commit your wife to a mental hospital?"

I could see him mulling it over. Looking grim, he finally said, "Okay, I'll go, but don't you utter a single word of this to anyone. Do you hear me?"

"I hear you."

In twenty minutes, he was packed, having completely cleaned out his closet and drawers. I shook my head in confusion. How had things deteriorated so profoundly?

After he slammed out the door, I surveyed my surroundings. Fortunately, he had only moved two chairs, a trunk and two side tables to the garage. With great effort and much perspiration, I dragged them back inside, after which I sank down into a chair, breathing heavily.

"Lord, I tried—I really tried to be the peacemaker, to do the right thing. But I'm confused, Lord. I don't know who I am anymore. I'm not a teacher and maybe I won't be a wife for long." With a dejected sigh, I added, "Help me."

After starting a load of dark laundry, I pulled a yellow legal pad onto my lap, looped an errant lock of hair behind my ear and began to make notes. I jotted down all the character qualities that make me who I am. Then I added a list of all the things Brian demanded I change. The only thing he hadn't gotten around to changing was the color and style of my hair and the makeup I wear. But perhaps given a little more time....

I scribbled a jagged line through his list and underlined my own. I would read this list everyday to reinforce my identity. I added all the activities and people I enjoyed. Then I wrote down my dreams for the future. No one could steal my dreams. No one could change my likes and dislikes without my permission, and I wasn't giving it.

And as much as I had always struggled with my identity, I refused to give up what little ground I had made. Instead of feeling devastated, I felt furious.

Opening my Bible, my eyes fell on the last four verses of Psalm twenty-eight.

"Blessed be the Lord, because He has heard the voice of my supplication. The Lord is my strength and my shield. My heart trusts in Him, and I am helped. Therefore my heart exults, and with my song I shall thank Him. The Lord is their strength, and He is a saving defense to His anointed. Save Thy people, and bless Thine inheritance; be their shepherd also, and carry them forever."

Tears filled my eyes as I pondered how the Lord had showed me the truth—that being a King's kid was all the identity I would ever need. I was secure in Him, even though my world had been turned upside down.

Not long after, I got up and started another load of laundry, realizing many of Brian's clothes were still there. No doubt, he would buy new to replace them.

In the kitchen a while later, I made Minute Rice and ate it like cereal, with milk and brown sugar. It tasted heavenly. Because I wasn't full, I made toast and topped it with peanut butter and jelly. I chased it with a glass of milk, enjoying every morsel. It hit me, just then, that I was doing everything Brian despised. Why had he married me in the first place?

Do I still want to teach? I asked myself as I placed my dishes in the dishwasher, and I knew immediately, the answer was no. I would not seek another teaching job. "Then what do you want to do?" I asked myself out loud, enjoying the sound of a human voice.

After a moment's thought, I said, "I want to write. I've always wanted to write."
After a beat, I added, "And paint. I want to try my hand at painting, just to see if I can do it."

My adoptive mother, whose name was Phyllis, was a talented poet and sculptor, but she had nixed my endeavors in that vein with one swipe of her hand. She had said gravely, "Your talents obviously lay elsewhere, my dear."

She had been wrong about a lot of things over the years, though I hadn't realized it until recently. Not only that, but she had made a verbal list of my talents. In the end, after eliminating what I wasn't gifted in, it was a very short list indeed. I recalled the conversation as though it were yesterday.

She had pulled me to her, surveyed me thoughtfully and said, "You have beautiful eyes, a tender heart, and you make a wonderful friend.

However, as far as musical or artistic talent goes, I deduce that your gifts lie elsewhere." Where, exactly—she had never quite *deduced*.

In spite of her nay-saying, I had successfully studied decorating books after moving into our home, and developed an eye for color, texture and line. I had decorated the space to my satisfaction and even now, take great comfort in its distinctive character and warmth. It suits me to a tee, and I feel pleased when others ask for the name of my decorator.

In fact, I had surprised myself many times, by simply pouring out in writing, what was inside me. Over the years, people had commented favorably, leading me to believe that perhaps my mother didn't have all the answers after all.

I studied my list of dreams and decided I could wait no longer to try my hand at everything at least once before I died. I turned the page over and made a new list of what I wanted to try. Writing topped the list. I would write, beginning immediately— things simmering inside of me, things I needed to dump. Venting should be therapeutic.

In the office, I checked my supply of diskettes, copy paper and all the reference books a writer needs. With nothing lacking, I would begin writing my novel tomorrow.

After changing the laundry and pulling out a

threadbare but soft cotton sweatshirt and khaki shorts, still warm and fragrant from the dryer, I had a yen to wear them. Their familiarity was somehow comforting in my present chaotic state of mind.

Dressed in my wonderful old clothes, I wrapped a headband around my hair. At that moment, I could hear the siren song of the computer, calling me to get my thoughts on paper. Without further prompting, I began to dump all the pain of the past few weeks, then of the earlier years, onto that screen. Page after page I wrote, feeling lighter just with the telling. I finally ran out of things to write at two forty-two a.m.

Re-reading some of what I had written, I realized that until the last few weeks, I had been satisfied with my marriage to Brian although he had been somewhat controlling and even arrogant at times. And until the partnership issue surfaced, I had relatively little to complain about. I shook my head, trying to understand how a promotion could've changed his personality so radically. Had I never really known him?

Finally unable to complete a rational thought, I climbed the stairs and slept in my soft, rumpled shorts and shirt.

In the morning, I woke to the ringing of the phone. With a glance at the clock, I saw that it was 8:20. Picking up, I heard the sound of my mother-in-law's voice.

"Jolie, where are you? You were supposed to pick us up at the terminal."

"Oh, dear. I'm sorry. I forgot. But honestly, this is really not going to work out, so please, have a cab take you to a hotel. Your son doesn't live here anymore."

With that, I gently replaced the receiver, before taking it off the hook and covering it with Brian's plaid silk-covered pillow. Both the pillow and receiver slid to the floor, where I left them as I drifted back to sleep.

I woke again at noon, feeling overheated, with the sun shining in my face through the skylight overhead. After rubbing the sleep from my eyes, I stood, made my bed up with often-washed, soft, clean sheets and slipped into the shower.

Not long after, I made a sloppy joe for myself and chased it with cherry Kool-Aid, from a twenty-year old packet I found crumpled behind some noodles in the pantry.

I knew I was doing everything out of spite, but it didn't seem to be hurting anyone, and it felt wonderful to be able to choose what I wanted to do, especially since I hadn't been able to do that in so long.

After finishing the laundry, I browned hamburger and made spaghetti and meatballs, thawed some French bread, planning to make garlic bread, and stuck it all in the fridge. I felt like I was coming home.

In the office, I pulled up the files I had written the previous night and glanced over my notes. I would let it all gel for a few days and go back later to make additions and corrections. Then again, feelings didn't need correcting, did they?

Opening a new file, I tried to recall some story ideas that had occurred to me in the not too distant past.

My imagination, according to my adoptive mother, had been very active at the age of three, when I dreamed up three imaginary friends, Benjy, Gadfry and Pete. When she mentioned it for the first time only a few years before her death, Mother seemed slightly embarrassed and wondered aloud why I had no imaginary *girl* friends. It had me wondering about the state of my mental health at three years of age, no less. Now I saw how dumb it was to even think about it. And instead of wondering about myself, it now had me wondering about *her.*

Chapter Fourteen

Without stopping to think up a title, I began to type, letting my mind wander and explore possibilities. I kept typing as long as the ideas flowed, finally stopping at page thirty-eight. For a mid-afternoon snack, I made a peanut butter and banana sandwich and drank more Kool-Aid, swiping the red mustache from my lips with the back of my hand. Then I went for a walk, wishing I had a dog for companionship. *Maybe I should get one.*

Maybe I would. Did I want a dog bad enough to risk Brian's wrath? That would take a bit of thought. I would jot it down on my legal pad when I got home. Maybe I would get a second hand, slightly used, clean but scruffy mutt at the pound. I smiled, liking the idea a lot.

Since I had no dog, I walked alone, drinking in the beautiful colors and sounds of spring.

Back home once again, I saved my story to hard drive, slipped out of my Nikes, and took a nap on my exquisitely soft, shabby sheets.

A phone call from Brian woke me at four. Angrily, he said, "I made an appointment for you at Mitchel Hardy's office. You've got a problem, and you need psychiatric help. Be there at nine in the morning."

I fortified myself with a deep breath and said firmly, "No, Brian. I am not the one with the problem here. I'm perfectly fine, loving my life, and I will not change it for you or anyone else. So you'd better decide how it's going to be. It's either me or the firm. Not both. Goodbye." I had said it gently but firmly, and I felt like shouting it from the housetops. Instead I whispered, *praise you, Jesus*.

I worked on my story for a while, then called Chrissy Dailey and arranged to pick her up to go garage saling the next morning at seven sharp. We both agreed: the early bird catches the worm and other wonderful delicacies.

By six, my stomach was begging to be fed, so I pulled out the spaghetti and garlic bread and warmed them up. Because I had made enough to feed a dozen people, I divided it into single serving zippered freezer bags and froze it for later.

"Hey, this might come in handy when I get hungry while writing, but don't feel like cooking."

Smiling, I nibbled that savory, crunchy garlic

bread and slurped up the long tomato-y noodle strands, chasing it with raspberry tea. I knew Brian would have a fit, but I was in heaven and didn't care who knew it.

I retrieved the newspaper from the front porch and tugged out the classified section, laying it flat on the kitchen table, searching until I found *Pets and Animals*. Scanning the column, my eye fell on a small ad. "Good home needed for small and gentle six-year old Yorkie mix named Shark."

I dialed the number and learned that Shark was a female, misnamed by the owner's four-year-old son. Shark sounded like exactly the kind of pet I was looking for, her name notwithstanding.

After parking beside the curb at the address I'd been given, I strode to the door of a tidy, mid-sized bungalow and knocked. Instantly a scruffy looking smallish dog appeared and stood on her hind legs, trying to get a better look at me.

A slender, middle-aged man opened the door and smiled. "This, if you couldn't tell—is Shark."

Once inside, I bent down and grinned. "Hi, Shark. You're adorable." Her hair stuck out seven ways from Sunday, but she was perfect. She would make me smile.

I ventured, "I'll bet you hate to see her go."

"Oh, sure, but I'm getting married and my fiancé is allergic to dogs."

"How much do you want for her?"

"Oh, I just want her to have a good home. And from the look of it, I imagine she'll be very happy with you." He chuckled, when Shark excitedly covered my hand with sloppy, wet kisses.

"I'll take her. Oh, she is potty-trained, isn't she?"

He laughed. "She's housebroken, if that's what you mean. She stands at the door, or scratches at it when she needs to go out."

"Ooh, she sounds perfect," I said, picking her up. She nuzzled her cold wet nose under my chin and promptly melted my heart.

"Well, have a wonderful life," said the man, smiling as he finished loading the trunk with fifty pounds of dog food and every doggy necessity known to man.

Shark and I chatted while we drove home, and I told her how much fun we would have together.

As I was bathing her a while later, I said, "Listen, Shark, we really need a new name for you. So what do you think?" I reviewed her choices, but she seemed apathetic until I said, "How about Wrigley—Wait. How about Cupcake?"

Her entire drenched frame trembled with excitement at the word *cupcake*. Had she eaten one? Oh, well. Perhaps if I called her that, she would always come when called.

"Okay then. Cupcake it is." I toweled her off and laughed at her wild, wiry hair. After spraying her with fragrant doggy perfume, I wondered how I would untangle her messy coif, but when I set her down, she gave her body a good, hard shake and suddenly, she looked like a rust-colored porcupine, with slightly stiff bristles no longer tangled, but standing at strict attention.

"Oh, you're wonderful," I murmured as I hugged her and reached under the cupboard for one of her doggy treats.

From that moment on, she followed me everywhere and plopped down on the floor beside me wherever I landed.

She curled up at my feet as I sat down at the computer and began to write a short time later. My story took shape, coming like a flood from somewhere deep inside me, and I realized, at that moment, I had finally figured out what I wanted to be when I grew up.

At eleven, I blinked and realized I had read the same sentence four times without seeing it.

Letting her in after her last foray of the evening, I said to Cupcake, "Okay, dog, I mean, Cupcake. We need to hit the feathers. Come on."

I had set her small plaid dog bed at the foot of my four-poster, but she eyed the big empty space beside me and instantly made herself at home, curling into the circle of my arm.

"Oh, dear. If Brian comes home, he'll have an absolute cow. Oh, well, we'll cross that bridge when we come to it, I guess." I liked holding her close.

The next morning, after letting her out to do her business, I said, "Okay, girl, you've got to stay here while I'm gone. Okay?"

As if psychic, she made a nest in the rug beside the bed, and went back to sleep. After my quiet time, I showered and dressed, filled the dog dishes, made coffee and finally jotted a list of things to do. After a slice of peanut butter toast and coffee, I got in my Oldsmobile and headed toward Chrissy's place.

Chrissy Dailey and I go way back. Ironically, we met while garage saling. I clearly remember my first impression. When I saw her with two small sons in tow, literally, one by the collar of his shirt and the other held tightly by the hand, I had to stifle a laugh. I knew exactly how she felt. Every mother of two small sons feels like shaking them on occasion.

She met my eye, and we had instant rapport when she said, "I see you know this story."

"Um, yup. My boys are in the car, threatened within an inch of their lives for squabbling. Why do they always have to fight when I'm doing garage sales?"

Shaking her head as if it were a foregone conclusion, she sighed. "For the same reason I can't get on the phone for five minutes without a major skirmish." From that moment on, the bond was sealed.

Chrissy's reddish blonde curls bobbed as she slammed the front door and locked it with her key, before turning her wide grin on me.

"You can't imagine how I've been looking forward to this. With mother in the nursing home now, and Mick recovering after knee surgery, I feel like I've been tethered to someone else's ucky life."

I frowned in confusion. "Wait. When did Mick have knee surgery?"

"About a week ago. Before that, he needed me to wait on him hand and foot. And I mean to tell you, it's not my idea of a good time—mostly because of his attitude. Remind me, if something ever happens to him, that I do not—I repeat, do not want to get married again, will you?

"I mean, who, in their right mind, marries in old age just so they can follow someone else around, who's growing more cantankerous everyday?" After a beat, she added, "Mick is only fifty-two, but boy, can he be a bear when he's in pain."

When I said nothing, Chrissy leveled her blue-eyed gaze at me and frowned. "Okay. What are you not telling me?"

"Brian moved out."

I backed out of her driveway, hoping she'd be distracted enough to let it go, but she stared at me, her brows drawn up into arches. "Say that again. I must not have heard right."

"You heard right."

"What on earth brought this on?"

"He's been made a partner."

"Yes, and…."

"And he's turned into someone I don't know. Honestly."

"So give, will you?"

I shook my head. "He came home a few days ago, saying he'd been named a partner to replace one that died recently. I mean, that seemed heartless enough, all by itself, but then he began to change and demanded I change, too."

"Change? In what way? I mean you guys have been married for thirty years. You're like old slippers, comfortable—a perfect fit. I just don't get this."

I shook my head. "You don't want to know. It will spoil a perfectly wonderful day."

She scrunched up her nose and gave me a sour look. "Are you kidding? I've had nothing but grumps on my hands for months, and you're going to deny me the pleasure of sharing your pain? No way, girlfriend. This is the first time I've felt human in—I don't even want to think of how long... Now give."

I frowned. "Maybe you'd better tell me where we're going first."

"Oh, Murphy's Ridge. You know, south of town. They're having their neighborhood wide garage sales. We should be able to find some great stuff, I hope."

I put on my turn signal and headed south.

"Well, my first clue that something was up was when Brian booked us to fly to Orlando."

She made a face. "You—fly? But you hate to fly. You hate to leave the city limits."

"Hey. It's not as bad as all that."

"Oh yeah? When was the last time you left town of your own free will?"

"Last summer. You and I went garage saling in Cinder Mills. Remember?"

"That doesn't count because I drove."

"Well…."

"Never mind. Continue."

I gave an audible sigh as I picked up my train of thought. "Anyway—oh, man. I've got so much to tell you. I mean, how long has it been since we've talked?"

"At least six weeks, and I've got to tell you, I'm running on empty here, kid."

"Well, remind me to tell you that I met my biological mother, okay?"

"What? When did this happen?"

"Never mind. That's only a small part of the story."

"I can't believe it," she murmured.

"Me either."

"So did you really go to Orlando?"

"Oh, yes, but not before I got fired from my job."

"Fired? You're not teaching anymore?"

"Nope. Cleaned out my locker and said adios."

"Hey, do me a favor, will you, and start at the beginning?"

I let out a deep breath. "Okay. Well, my mother, I mean my real mother called a couple of weeks ago and asked if we could get together. It was an odd conversation, short and sweet, and made me wonder what was up. I mean, it was curt, almost business-like."

"So what happened?"

"I was right. It was only business."

I parked the car just then, and turned to watch throngs of shoppers wandering up and down Mint Julep Road.

I said, "Come on, before all the good stuff is gone."

"Okay, but keep talking."

We walked as I talked. "She needed a bone marrow transplant. She was dying of leukemia."

"That's it? She wasn't glad to see you after all

these years?"

"Um…nope. She told me point blank that she had no use for me in her life at this late date, just needed a body part."

"Well, don't keep me in suspense. Did you donate or let her die? No, don't tell me. You could never do a thing like that. You donated, right?"

"Yup. That very night, in fact. She went into crisis and needed a transplant ASAP."

"Wow, when it rains, it pours, huh?"

"Yeah. I had barely even come to grips with the idea of having a huge needle stuck in me and there it was."

"Then what?"

"Well, I didn't bounce back quite as quickly as I'd hoped, and well—suffice it to say, Brian wanted to whisk me away for a break."

"To Orlando. Okay, go on."

"Well, you know how I hate to travel?"

"We already covered this ground."

"I know, but I was just going to say that Brian has always loved being home as much as I have. But now, he's got this wanderlust a mile wide, like a contagious disease or something. Probably from hanging out with guys who think you haven't lived, until you've parked your fanny under every banyan tree in the Caribbean."

Chapter Fifteen

Chrissy laughed. "You're funny. Do you know that?"

"Well, it was no laughing matter when it happened."

"Okay, so you went to Orlando. It couldn't have been that bad, could it?"

"Well, I guess Brian failed to check the weather channel before we left. They were in the middle of a heat wave of catastrophic proportions. I mean, it was one hundred twelve degrees in the shade and none of the air conditioners worked—brown out."

"Oh man. Bummer."

"No kidding. Listen, you know what a diehard golfer Brian is? Well, the heat was so bad that he quit golfing at the second hole. Now remember, this is the guy who's never played less than eighteen holes before quitting, even when he was sick as a dog."

"Man. I can't even imagine it. So what did you do?"

"I had heat exhaustion and fainted at the hotel manager's feet."

"You didn't?"

"Yup. Ended up in the hospital. And we'd still be down there in the sweltering heat if Brian hadn't been ordered to bring me home. I even had my very first asthma attack while I was there."

"No kidding."

While I surveyed a table of someone's excess wedding gifts, still pristine in their original boxes, she said, "So go on."

"Well, Brian acted like it was my fault that we had to come home early, and I mean, he—well—he began to change before my very eyes."

"How?"

I sighed and grimaced. "He told me he could no longer eat instant rice."

She laughed. "So what's wrong with that?"

"Just wait, girlfriend. You haven't heard anything yet."

She set down the stack of pleated mauve placemats in her hand and waited with her gaze fixed on me. Another woman snatched them up, leaving Chrissy glowering after her.

With a smug smile, the woman retorted, "You laid them down."

Chrissy looked at me and frowned. "Listen, keep talking, will you? I'm losing some good stuff, trying to keep you on track here."

"Sorry. He told me he couldn't eat ground meat anymore, or garlic. It's too ethnic. He said that from now on, I had to cook with onion and cilantro. And you know how I hate cilantro. Ack."

"Yeah, but what does all this have to do...." Her concentration was fixed and her eyes glazed as she intently studied the tables in front of her.

"Just wait. I haven't gotten to the good part yet."

She nodded.

"Well, he cleaned out his closets and told me he was getting all new designer clothes. Not only that, but he told me I needed to dump all my favorite clothes, too."

"You mean your soft, frumpy stuff?"

"Yes. And he said it was not proper for a partner's wife to work for money, so it wasn't a problem that I was losing my job."

"Oh, yeah. What was that about anyway? I mean, you loved that job, didn't you?"

At that moment, a harried-looking young mother, with four small children in tow, wandered into the garage. An infant boy in a navy backpack screamed open-mouthed, and a little girl about a year old, whose hand the Mom held in gridlock, kept repeating the words, "Eat--me eat." A slightly older boy, who held Mom's other hand, complained, "I'm tired, Mom. Can't we go home?"

My gaze met Chrissy's, and she held up her finger, meaning to wait.

The Mom responded, "I've got to find the kids clothes. They've got to be around here somewhere."

The middle-aged male garage sale host gave her a tired smile. "Sorry, ma'am. Kids clothes are down the block." He pointed to his left, before adding, "Our kids are grown and gone and haven't given us any grandchildren yet."

The woman nodded her thanks and ferried her brood on to the next sale.

"Okay," said Chrissy, "now what were you going to say?"

"I was going to say I loved my job, but I was getting worn out with the politics of the whole thing. It turns out that Hested fired me for lack of written notice that I wouldn't be in, after I told him about our trip. The thing is, I was already off work on sick leave, because of the bone marrow transplant."

She made a face. "That seems a little severe."

"Yeah, well, I'm thinking that wasn't the real reason I'm gone. I torqued him off big time when I refused to teach a sex education class to second graders."

"Second graders? What do they need to

know about sex?"

"My question exactly. Anyway, they needed a sub for two weeks while the regular teacher was recovering from a back injury. It seems she slid on some peas in the cafeteria and ended up in traction."

"Bummer."

"Yeah. Well, when we got back from Orlando, I had a message on my machine, saying I was canned."

"Wow. How did you feel about that?"

"Awful. For about five minutes. You know, as much as I loved my kids and the other teachers, I think I'm in burnout."

"I wondered about that."

"I think I'm ready for a break."

"So you agreed with Brian after all, huh?"

"Well, I told him I wanted to write a novel—you know I've always wanted to do that, right?"

She nodded. "You've been talking about it for years."

"Well, he said partners' wives aren't allowed to be artsy, so he nixed the Great American Novel toot de suite."

"You're kidding."

"Nope. Also told me I couldn't garage sale anymore. He says partners only buy new." I chose not to mention that he also had no use for my friends of Irish descent.

"Not garage sale? What's that about? Doesn't he know that's who you are?"

"Yes, he knows. But it's his business, now, to turn me into the firm's ideal partner's wife." I made tiny quotes in midair with my index fingers.

"I can't believe this," she said, meeting my gaze for an instant, before spying an exquisite periwinkle J. Bonaventure all-weather coat. I saw it at the same time.

"So how come you're with me, doing this, if he said that?" She slipped into the coat and turned, modeling it for me. I nodded and smiled.

"He moved out. After I gave him an ultimatum. He was tossing out all my wonderful living room furniture."

"What? But there's nothing wrong with it. It's perfect."

"You're right, but that has nothing to do with it. It's used, and he doesn't *do* used anymore now that he's a partner. He'd hauled it to the garage before I knew it, and said he was giving it to a junk man this morning. Well, that was the last straw. I was livid."

"So what did you do?" She slipped out of the coat and draped it over her arm.

"I started to walk out, but then I made him leave. I mean, it's my house, too."

Her brow furrowed as she waited for me to speak.

"I was so angry that he restrained my arms

and said he was going to have me committed if I didn't stop being hysterical."

Her hands fluttered in midair. "I can't believe this."

"Me either."

"But how did you actually make him leave? Pick him up and throw him out bodily?"

"Nope. I threatened to tell his boss about his coercive behavior."

"And he went for that?"

"Only after I said I'd tell how his wife is a mental case that he threatened to commit. You should've seen his face. It was the ultimate perfect threat. He couldn't dare let that get to the partners, or he'd be history." Suddenly, I felt ashamed of myself and said, "Listen, I shouldn't be talking like this. I mean, I really love the guy. I just hate what he's doing to us."

"Wow, you really have had a wild ride this past month, haven't you?"

"Now that Brian's gone, I've already started doing things differently."

"Like what?"

She paid for her raincoat and carried it to the car, before turning to survey the sale across the street.

I said, "I got a dog."

"You did?"

"Yes, a cute, scruffy Yorkie-mix. Her name is

Cupcake."

"Oh, man. You're walking on thin ice, girl, doing that without Brian's consent."

"I know. But I'm willing to risk it. I also started my novel last night. And I'm going to garage sale to my heart's content."

"Have you made your funeral arrangements yet?"

I stopped abruptly in front of her, causing a minor collision. "What?"

"He's going to kill you when he finds out, you know."

"No, he won't. Not if I come up with a few more creative threats. I mean I hate to do it, but what options do I have? I actually gave him an ultimatum, but I guess I said that already, didn't I?"

"Yes, but you never said what it was."

"I said it's the partnership or me. So we'll see what happens next."

She stared at me, frowning. "Are you really prepared to let him go if he chooses his career over you?"

"Yes. He wants me to change who I am inside, and I told him I won't do it. I did that to please my parents, and it's a crummy way to live. It doesn't please the Lord, either, so I'm sticking to my guns on the subject. In fact, I wrote down who I am, and what I like and dislike, as well as my dreams and plans. And everyday, I'm going to read it just to reinforce my resolve."

"Wow. I've never seen you like this," she said, looking at me with frank admiration.

"I've never had to be this way before." Don't tell her, but I felt shaky even imagining my life without Brian . "I still do love the man."

"I know—push comes to shove."

"Ain't it the truth?" I said forlornly.

At the next garage sale, I met several teachers I had said goodbye to the day before.

"So," I said to them wistfully, "how's every little thing at Hershel B. Walker Elementary?"

Fifth grade teacher Marsha Greenfield shoved wayward tendrils of curly red hair from her porcelain, heart-shaped face. "You know, I wish, like anything, that I could just kick over the traces and shove that job. Unfortunately, we can't live on what my husband makes. And now I make too much to quit. Lucky you," she added sincerely.

Slightly built Prissy Parks said, "My sentiments exactly. I'm green with envy." She taught kindergarten.

"I'm going to miss you guys," I said, blinking back hot tears that burned behind my eyes.

"Keep in touch, okay?" asked blue-eyed Marsha, squeezing my hand.

"Sure," I agreed, knowing it would never happen.

Chrissy motioned me on toward the next

sale. My eyes grew wide, seeing country furniture and antiques. We browsed, too deeply immersed in our own thoughts to converse. I tried to figure out where I would put the wonderful items I saw, but I already owned most of it and couldn't accommodate much more.

One thing I absolutely couldn't resist—a small, slightly beat up chalk dog, with some of his paint worn off. Smiling, I picked him up and hugged him to me. "You can keep Cupcake company, okay?"

I paid for my prize and watched Chrissy lay down a huge stack of Country Living magazines. She got out her wallet and handed the woman some bills.

"Don't you already have all those?"

"Nope. These are the old ones. The ones with hardly any advertising and lots of great ideas."

After stowing our stuff in the car, I said, "I'm thirsty. Want to go get something to drink?"

"Actually, I'm starved. Didn't take time to eat breakfast."

"Really? How come?" With a glance at my watch, I saw that it was eleven, and the restaurants had opened for lunch.

"My mother-in-law was on the phone, driving me crazy again. These days, she can't remember whether or not she's taken her pills. The thing is, the nurses are giving them to her, so she doesn't have to remember."

"Then why does she call?"

"She can't remember that she can't remember, with her increasing dementia, whether she's actually taken them or not, so I just go through the same routine over and over again, telling her "Yes, you have, Mother. So go take your nap. After I say that, she settles right down. At least now we have it down to a routine. There for a while, it was an ordeal. Now I just say the magic words and it's cool."

I nodded.

Meeting my gaze over gold wire-framed glasses, she lowered her chin. "You haven't mentioned your mother-in-law for a while. How's she doing?"

"Oh, all right I guess. Wait, no. Shuck that. She'll probably never speak to me again. I was supposed to pick them up at the airport yesterday and I forgot. When she called me at 8:30, I had only been in bed a few hours. I told her to get a hotel—that her son didn't live there anymore."

"You're kidding. What did she say to that?"

I made a face. "I didn't give her a chance to say anything. I hung up."

She shook her head in awe. "I can't believe you. You've never done this kind of stuff in all the years I've known you."

"You're right."

Chapter Sixteen

After waiting ten minutes among an antsy crowd, we ate at the China Delight Buffet. We listened to the four Hispanic people at the table beside us, who struggled to make themselves understood, evidently unable to speak a word of English. For some reason, it intrigued me that they would like Chinese food, but even more, that they couldn't speak the language. What is it with that anyway? Whatever happened, to 'when in Rome'?

Slowly I nibbled my way through tender sweet and sour chicken, fried rice, Crab Rangoon, broccoli and cashew chicken and finally, a fortune cookie. She and I don't believe in that fortune stuff, but we still get a kick out of seeing what they say.

Chrissy broke her crunchy cookie in half and pulled out her fortune. She chuckled, "Don't get discouraged. Things are looking up."

I swallowed a bite of cookie and said, "Listen to this. 'You have the heart and drive to someday be a famous author.'"

She gave me a knowing smile as I stuck it in my pocket, planning to tape it on my dream list.

In the restaurant parking lot, we stopped short at a vehicle in which a small infant slept unattended. Irate, Chrissy tried the door, but found it locked. "How can people do this—leave a baby alone for any reason?"

Frowning, she headed back inside the restaurant to call the authorities while I kept an eye on the baby. A few seconds later, Chrissy rushed out, followed by an irate and huffy woman, whose eyes blazed fire. The twenty-something woman wore her blonde hair in cornrows and her face heavily made up, black eyeliner making a quarter-inch wide horizontal exclamation point over each eye. Didn't she know that less is more?

"How could you have called the cops on me? I was only going in for a second—to get takeout. The baby was sleeping, and I saw no harm in it."

"Listen," Chrissy flounced around, hands slamming to her hips, to face the woman. "It's illegal to leave an infant in a vehicle unattended—for any reason."

The two continued to stare at each other, unyielding. The police ended the standoff when they approached the woman, who gave Chrissy the evil eye as she turned to leave.

I sighed. "Boy, I'm glad the cops finally came. If looks could kill, girl, you'd be a goner for sure."

By three-thirty, we had both seen enough of other people's things and finally headed home.

We sat in the car for a long time, just visiting, until she finally tilted her head.

"So what do you think will happen now? Think he'll dump you for the sake of his career?"

"I don't know. I'm sure it happens. You know, if he would only stop long enough to take a good look at what's happening, I think he'd come to his senses. I mean, what he's doing now is exactly what he and I have despised all our lives. You know, brown-nosing, being something you aren't—to get something you want. It's lousy. It really is."

"Listen, you won't hear me arguing that point. I hate that stuff. In fact, did you know there are even those who are so high and mighty that they refuse to associate with those of us who are Irish?"

I blinked, saying nothing, and she frowned. "Why are you looking at me like that?"

I shrugged and lowered my gaze, but she had nailed it already. "Oh, man. I get it. He told you not to associate with me anymore, didn't he?"

"Yup. And I told *him* to jump in the lake."

"Good for you. Thanks, kiddo," she added thickly, with moist eyes.

"Listen, you and I have been best friends for twenty-five years, Chrissy Donovan Dailey, and nothing, I mean nothing, is going to change that now, y'hear me?"

"I hear you," she said, with a silly lopsided grin.

Chagrined, I said, "I wasn't going to tell you. I can't imagine living the way he's dictating. Not going to happen, and that's all there is to it."

She hugged me before we hauled all her purchases inside.

Because it was a big part of the garage sale ritual, I fussed over her beautiful new raincoat. "Listen girlfriend, this thing is a steal. Really, where are you going to get something this great for only three dollars?"

"I know, and I could see that you wanted it, too. Thanks for not saying so."

My own eyes felt hot with unshed tears. "Oh, sweetie, you're welcome. I'm so glad you're my friend. Don't know what I'd do without you, you know?"

"I know. I feel the same way."

I brightened. "Okay, well, see you. Same time next week?"

"Sure."

"Good.

At the door, she turned to face me. "Listen, I'll drive next time, okay? Pick you up at seven?"

I nodded and waved, walking backwards to my car.

Because I wasn't looking where I was going, I didn't see what was coming. Before I knew it, I was sprawled unceremoniously on the ground, tangled in a retractable nylon tether, looking into the massive jowls of a drooling St. Bernard.

I screamed and found myself being helped to my feet by a husky blond man, wearing a blue and green nylon running suit. His cologne scented the air around him with a pleasant spicy fragrance, like cloves.

"Oh, dear. Are you hurt?" he asked, his middle-aged blue eyes looking apologetic.

"I'm okay. The only thing bruised is my vanity, I'm afraid," I said, dusting myself off.

"I'm terribly sorry. I was listening to my Walkman, so I didn't notice you until it was too late. Are you sure you aren't hurt?" I could hear just a twinge of a British accent when he spoke.

"Listen, I'm fine. Sorry I wasn't watching where I was going."

"Well, all right, if you're sure. Take care of yourself," he said, as if hating to see me go.

By then I was flushing twelve shades of red, wishing the earth would open and swallow me whole.

Since that wasn't going to happen any time

soon, I smiled inanely, hurriedly slipped behind the wheel of my car, slammed the door and drove off, thinking what a kind man he was and what an idiot I was—as tears filled my eyes.

Funny—how even the smallest kindness could reduce me to tears these days.

At home, I pulled into the garage, and began unloading my treasures. My stash included a small hand-painted celluloid stationary box from the 1800's with beautiful faded flowers on a pale gray-green background that had aged to a soft patina. I examined it, turning it over in my hands and saw the initials of its maker etched on the bottom. The letters E and M in fancy script.

A flower-etched ceramic pedestal, with a scratch on the top was my buy of the day for a dollar. I could touch up the scratch with tooth-paste, and no one would ever be the wiser.

The chalk dog looked right at home when I placed him in front of a large basket of dried flowers on the fireplace hearth.

I opened a quart sized zipper bag and removed several finely woven, lacy tatted collars, worn in an earlier, simpler time. I gently ran my fingertips over the delicate lacework and wondered about its origins. Someone had put her heart and soul into creating these beautiful things, and I would never take that for granted. In the entryway, I arranged them, fanned out in an antique trunk, displaying other fine examples of handwork.

A pair of white doeskin gloves, slightly yellowed over the years, felt soft under my touch. After sniffing their faint leathery scent, I held them beside my larger hand. It was clear they had belonged to a fine-boned woman of culture. I tucked the gloves into the open stationary box and set them on my dresser.

A colorful and ancient, painted cookie tin held old wooden spools and medicine bottles with their labels still attached. Faded with time, I could still read, "Dr. Hervey's Anti-fat Elixir. Take one tablespoon before meals." They were still selling this stuff; only the names had changed.

Smiling, I added the bottles to those arranged on my wide bathroom windowsill.

In a bag that held beautiful old textile remnants, I found several of Chrissy's Country Living Magazines. She had jotted a note on the back of the top one. "Knew you loved them, too. Enjoy! Love, C."

I smiled. Those Irishmen really knew how to show love.

Cupcake's entire wiry body shuddered with glee when I finally remembered her and opened the laundry room door, where I had tucked her for safekeeping. No need to invite Brian's ire by asking for trouble. With wild hair bouncing, she eagerly availed herself of the outdoor facilities, ie; the yard, and shortly ran back inside, where she danced around my feet until I bent to pick her up. She licked my ears and face, my neck and hands in her excitement, making me laugh.

"You crazy little mutt. I already love you."

I set her down and offered her a doggy treat, which she promptly carried onto my white dining room carpet before she finally indulged.

The message light blinked on my machine, and I picked up to hear the voice of Leo Hested. With my mouth open in surprise, I pushed *rewind*, then *play*. "Listen, I have a favor to ask. We need a sub for Amy Milhouse. She's six months pregnant and needs to be on bed rest for the rest of her pregnancy. I need you to take her second grade class for the rest of the term. I'll expect you here at seven tomorrow unless I hear back from you." *The nerve of some people.*

I pulled up Leo's number from the phone's memory, and pushed MEM and the number four.

After three rings, I was irritated enough to hang up, but Leo picked up just then.

"So, ready to come back to work?"

"Nope. You need to find someone else."

"What? How can you say that? I should think

you'd be grateful to get back to work, under any circumstances."

"Listen, Leo. I think you have colossal nerve, thinking I'll dance right over there to help you out when you just fired me. Excuse me, but I like being retired. In fact, please don't call me again."

He huffed just before I gently but firmly hung up on him. After the fact, I wondered if I should've taken the work, since who knew what would happen with Brian and me.

I couldn't believe I wasn't more upset by all the losses in my life. In the past, they had always left me devastated, but now it seemed that I could simply take God at His word, and relax.

I whipped up a pot of broccoli cheese soup, made some garlic bread and sat eating it on the deck, savoring the soup's creamy texture. The wind whipped my hair into a bird's nest as I nestled under the umbrella with only my legs soaking up the warm spring sunshine.

I usually only fixed my favorite soup when I had friends over, because Brian wasn't keen on the odor of cooked broccoli—said it made him nauseated.

I stepped into the kitchen, returning to the deck with my yellow tablet and pen, and listed all the things I was doing that I really enjoyed— things I couldn't do around Brian.

"Listen, Lord, is it all right to have this much fun?" Somehow, as much as I enjoyed doing my own thing, it also felt sinfully indulgent and made me feel a little guilty.

After cleaning up the kitchen mess, I wandered around the yard for a while, tidying up the flowerbeds and watering the budding plants. I chuckled as I watched Cupcake leap into the air after a butterfly.

"You funny girl," I said, scratching between her ears when she came to me a minute later.

I had just pulled the mail from the box on the porch, when the phone rang again, and I picked up to hear Brian's voice.

"Jolie, you and I need to get together and talk. I want to meet you for dinner. Let's meet at The Steel Magnolia at seven. See you there," he said, without taking a breath.

"Wait, Brian. I agree that we need to talk, but I want to talk to you here, not in some restaurant."

"No. Be there. Steel Magnolia at seven sharp." He was gone before I could say another word.

I grew anxious as I showered, wondering what Brian would say. Did he want a divorce? In my wildest dreams, I had never imagined us struggling with these kinds of issues. I tried to turn off my mind to the potentially frightening outcome of the evening.

At six twenty, I switched handbags and slipped into black patent pumps. I wore a black crepe dress and a blue and green opaque duster over the top. I struggled with my anxious thoughts. I hated The Steel Magnolia, where all the beautiful people made a point to be seen.

The place was cold, done in stark modern lines, black, white and silver, with nothing warm or inviting to soften the look.

Brian was already seated, waiting for me when the host led me to our table. Brian wore a new gray pinstriped suit, Armani, if I didn't miss my guess—with a dove gray dress shirt and a gray and burgundy tie. With a furrowed brow, I decided he looked no better or worse than he had any other time he dressed up. I mean, it was a great-fitting suit, but so were his other suits, which had been custom-made by a local tailor. So much for Armani.

My husband eyed me critically before standing to seat me. After sitting back down, he pulled a silver pen from his pocket and began clicking it distractedly.

"So have you given any thought to what you'd like to eat?"

"Not really. I guess I could get my old favorite, shrimp scampi."

He nodded. "All right. Would you like some wine?"

"No, thanks."

"Well, listen, you're probably wondering why I asked you here."

I shrugged. "The thought did cross my mind."

He perused his menu thoughtfully as he spoke. "Well, I've been thinking. I know you can't be happy in that huge house all by yourself, so I've decided to make you an offer that suits you better."

I was wary of his condescending attitude. "What kind of offer?"

"I'll take the house and find you a condo you'll be able to manage more easily."

"What? No. I'm not leaving my home. I told you that."

"Come on, honey, be reasonable. I can't imagine you clattering around alone in a five-thousand-square foot space. Let me find you something small and efficient, something where you won't have any upkeep. What do you think?"

"Sorry, Brian, but if that's what this meeting is all about, you can keep your dinner and your money. I'm staying in the house—and don't call me *honey*."

I got up, excused myself, and quietly exited the restaurant. Tears burned my eyes as I turned into my driveway a short time later. He obviously wasn't planning on coming home any time soon.

I slept badly when I finally went to bed, and eventually got up, sat down at my computer and let my story evolve one precious word at a time.

By four thirty, I was exhausted, and sat there blinking, knowing I still wouldn't sleep, even if I went back to bed.

Getting up, I paced the length of the house, back and forth, thinking about our life together. Was he so enamored of his new career path that he would dump everything we'd held dear for thirty years?

Chapter Seventeen

The next morning, I let the dog out and decided I needed to go buy art supplies so I could try my hand at painting.

After starting laundry and taking care of household chores, I finally drove to the mall.

Wandering around in Paints Etcetera, I took in a dizzying array of art supplies. Not sure what I sought, I consulted the thirtyish female clerk, who asked appropriate questions before finally saying, "Well, listen. If you're just trying it on for size, I'd suggest you start with acrylics. They're quick-drying and easy to use. Want me to set you up with all the stuff you'll need?"

Nodding, I gave her the go-ahead, and watched as a stack quickly accumulated on her counter.

She nodded and her curly blond hair bobbed

up and down in agreement. "Okay. That should do it. There's one other thing that might help." She held up a book. "This book, if you're a beginner, will teach you the basics. Are you a visual or an auditory learner?"

"Visual, I think."

"Well, then this book is for you."

"Okay, great," I said as I handed her my debit card. A butterfly of excitement fluttered about in my middle as I thought about my upcoming foray into the world of art.

At home, I shoved all the guest room furniture to the side of the room, covered it with old sheets, and set up tables, an easel and my paint supplies. I found an office chair that I could be comfy in, and settled down with the book, studying the technique.

Within an hour, I was ready to try my hand at painting when the phone suddenly rang.

"Listen, Jolie. This is Jeanette. I need to see you."

"Is everything all right?"

"Not exactly."

"Okay, when do you want me to come?"

"As soon as possible."

"Well, okay. See you shortly."

My mind could no longer retain the intrica-

cies of painting, so I closed the book and turned
my mind toward my meeting with Jeanette.

"What's going on, Lord?"

I wondered if her transplant had failed. If so,
I wasn't sure I was up to donating again.

I was restless over the unknown and hurriedly
showered, changed and got ready to leave. Praying
in the spirit, I couldn't help but wish she and I
could have what I had always dreamed of—a
normal mother-daughter relationship. Shaking my
head, I decided not to hold my breath.

When Jeanette met me at the door an hour
and a half later, I could see she had been crying;
her eyes were red and puffy.

I tilted my head and studied her face. We
both sank into chairs, and I noticed her hands,
nervously fluttering about on her lap, picking in-
visible lint from her slacks.

"Are you okay? What's wrong?"

"My sister, Ruth, was diagnosed with Parkinson's disease a couple of years ago, but she has
managed to live alone and care for herself until
now. It's now clear—she can't live alone anymore,
and Steven won't let me move her in with us. He
says it would be too much for me, taking care of
her. But how can I know unless I try?" She had
said this in a single breath and now inhaled
raggedly. The woman she referred to, it occurred

to me just then, was my aunt.

"Well, what can I do to help?" I couldn't help saying it, because I wanted her to clarify where this relationship was going.

She gave me an odd look, a slight frown flitting through her eyes. "I just—thought—well, I guess I thought you'd listen to me talk about it. I mean, I don't expect anything really." Her hands moved fretfully by her side, as if punctuating her feelings of frustration. "I mean, you will listen to me, won't you?"

"Of course I will. Why don't you tell me what's been going on."

I took in her appearance. She bore absolutely no resemblance to the put-together, sophisticated woman I had met only a couple of weeks earlier. Her hair stood on end as though she had missed a style session at her beauty parlor. Her pale baby blue pantsuit, now wrinkled, had a water spot above the right breast. The living room even looked a bit dusty, and I pondered whether the woman in the chair had actually aged twenty years or if I should blame it on her lack of makeup.

I reached over and took her restless hand, tilting my head and smiling. She relaxed just a bit before I said, "May I make you some tea, Jeanette?"

"Oh, yes. That would be lovely. Maybe calm my nerves." I followed her to the kitchen, and glanced around at its framed watercolor art surrounded by a sea of white. White ceramic floor, stark white walls and cupboards, the only relief coming from the pastel watercolor border at the ceiling and a few well-placed pastel plates, hand-painted with delicate flowers in the same palette.

It had the minimal look of an expensive decorator, but lacked warmth. I hoped against hope that she hadn't spent big money on such minor design input.

I pulled the white china teapot from the stovetop and filled it with water. "Where are your teabags?"

She pointed, which I was sure she never did. "Cupboard left of the stovetop."

I fished them from among myriad boxes of specialty coffees and herbal teas. "Plain tea okay?"

Without inflection, she said softly, "Of course, if you add cream and sugar."

"I can do that. So tell me what's been going on," I urged again.

"This morning, I got a call from Ruth, who was very upset. Sounds like she's going to have to go into a nursing home."

"So she's been managing on her own up until now?"

"Not well, but managing. Lately, though, she's been falling, dropping things, forgetting her medications and feeling paranoid…."

"And she has no one but you to handle her affairs?"

"Her husband, Franklin died ten years ago. Her children, a son and a daughter, are off, busy with their own lives, and rarely even call, let alone take an interest in her welfare."

"And you have no other siblings?"

"No. It's always been just the two of us against the world."

"Sounds like you're very close."

"We are. If only her children would take an interest. Perhaps she could live with one of them if they would allow it. At least for a while." With a deep sigh, she added, "I'm dreaming, of course. All they want from her is money. Ne'er do wells, both of them. At least they were before they finally found good jobs. Nearly sucked her dry, leeching off her. You'd think they'd try, especially now that they're making good money, to pay her back what they borrowed, but that will never happen."

I removed the kettle from the flame and turned off the burner. After pouring water over the teabags, I hunted up her cream and sugar containers, unwilling to interrupt her train of thought.

A minute later, I set the tea in front of her, but she seemed lost in a world of her own.

"I could take care of her. I know I could, but

Steven refuses, says he didn't marry me to end up losing me to my sister. How can he be so cruel? Doesn't he understand I need to try this? I mean, maybe it wouldn't work out, but I simply have to try."

"Does Ruth have a caseworker?"

"Oh, yes. She's considered disabled, has been for several years, so because of that, they assigned her a caseworker. Not that the woman takes much interest. I think she makes a short phone call at least once a year. Probably compulsory—so she can collect her paycheck," she added morosely.

"Well, maybe they could find her a live-in aid to help her stay at home."

"No. She's barely able to feed herself anymore, and she'd rather die than let anyone clean her—you know..."

I did.

She stared into midair, seeing nothing. "I hate the idea of getting old, if this is what we're reduced to. I mean, I've always had my health, and in fact, so has Ruth, until recently. We thought we'd grow old together. She's two years older than I. Anyway, we thought maybe we could travel together, you know, do all the things you dream of when you're younger."

I said nothing, but rested my chin on my palm. She met my gaze and then noticed the tea in front of her. She nodded her thanks, picked up the cup and promptly spilled hot tea down the front of her periwinkle shirt.

"See?" she said, bursting into tears. "This has me so upset that I can't do anything right. I mean, I'm a wreck just thinking about Ruth in a nursing home."

I handed her a napkin and she dabbed at the new stain that covered the old.

Suddenly she stood and flushed a bright pink. "Listen, I didn't mean to bother you with any of this. I shouldn't have called. You may go."

I blinked in confusion. Had she just dismissed me?

I slowly stood and tilted my head. "Jeanette, it's okay. I'm here, and I'm not going anywhere."

That simple statement seemed to shatter the rest of her reserve, and she fell into my arms, sobbing inconsolably.

I held her and patted her back, amazed that she would even touch me.

Shortly, she looked up, wiped her eyes on the backs of her hands and surprised me by softly saying, "I can't believe I gave you up."

I couldn't believe my ears. "I beg your pardon?"

Softly, she repeated, "I can't believe I gave you up."

"Really?"

"Yes. I watched Ruth struggle with her kids over the years. The two of them have been tough to raise, greedy and self-centered, and I hated what they put her through. Because of that, I guess I lumped all children together, thinking they were all the same, but you're not like that, are you?"

I shrugged. "I should hope not."

"No, you aren't. If you were, you wouldn't be here right now listening to me blubber on like this."

She was still in my arms when I pulled her close and hugged her close on a whim. She didn't flinch or balk, but neither did she respond to hug me back, at least not for several seconds. Then she let new tears slide down her already wet cheeks, smiled and lifted my hand to kiss it before she hugged me tightly.

Just as quickly as it had begun, the hug ended and she backed out of my embrace. "Well, I need to go change. Going through lots of outfits these days as you might well imagine." Looking uncomfortable, she disappeared through the doorway.

I prayed in the spirit, asking for wisdom, and knew I was not to take to heart any of her words—yet. *Just wait and see. That's the ticket.*

When she returned after several long minutes, she had rearranged her hair, made up her eyes and lips and changed into a soft peach knit lounging outfit.

"I looked a fright and you were just too nice to say anything."

"Never mind how you look. You're going through a difficult situation right now."

She tilted her head and studied my face. "You've done this before, haven't you? Come alongside to comfort someone?"

I nodded. "If you live long enough, you have pain. That's what it all boils down to."

"I guess you're right. Ruth and I have been lucky. Except for losing our parents, with whom we were never really close, the only loss we've endured was her husband. Neither of us was ever ill or particularly needy until recently. And I suppose it might seem odd, but we never hug or touch or anything. I guess we never learned how." Why was I not surprised?

She went on. "But it feels awfully good to have that support, doesn't it? I never realized just how good…."

When her gaze met mine, she flushed again. "I'm not very good at this—I mean, expressing myself or my feelings. Steven wouldn't know what to do with me if I did."

"He might surprise you."

"You think so?"

"I do. More tea?"

At her nod, I poured out her cold tea and

added steaming water, looking up with a question in my eyes.

"You can use the same teabag. Usually I don't. Usually I'm a stickler about such things, but what's the point? What's the point of getting upset over stupid things like that?"

I nodded and added her teabag to the cup.

She sank into her chair, sighed and closed her eyes, looking fatigued and fragile.

Once again, I set the cup in front of her and she dunked the bag a few times before carefully wrapping the string around her spoon and squeezing it. She untangled the spoon, set aside the teabag and stirred the dark liquid before adding cream and sugar.

Jeanette met my gaze. "You're a comforting soul to be with. Do you know that?" She paused before continuing, "You don't mind long pauses in the conversation. They usually drive me crazy—make me uncomfortable, I guess. Maybe I'll have to take lessons from you," she added, before sipping her tea.

"Listen, Jeanette, do you have anyone to help you tour and choose a nursing home for Ruth?"

"No. Steven has no desire to be part of this decision. I can barely imagine doing it myself. It's like I'm being dragged, kicking and screaming, through this process…."

After a second's pause, her voice shuddered

as she added, "I don't know if I can do it."

I put my hand gently over hers. "You're going to do just fine."

Her gaze held a question; I knew what was coming.

"Will you go with me?"

After only a second's hesitation, I replied, "Of course I will."

"You will?" she asked as if she couldn't believe I had agreed.

"Just let me know when you're up for it, and I'll be here."

Her eyes filled with tears that slipped out and trickled down her chin. "Thanks," she whispered thickly.

"It's okay. Really. Do you think you need a few days to gear up for this?"

"I'll talk to Ruth. I think she might want to be the one to make the final decision, don't you?"

"Yes, and I'd love to meet her."

"Really?"

"Of course. She's my aunt as much as your sister, you know."

Jeanette's face broke into a wide smile. "I think I'm going to enjoy spending time with you."

I returned her smile. "I'm going to take that as a compliment."

"Good."

I turned and walked toward the front door, picked up my handbag and then turned back to her. "I'll be praying for you. I know this isn't an easy thing to handle."

"You're very kind." Her tone was detached again. I guessed it would take her some time to let go of the distance she had clung to for so long.

I smiled as she opened the door for me.

"Let me know when you need me, okay? Maybe you and I can treat Ruth to lunch somewhere."

She frowned. "We'd have to feed her. Remember?"

"We could do that."

"We could?" She sounded surprised, as if the thought had never occurred to her.

"We could find a quiet corner of her favorite restaurant, facing away from other people and just enjoy ourselves."

She nodded with upraised brows, as if thinking it over and liking the idea.

I waved as I walked to my car. I thought we had turned a corner, and I could only feel excitement at what would come next.

Chapter Eighteen

At home, Cupcake did a delighted jig at the sight of me. I hugged her and let her out to romp in the privacy-fenced backyard.

I wasn't prepared to hear the phone ring and flinched at its piercing sound. Picking up, I heard the voice of my husband.

"We need to talk. Can we get together?"

"I don't think so, Brian. At least not if it's a repeat of last night's conversation. What do you want to discuss this time?"

"Getting back together." My brows danced upward and then down in a frown.

"Why?"

He demanded, "What do you mean why? Don't you want to get back together?"

Feeling a little unsure of myself I stammered, "Well, uh—under the right circumstances, yes.

Otherwise, probably not. At least not right now."

An uncomfortable silence hung in the air between us.

"What circumstances?"

After a short pause, I said, "That's what we need to discuss, I guess."

Without preamble, he ordered, "Meet me at Monroe's."

"No. I'd rather you came here—please."

"I'm not comfortable with that."

I held my ground. "Well, I'm uncomfortable in your fancy restaurants. In fact, how can you be planning to move home if you can't even come here long enough to talk?"

He gave an audible sigh. "Touché."

"So when do you want to come?"

"I'll be there in ten minutes."

I spent an anxious ten minutes, tidying up and primping automatically. Unnecessary for me, but very necessary for him, I was certain.

When he showed up at the door, he rang the bell. Showing him in, I felt my heart racing, pounding loud enough that it drowned out his words.

"What?" I asked.

"I said you look nice."

"Oh. Thanks." *I think.*

After leading him to the library, where we stood awkwardly, I asked, "Want anything to drink?"

"No. Just sit down and stop fidgeting, will you please?"

"I'm fine," I said, forcing myself to be still as I sank into a chair.

He let out a huge breath, steeled himself visibly and stared at me.

"So how are you getting along here alone?"

"Oh, fine. I mean, it's different, being alone, but I'm okay." Before I realized it, I stumbled on, "and I'm not exactly alone."

His left eyebrow flew up and he frowned. "What do you mean, you aren't alone?"

"Oh, dear. Don't look at me like that. I don't have a live-in boyfriend, if that's what you're thinking. I just bought a dog."

"That's even worse."

I shook my head, unable to believe the man.

His glance took in the perimeters of the room. "So where is he?"

"*She* is out in the backyard. Want me to get her?"

"No. I just want a look at her. You know I don't do dogs."

"Yes, I do know, but you're not here now, and I needed a dog."

With a glance out the dining room window, he shook his head. "You bought a mongrel?"

"Never mind the insults. I love her, and we're

getting along great."

Changing the subject, he asked, "So what are you doing with your time, now that you no longer have to take care of me?"

"Oh, well—I've been garage saling with Chrissy, went to see my mother, started my novel, took up art, painting actually...."

"In other words, doing everything the firm despises?"

"I don't know what the firm despises. I just know what I like, and I am doing the things *I like*."

With another sigh and a glance at the floor beneath his feet, he said, "I thought we could work something out. I really did, but I can see you've decided to be stubborn and disobedient about everything, so maybe I should just leave."

"Whatever you want...." I said airily, not wanting to argue. I followed him out of the room.

Suddenly, he pulled up a dining room chair and sat down hard. "Don't you know you're making things harder for me? Here I am trying to please them, make a good impression and...I mean, the firm does not approve of couples who separate or divorce, so those things are simply not an option."

"Well, I guess that's a good thing, isn't it? We've always said we believe in the institution of marriage, haven't we?"

He looked glum as his mouth worked in concentration. "Why can't you just agree with me and make my life easy here?"

Slowly, I shook my head. "It's not my job to make your life easy. It's my job to live my life to the fullest, to do what the Lord intended me to do."

"That sounds very independent."

"And what? You don't like independence?"

"Not particularly."

Softly, I said, "I'm not trying to be independent, at least not on purpose. I'm just trying to be what I am. If that goes against your wishes, then it goes against your wishes, but I can't—no—make that, I won't—conform to what you and the firm want, if it means denying who I am inside."

"You said that before."

"And I mean it. I will not change who I am to suit them or you, so you'll have to decide how it's going to go."

"You're purposely trying to wreck my chances with the firm, aren't you?"

"No. I'm really not. If you could be a partner and simply let me be me, I would have no problem with your promotion."

"Well, that's just not how it works."

I couldn't help myself. "Oh, that's right. You have to exchange your very soul for this status, don't you?"

He frowned, shook his head and puffed out a breath in frustration. "You're just trying to goad me into a fight. Well, it won't work."

"I don't want to fight. But I also do not want to change."

"Yes, you mentioned that before," he said with deeply etched sarcasm.

At loggerheads now, my tendency was to back down, but I lifted my chin higher, knowing my capitulation was exactly what he wanted. This issue was too important to concede.

I could practically see his mind whirling, trying to think of another tack.

Finally, he said, "Listen, maybe I will have that drink. A cup of coffee?"

As I turned away from him, I rolled my eyes, wondering what he would do next.

I filled the coffee filter with French roast, the only kind he would drink, and added water.

He was still standing, leaning against the door jam when he commented, "You know, we need a better coffeemaker. Bunn makes a fabulous product, one that turns out a world-class cup of coffee."

I shrugged. Coffee was coffee, and I wasn't even all that fond of it. Only drank it out of habit.

"So, tell me about Jeanette. What's up?"

Turning to look at him, I frowned. "I thought the firm didn't like diluted bloodlines."

Perturbed now, his brows furrowed into a fuzzy straight line across his forehead. "Just answer the question, will you, Jolie?"

Shaken by his tone, I asked lightly, "What was the question again?"

"Jeanette. We were talking about Jeanette."

"She's upset. Her sister has Parkinson's disease and is no longer able to manage on her own. Why do you want to know?"

"Just interested, I guess."

Just interested, my foot. I said nothing, waiting for him to speak.

"So why did she call you?"

"She has no one else."

"What about Steven?"

"He isn't interested in supporting her right now, because she'd like to take her sister into their home and care for her, and he's put his foot down."

He made a motion of clapping his hands together. "Well, good for Steven. I hope he sticks to his guns. I can just imagine how it would look to have a messy, helpless invalid in the house. That's one thing on which the firm and I heartily agree."

I had to bite my tongue to keep from firing back an angry retort. At least now I knew where he stood on the issue.

I poured his coffee and set it on the table in front of him.

Brian stood staring at me, as if waiting for me to speak. Finally I could bear the silence no longer.

As he sat down, I asked, "Anything else, Brian? If not, I really need to get busy on my novel."

Angry now, he stood, his coffee forgotten, and began to pace with his hands clasped tightly behind his back. "Oh, yeah? It looks to me like you're throwing that in my face."

"Funny," I said, with cynical laugh, "Have you noticed how it's all about how things *look* now?"

"Of course it is. That's all it was *ever* about."

"I beg to differ. Now if you don't mind, I have things to do and places to go."

He stopped pacing and turned to face me, resolute. "I'm not leaving until we discuss this and come to some kind of mutual agreement."

"Mutual? Oh, no. You don't want a mutual agreement, because that would mean we'd both be happy. You want me to swallow your party line—hook, line and sinker. Well, if that's what you're waiting for, please don't hold your breath." I gestured, then followed him toward the door. He stopped midway and glared at me.

"I'll fight you on this, Jolie. I'll have you

committed as the unbalanced woman you are."

"Yes, I think you might've mentioned that a time or so. But as I said before, I'll draft a letter to the partners, explaining how your wife is now a raving lunatic, whom you feel must be institutionalized."

"You wouldn't dare. It would jeopardize your entire way of life." He had turned toward the door again and was stomping ferociously, as if to threaten me.

"Who cares? I could live in a two-room cottage and be happy if it allowed me to be myself. Besides, you're the one jeopardizing my way of life. Right here and now."

Abruptly, he turned to me, and I bumped into him. He took hold of my shoulders and turned my face up to meet his gaze.

"So what's the answer to this? What do you want me to do?"

"I want you to give up the firm. Start your own law practice. You're sharp, capable and a class act. You could do it, Brian. You'd be great. We'd be great."

After a thoughtful pause, he sighed. "You're dreaming. We'd be starting over from scratch. Do you know how much effort it would take at this age to make it work?"

"But you always said anything worth having is worth working hard for, didn't you, Bry?"

"You know," he said, really communicating with me for the first time in weeks, "if I actually believed you would be behind me in something like that, I might just do it."

"You know me better than that, Brian. I would back you 100%. I'd drop everything to help you. Be your secretary, your gofer—you name it, I'd do it. That is, if we could go back to being who we really are, with no compromise."

He tilted his head and looked into my eyes. "You're serious, aren't you?"

"Deadly."

He sighed and let his shoulders slump. "I can't do it. It would be throwing away my dream."

"My nightmare."

He gave me a sad smile. "You're funny. Do you know that?"

"I'm not trying to be funny. I'm being honest." After a brief pause, while I let my hope die, I added, "Listen, Brian, if you ever decide you want me and our old life instead of this…nonsense, you let me know, and I'll be there for you, okay? Really."

He nodded, looking forlorn, and it brought to mind the scripture where Jesus asked the rich young ruler to give up all he had to follow Christ. The man refused and went away rich, but sad and empty, just like my husband.

As Brian opened the door, I pulled him down by his lapels and gently kissed his cheek. "I love you, big guy. Always have. Always will."

Looking uncomfortable now, he waved and left. I felt tears sting the back of my throat as I closed the door behind him. It was like he was caught in the quicksand of so-called success, and couldn't pull free even if he wanted to. Well, the Lord and I would have something to say before letting him sink into oblivion.

Cupcake indicated, with a scratch at the back door that she was ready to come in, so I opened the door. But instead of the dog waiting to be admitted, a man I hadn't met stood there. My heart leaped in fright as I stepped back, ready to slam the door.

Chapter Nineteen

"Wait!"

Frowning in confusion, I asked, "Who are you?" Before he could answer, I continued, "And why did you come to the back door? How did you get through the gate?"

"Never mind. Just allow me to introduce myself." He held an ID badge in his hand, which he flashed in my direction. It looked official from what I could see.

He was tall, thin and business-like as he extended his hand to shake mine.

"I'm Jergen Hittner. I need to speak with you, if I might." Uncomfortable admitting him into my home, I exited onto the deck, sank onto a patio chair and gestured for him to join me.

"All right," he said, as he turned his chair to face mine. In the waning sunlight, I could see he was older than my first impression had led me to believe. He had tiny wrinkles around his mouth and eyes and a newly receding hairline if I didn't miss my guess. He had to be in his fifties. But what did he want with me?

His serious gray eyes studied mine as I took in his appearance. He wore a gray pinstriped three-piece suit, with a dove gray shirt and a black and white tie. His ring finger was bare.

I shook my head. "Listen, Mr.—Hittner, is it? Please. I don't understand what you need from me."

"I know. Let me explain. I'm with the Justice Department. We are the law enforcement arm over the ATF, the Department of Alcohol, Tobacco and Firearms. Ever hear of us?"

"Of course, but what do you want with me?"

"To make a long story short, we think your husband's firm is involved in illegally supplying arms to radical right wing organizations in war-torn foreign countries. I just need to ask you some questions."

I shrugged. "Okay, but I know practically nothing about what he does at work. And now that he's a partner, he's like a complete stranger. What is it you want to know?"

"Has your husband ever mentioned any of his cases? Anything that made you wonder about his work?"

"Never. He rarely spoke of it even before his

promotion. I mean, he never discussed any particular cases, except on rare occasions. In fact, I can probably count them on one hand."

"Oh." His mouth twisted in disappointment.

"Listen, I know you've said what they're doing is illegal, but will anyone get hurt?"

"Undoubtedly. What they're doing will endanger the lives of Americans living in those countries, and in some cases, the lives of our military personnel as well."

"In what way?"

"People like those in your husband's firm don't like the agendas of certain government regimes that rule the world, many times because of their trade policies, and because of that, they will support the other side of a war effort. The thing is, in most cases, neither side is especially congenial toward Americans. And sometimes they can be downright hostile. Given weapons, they can become enraged over what they consider even the slightest affront by an American, and in some cases, they simply beginning shooting. So you see why we want this stopped."

"Of course. I see."

"Do you agree with our mission as I've explained it?"

I frowned. "It sounds like you're trying to recruit me or something."

"I am. In fact, I really need someone who can

get inside that office."

"I have no access to the office."

"Why is that?"

"My husband isn't even living here right now."

"Oh, I wasn't aware of that. So there's no chance of your reconciliation?"

"I don't know. We're at a standoff right now."

"Listen, I'm going to give you my card. If circumstances change, please give me a call."

He exited out the back gate without so much as a backward glance, leaving me puzzling over his words. Would I dare to spy on my husband's firm even if I had the means?

Because I desperately needed to clear my head, I pulled the leash off the hook by the back door and called Cupcake to me.

"Want to go for a walk, girl?" I tilted my head in question. "Hey, why didn't you bark when you heard someone break in through the back gate?"

She wasn't saying. Sighing, I clipped the leash to her collar and went to the gate, trying to see how the man could've broken through so easily. The padlock was locked, and even I couldn't exit without using a key, which I didn't have on me. Still shaking my head, I urged my wonder dog through the house and out the front door.

"Listen, you—you dog. I didn't take you in simply for your pretty face. I expect you to protect this place. So what's the deal here, huh?"

She meandered off track to do her business, blithely unaware of how insecure I felt, knowing just any old Tom, Dick or Harry could walk through the gate to mess up my life.

Back at home, I wondered about Brian's involvement in a gun running operation. Unable to stifle my curiosity, I went into his office and locked the door behind me. I was sifting through the things in his desk drawers and suddenly laughed out loud, realizing I was getting paranoid, locking doors when I was alone.

After searching the desk and finding nothing, I booted up his computer and wondered then, why he hadn't moved his office out of the house. Probably because there was nothing of any value here.

Among his computer files, I found one that needed a password to access. I licked my lips, trying to imagine what was important enough to be hidden behind a password. In deep concentration, I tried all the words I could think of and came up empty, before I finally recalled our first phone number, which we tended to use as a password years earlier. Pressing in the numbers, I held my breath.

The melody of a file opening sounded and I watched as the title, in a fancy font I didn't recognize, appeared at the top of the screen. I read, "Enter At Your Peril."

Is this Brian's idea of a joke? I hoped so as I began to read. Before long, I realized it was certainly no joke.

Before I had finished reading the first page, it was clear that Brian had stolen company files and stored them here, but for what purpose? From what I had read, it was clear; they weren't even his clients. *What on earth?*

As I read on, I had trouble pronouncing the names of the clients, whose addresses weren't even in our hemisphere or on our continent. What was Brian up to?

The list was long, including probably seventy client files. The accounts were those involving only the company's three top partners, including the late Ted Pardee, who had died in the mysterious plane crash over Denver a couple of months earlier.

My heart jumped to my throat when I realized Brian could've used this information to blackmail his way into a partnership. Was this the information Jergen Hittner was looking for?

I pulled his card from my tee shirt pocket and looked at it. A cell phone number was penciled in under his office and home phones. I dialed the cell number and heard him pick up on the third ring.

"Sorry to keep you waiting. Hittner here. How may I help you?"

"This is Jolie Stevenson. You were just here—in my backyard?"

"Oh, of course. I'm sorry. I'm just surprised to hear from you so soon."

"I found something in my husband's computer files that may be what you're seeking. I mean, I've got it open, but I can't tell exactly what it is."

"Listen, keep it open and I'll be there in fifteen minutes. All right?"

I hung up, wondering if I was doing the right thing. How could I know what the right thing was in this situation?

When the doorbell sounded only a minute later, I felt suddenly anxious, knowing it couldn't be Jergen Hittner.

Getting up, I turned off the monitor and closed the door behind me. Telling myself to calm down, I took several slow deep breaths and looked through the security hole in the door. Brian stood on the other side. I felt tiny droplets of perspiration form on my forehead and in my hair just before they trickled down the back of my neck. Sweeping my hand across my face, I wiped the dampness away and opened the door.

"What took you so long?" he demanded tersely.

"I'm sorry. I'm not feeling well. I was in the middle of something when I heard the bell."

"So aren't you going to invite me inside?"

"Please, Brian. I don't want to talk about this

anymore."

"Talk about what? Are you second guessing me now?"

"No. I…."

"Well, why don't you just let me speak, and you'll find out why I'm here."

"Go ahead."

"I just realized I need some things from my office."

I had to clasp my hands together to keep them from shaking. "Listen, could this wait until a more convenient time?"

"No. It can't wait. Why would you care if I take what's mine?"

Reaching for a reason, I said lamely, "For one thing, I'm not feeling well, and I get upset when you come, because you aren't coming home to me. You just come and talk, and nothing is ever resolved.

That's the pattern and it's—well, it's hard for me."

He tilted his head and pursed his lips. "I thought you didn't want me to come back."

"I don't if things stay the way they are now, but hey—if things could go back to the way they were. Well, then…"

"That's not going to happen, so just let's get this over with, please?" he said, stalking past me without waiting for a reply.

Grasping for some way to distract him, I began wheezing and choking, let my hands fly to my throat as my eyes rolled back in my head, and I slid to the floor.

After a slight hesitation, he knelt beside me. "Jolie. Jolie, what's going on?" He checked the pulse in my neck and felt my cheek.

"Jolie. Honey, wake up."

I kept my breathing shallow, knowing my heart raced in my chest. I actually felt lightheaded enough to pass out if I weren't already in a heap on the floor.

He took off his tan Armani jacket, folded it and placed it under my head. *Hey, maybe he loves me after all.*

A second later, I heard him pick up a phone and dial 911. *Oy vey, I'm in trouble now.*

Brian stood to his feet. Now terrified he would go into the office, I began to moan.

"I'll be right back, babe. Just let me get a cool damp cloth for your face, okay?"

My only response was another soft moan. A moment later, he was bathing my face, neck and hands with a cloth and his touch felt wonderful. By now, I wanted him back in my life so much I could taste it.

· The doorbell rang, and when Brian answered it, I could hear Hittner's voice through the portal. *Oh, man.*

"Well," said Brian, "it's not really a good time. My wife blacked out a few minutes ago. I don't know what's wrong, and I'm worried about her. The rescue unit is on the way."

"Well, maybe I should take a look at her. I'm a physician," he explained.

Brian evidently fell for it, because I felt the two of them hovering over me, while Hittner took my pulse, checked my eyes and said, "She doesn't seem to have a fever."

"I know—that's what's got me puzzled."

"Did she say anything before going out on you?"

"No, just said she didn't feel well, just before she started to choke and wheeze."

"Does she have asthma?"

"No. Nothing like that. Wait, yes, she was diagnosed with asthma a couple of weeks ago when we were in Florida."

"Well, sometimes we see sudden onset cases in response to certain allergens, that sort of thing."

Just then the ambulance, sirens blaring, screeched to a halt in front of the house and within seconds, two more men were talking quietly and calling my name, checking my vitals, and I had to stifle a sudden urge to scream when one of them started an IV without telling me.

Chapter Twenty

I was still moaning softly and wheezing when they lifted me onto a stretcher and wheeled me out to the ambulance.

As Brian and Hittner followed the gurney, the ATF agent offered, "Listen, you need to be with your wife. I'll lock up the house for you. How would that be?"

Brian, sounding worried, readily agreed, and I knew Hittner had found his opening to copy the files.

The paramedics told Brian to follow in his car, just before closing the door behind us. After taking more vital signs including my blood pressure, one of them said, "This is obviously some kind of an acute allergic reaction. I think we need to give epinephrine. Call it in, will you, bro?"

"Go ahead and give it," called the driver after

speaking briefly on his radio.

I slowly opened my eyes just then, and met the gaze of the tech standing over me.

"Listen, you're having a reaction of some kind, so I'm going to give you epinephrine."

"Please don't. I'm okay."

"Now you just let me take care of things."

"Stop. Please. I said I'm fine."

He cocked his head, studying my face. "You had an allergic reaction of some kind. At least that's what we think happened. You were struggling to breathe."

"But I'm fine now. I'm just embarrassed that I bothered you."

"You didn't bother us. This is what we do. Now let me ask, do you have asthma?"

"Yes. At least that's what one doctor said."

"What about allergies?"

"I don't know. I think I'm allergic to cleaning products and maybe—vinegar."

"Oh. And were you using any cleaning products before your fall?"

"I don't know. I can't remember."

He pumped the cuff on my arm, then listened to my heart and lungs.

Looking slightly puzzled, he said, "Well, listen, you just sit tight, and we'll let the docs decide what to do next."

"No, really. I'm fine now. I just want you to

stop this thing and let me out, okay?"

"Are you crazy? We can't do that. You can go home after the docs clear you to leave, understand?"

In the emergency room, several people began asking questions that I had already answered, and after a time, they finally agreed that the crisis was over, and Brian could take me home.

At home, he seemed reluctant to leave me, but I could only wonder—had Hittner found the files I left for him?

Some time later, the phone rang, and I scurried to pick up before Brian could reach for it.

Jergen Hittner said, "So how are you feeling?"

"Better now, thanks."

"Good. Is your husband listening?"

"Yes."

"Okay, then just let me say I have what I need. Just wanted you to know, so you could rest easy. By the way, that was some very good acting on your part. I take my hat off to you."

"Thanks so much for your kindness."

"Who was that?" Brian asked, looking puzzled, after I hung up.

"Some man who said he was here when I was down. I think he mentioned his name, but I can't remember it."

"I think he said he was a neighbor. His name is Jergen Hittner. So what did he say?"

"Just that he hoped I was okay."

"Are you?"

"Am I what?"

"Okay?"

"I'm fine."

"Good, then let me get what I need from my office, and I'll say goodbye."

"Whatever," I said, sounding resigned.

"We'll talk again, just not tonight. Maybe I'll bring Chinese tomorrow night. What do you say?"

"Only if you don't pressure me to change my mind."

"Okay, then forget it. Why else would I come?"

"To check on me perhaps?"

"You said you were fine."

I said nothing, just flopped disconsolately on the sofa and closed my eyes. He would do whatever he would do, and there was nothing I could do to stop him.

After he left a short time later, I pulled the card from my jacket pocket and phoned Hittner. "Just wondered if you've looked at the files. I want to know if my husband is involved in anything illegal."

"Without studying them in depth, I can't say for sure, but it looks like he used the information to blackmail someone. Do you suppose that's possible?"

"I wondered that myself, but I can't imagine him doing something like that."

"You know, it occurs to me—he could've turned his evidence over to the feds and gotten a nice big reward."

"That's not his style. But then again, I didn't think blackmail was his style either. I honestly have no idea what's going on."

"Listen, let me get back to you, okay? Has he decided to move back home?"

"No."

"Oh, I thought perhaps because of the blackout incident, he might have changed his mind."

"No such luck."

"Well, all right. Take care of yourself, and thanks for the file. I'll let you know what I find out."

After hanging up, I got busy and forced myself to do household chores. Even without Brian to mess it up, things tended to deteriorate. Now I would blame it on Cupcake.

I changed the laundry, then set the kitchen timer so I wouldn't forget it, before turning my attention to dusting and vacuuming.

Some time later, I went to the fridge for an apple and was horrified to see that the vegetable bins were growing furry green things in the bottom.

When, an hour later, I let Cupcake out for the fourth time, I noticed that the lawn needed mowing. Where on earth was the hand mower?

Could I figure out how to use a push mower, even if I did unearth it from the black hole of our garage?

After exiting through the kitchen door, I veered toward the twenty-foot section in front of where Brian's car usually sat.

Among other things, I found broken bicycles, one bowling ball in its open bag, tucked beside a pair of worn bowling shoes, stuffed with rancid socks. *How long have these been here?* Thinking back, I realized no one in the family had bowled since 1979. With only my fingertips, I tossed the socks in the trash and continued my dig.

Feeling like the explorers of old must have felt, I needed to forge a path to where I imagined the mower would be. Brian always used the John Deere rider and always made it look easy. But since I had no clue how to operate that monster, I continued my trek toward the nether regions.

Stepping over a small but heavy box of rusty tools and around a Dirt Devil vacuum on its last legs, I came upon two worn tennis rackets and one pair each of metal roller skates and water skis, both of which hung neatly suspended from the ceiling, ready to decapitate any unsuspecting trespasser. They came this close to making minced meat out of me.

I tripped then, nearly breaking my neck as I fell over a fertilizer spreader with a rusted out bottom. A little beyond that, I fished out a rag-filled garbage bag, a box of old fishing tackle and two bent cane poles. At that point, only a stack of firewood stood between me and my goal. Perched on top of the wood was a plastic gerbil cage abandoned when Cade was six.

I shook my head at the mess. I knew Brian didn't cotton to soiling his hands, but this was ridiculous.

Finally, I could see the window, under which sat my prize, a gas powered Sears push mower. Glancing around me, I could see no way of digging it out, short of bulldozing the entire structure.

Cupcake stared at me from a spot six feet away, as if hanging on every word.

I shrugged. "Listen, just forget it. I'll hire someone to mow. Come on, girl. Let's go have some ice cream."

After scrubbing my yucky hands, I dipped up a tiny bowl of vanilla and set it on the floor in front of her. For a brief moment, she stared at it, then at me before finally deciding it was worth a try. Obviously no one had ever offered her anything quite so delectable before. In less than a minute, the bowl shined, and I sat down to my own small bowl, over which I dumped chocolate fudge topping, in spite of what Brian would think. I savored its dark richness, closing my eyes as I let it melt on my tongue.

A phone call from Jeanette made me swallow a second frozen bite without letting it melt, sending a stab of pain up my forehead. I coughed, grabbed my head, and said, "Just a minute, okay?" I took a couple of deep breaths, swallowed some water and tried to regain my composure.

She asked, "You okay?"

"I'm fine. What's up?"

"You told me to phone when I was ready to go shopping for nursing homes. Well, I talked to Ruth about it, and she wants to go tomorrow. Get it over with."

"Are you sure? It's awfully sudden."

"She's afraid she'll fall and not be able to get up. She's terrified of dying alone and helpless, and we both know that's where this is headed, so I think it's best to get her situated before she gets any worse."

"Okay, what time?"

"Will ten work for you?"

"Ten it is."

"Thanks. I really appreciate it."

With a glance at the calendar, I saw that I had a doctor's appointment for my annual Pap smear the following morning. After penciling in my date with Jeanette, I crossed through my doctor's appointment and picked up the phone, feeling grateful for a reason to cancel. *Maybe another time?*

I knew Brian would have a fit, but Brian wasn't here to argue the point. Besides, my mother needed me.

With no appetite for supper, because of my ice cream blitz, I got into Brian's computer, pushed the password and waited. Nothing happened. I tried again, but the file was deleted, with only its title remaining. I was floored. Did Brian delete it, worried that I would find it?

I searched his other files, none of which had passwords, but found nothing that caught my eye. Suddenly worry set in, when I realized he could be in danger if he had actually stooped to blackmail.

The jangling of the phone set my nerves on edge and I took a slow deep breath to calm down before answering.

"Hey, Buzzy, you never got back to me the last time I called. Or maybe you didn't get my call? Anyway, I wanted to ask if you would invest in my dog grooming business."

"Well, listen, maybe another time, okay?"

She argued, "It's going great. I mean, I hired a twenty-year old animal lover to do the grooming. I pay her ten dollars per dog and I charge the people twenty and thirty, depending on the size of the animal. I mean, it's win-win all the way around."

"Well, I thought *you* were going to groom the dogs."

"I tried it, actually with a dog in your neighborhood. A St. Bernard. She and I had a pact—live and let live. Which meant, forget it. That's when I hired the helper."

"I see. Well, I'm glad it's working out for you."

"So how much can you afford to invest?"

"Listen," I said after brief deliberation. "I've heard it's not good to go into business with family members, so I think I'll have to decline your kind invitation."

"But hey, this is a cinch to make you rich."

"I don't want to be rich."

"What is the matter with you anyway? Who, in their right mind, doesn't want to be rich?"

"Me. That's who. Goodbye, Elly."

I sat down at my pc to work on my novel, but the house seemed eerily quiet, making the hair on my neck stand at attention. Getting up, I turned on the stereo, shoved in my favorite Mozart CD and began to type in earnest. At one point, I thought I heard some noise from the garage, but I knew I had to be imagining things, since Cupcake didn't bark an alarm, and Brian wouldn't be coming home on a bet.

The characters in my story were capturing my heart, and I could picture them walking through my life, living, breathing and doing things I would never dare to do.

The great thing about writing is playing the part of the creator, letting these crazy characters, inventions that exist only in my imagination, do their own harebrained thing, while I jot it down for the record. And the best part is, no one ever tires of stories.

By eleven, I was struggling to stay awake. I roused the dog from napping by my feet and let her out the back door. I thought it odd when she set up an immediate, piercing howl, turning my blood to ice. She'd never done that before.

Seconds later, the lights went out, leaving me in total darkness, feeling suddenly terrified when I saw the rest of the neighborhood had lights. Something was wrong.

Cupcake had still not shut up, and for some reason, resisted the idea of coming inside no matter how I begged. Now terrified, I ran out, picked her up and stuck her in the front seat of the car. After closing the door, I hurried back inside, slipped into my shoes and grabbed my purse and keys.

In less than a minute, I pressed the foot feed to the floor and raced from my neighborhood like a crazy person, heading for the nearest police station.

Our neighborhood is flat, for the most part, but sits on a rise, with three tight curves and several steep, descending hills that lead out of the area.

In my angst, I sped through our residential neighborhood and was approaching the edge of the lake, nearing the first tight curve that hugged a huge stand of dense pines. When I pressed the brake, I felt no resistance at all. In a panic, I pumped it repeatedly with the same result.

Suddenly frantic, I tried to slow my breathing and think calmly of my options. I tightened my grip on the wheel and steered, the centrifugal force shoving me against the driver's side door. After the curve, I righted the wheel.

Whew. I would have only seconds of breathing time before the next critical turn.

Out loud I ordered myself, "Okay, girl, think. What next?" After a brief second, I answered, "Pull the emergency brake." A hard tug did nothing to stop the car, and in fact, the cable pulled out of its holder and flew into the back seat.

"God, help me! Please!"

Instantly, I recalled hearing that if you put the car into park, it would sometimes stop. I did that, but nothing changed. Moving the gear lever from park to second to drive and reverse made no difference at all. What on God's green earth was going on?

"Okay, now think. There must be something else you can do."

I nodded. "Turn off the car. Turn off the ignition."

By now, the car was hurling itself at a high rate of speed toward the second tight curve, and my heart beat like a tom-tom in my throat, loud enough to echo my fear throughout the space.

I turned the key, but again, nothing happened. It was like every control had been severed. Steering wildly to the right, hugging the curve, I realized I was losing power steering. The thing responded like an antiquated Sherman tank, sluggish, making me break out in a sweat as I tugged and pushed the wheel.

Just over the rise was a treacherous, tight curve that had already claimed the lives of several winter drivers taken unawares.

I briefly frowned at the sound of Cupcake's plaintive whine and watched as she jumped to the floor and cowered against the seat.

After forcing my attention back to the road, the car took flight for a short second before landing again, hard, and continuing its downward plunge, and I knew it would take superhuman effort that I didn't possess, to keep it on the road.

Praying, I turned that wheel as hard as I could, following the curve, but immediately saw something that took my breath away. To my left, if I couldn't make the curve, was a drop off—a drop off I had never noticed before. Several trees blocked the path in front of it, but either way I went, toward the trees or the cliff, I—*we* would surely die.

Without thinking, I closed my eyes and gripped the wheel hard, unable to recall if I was seat-belted in.

Instantly the sedan slashed narrowly between trees with spoke-like branches, and the sound of scraping, crunching metal and shattering glass made me cringe before we finally slammed hard into a third giant pine. As the windshield collapsed and the door caved inward, I felt pain and a terrifying sense of dread just before I knew nothing at all.

Chapter Twenty-one

I opened my eyes and blinked in confusion, trying to remember what had happened. In an instant, it all came back.

The sky, still a deep inky black, let not a single shred of light through the thick cloudy haze. I felt weak and dazed, with pain in my head and chest as well as in my left forearm, right shoulder and my left leg and foot. A warm trickle of blood seemed to be wending its way from behind my right ear, down my neck. Try as I might, neither of my arms would stop shaking enough, or move freely enough to let me staunch the flow of blood.

In the dark, I struggled to see the condition of the car to determine the best way out. The driver's side seemed to have crunched like an accordion, effectively lowering the roof to just above my head. The passenger's side door was badly dented, but of the two, certainly seemed the better option.

All or a sudden, I remembered Cupcake. I said between teeth gritted in pain, "Cupcake. Girl, where are you?" Now twisting to get out from under the mangled steering wheel, I realized my left foot and leg were pinned into the corner and would not yield, no matter how I tried to get free. With my right hand, I tried to reach out for Cupcake, but screamed in agony, when white-hot lightning shot up my shoulder and into my jaw.

Flashing dots of white and black danced before my eyes, and I knew I was going into shock. With my last conscious breath, I thanked God for my wonderful life and asked him to take care of my family.

At some point, I dreamed that a weeping Brian stood beside me, telling me not to leave him.

It was some time before I woke again, wondering where I was. The space was a shimmering white, making me think of heaven, but the smell was too medicinal. I briefly puzzled over that; they didn't need medicine in heaven, did they?

I woke later, hurting in places I didn't know I had. Because my chest pained me with every breath, I took slow, shallow breaths. A blinding headache throbbed behind my eyes, in a head that felt hugely swollen, under a thick, rather too snug bandage. My right eye was nearly swollen shut, and the vision in my left eye was indistinct, making me want to blink repeatedly to clear it. A youngish nurse appeared at my side and smiled.

Even in my foggy state, I could tell she was pretty, with dark, nearly black, shoulder length hair.

"So, you finally decided to put in an appearance, huh?"

"What happened?"

"You were in a car accident. Don't you recall?"

"Vaguely."

"You're a very lucky lady. If you had been trapped much longer, it would've been too late."

She adjusted the IV drip and then frowned, studying the needle in my hand. "I sure hope this IV site holds, because you have terrible veins."

Pulling up the tape that held the needle in place, she moved it around, causing me to cringe with the digging.

"No, now don't move, all right?"

"When do I get to go home?" I knew the question was stupid even as I said the words.

She laughed. "Are you kidding? Any way you look at it, honey, you're going to be here for a while, so you'd just better get used to the idea."

"Does my husband know?"

"Yes, he's down getting a cup of coffee, if I'm not mistaken."

I turned to inspect my injuries, but immediately thought better of it.

"You hurting?"

"Yes." I stifled the impulse to roll my eyes.

"I'll add something to your IV, and we'll have you more comfortable before you know it."

She disappeared momentarily and returned with a syringe, which she injected into my IV. In less than a minute, a warm flush of comfort radiated through me, relieving my pain but also making me too drowsy to stay awake.

Fighting sleep, I moved my hands and realized my left hand was splinted and wrapped. My chest also seemed to be tightly encased in layers of bandages.

My left foot and leg were suspended in a metal and canvas contraption several inches off the hard bed, and my right arm lay against me, covered by a blue cotton sling.

Out of the corner of my eye, I saw movement, and recognized, through the blur of medication, the familiar figure of my husband. My heart did a little flip just before I slid into a hazy, narcotic dream world.

When I woke again, the sun was coming up just outside my window, and Brian stood beside my bed, gently stroking my cheek.

"Hi, babe. Waking up?"

I blinked and tried to smile, feeling relieved that I could see through my left eye.

"How you doing, honey?"

"Could be better," I said thickly, through a dry mouth.

"Here. Let me swipe your mouth with this. It will make it feel better." He used a lemon-flavored swab and moistened my dry lips and tongue.

Turning to look at Brian, I asked, "Is Cupcake dead?"

"The pup? Oh, honey. I'm sorry. Really."

Tears slid down my cheeks.

Stroking my battered forehead, he crooned, "Listen sweetheart, I'm just grateful you're all right. And hey, we'll get another dog if you want. How about that?"

"I just feel so bad. If I'd left her home, she would've been safe."

Suddenly, a man, dressed in a navy three-piece suit, appeared at the door, and knocked. Brian turned, gestured for him to enter and watched him walk into the room.

The newcomer studied my face as he reached out to shake, first Brian's hand, then mine. When he saw the sling on my arm, he simply nodded, letting his hand fall to his side. "I'm Detective Ross Haggerty, and I'd like to ask you a few ques-

Garden of the Gods

tions if you feel up to it."

Haggerty stood just a little less than six feet
tall, had gray hair and deep gray blue eyes. He had
aged well, kept a slender figure and exuded an air
of class even in what I guessed to be his early sixties. His eyes were savvy, but not suspicious, and I
felt ridiculously grateful at the realization.

When I nodded, he said, "Do you remember
pressing on the brakes before you hit the tree?"

"Yes, several times, but they had failed completely. I—even tried pumping them, then turning
off the ignition, shifting to a lower gear and setting the emergency brake. Nothing worked to
slow it down, and instead it seemed to speed up."

He nodded. "That fits with the facts. After
thorough inspection, we've discovered that your
car was tampered with. The brake line was cut
and the transmission and power steering fluids
had been drained."

I blinked, suddenly restless, trying to think. "I
thought I heard something, scraping noises in the
garage not long before I left the house, frightened. And Cupcake sensed something, too, set up
a howl, refusing to come inside."

Brian's face paled as he turned to look at the man.

"You mean someone tried to kill her?"

"Looks like it."

Brian frowned. "But that's ridiculous. Why
would anyone do such a thing? She has no enemies."

Haggerty tilted his head and stared at Brian. "What about you? Could someone have been trying to kill *you*?"

Brian swallowed nervously before stammering, "I d-don't think so."

Even in my altered state, I discerned my husband's lie.

"Listen," the detective said to Brian, "I think you and I need to go somewhere and talk. How about it? I'll buy you a coffee."

Brian reluctantly agreed and followed the other man out the door. He turned then, and said, "I'll be back shortly, sweetheart. You rest, okay?"

He didn't have to tell me twice. I slept until some time later, when I felt him kiss my hand.

He smiled. "I love you. Do you know that?"

"You do?"

"Yes. Very much. I know I haven't been very loving lately, but I'm just sick that you were so badly hurt. And the thing is, it was *my fault*."

"Your fault? What do you mean?"

"Hittner was just here and spoke with the detective and me. He says he knows I blackmailed the firm to get the partnership." He shook his head as tears glistened in his eyes. "He said you knew, too. Is that right?"

I nodded. "I wondered about it."

He continued, "I'm so sorry, honey. Can you

ever forgive me?" I nodded, pulling his hand toward my lips, where I softly kissed it.

Blinking back tears, he added, "I can't believe I did it. I guess you were right. I was ready to sell my soul to the devil in exchange for a partnership."

"But what did you mean—the accident was your fault?"

"I think whoever tampered with the car was planning to kill me, not you, and I'm pretty sure they were hired by the firm."

"Oh dear. Will you be charged with anything? I mean, are you in trouble?"

"Technically, there's no crime, because the partners never reported it. I had proof of their involvement in illegal activities, but there's nothing tying me to it in any way. Obviously, just between you and me, it was ethically and morally wrong. I'm not foolish enough to believe otherwise. I know what I did."

"So what does that mean?"

He sighed. "I'm trying to tell you that I won't be going to jail."

I whispered, "I'm so glad. I can't imagine my life without you."

He gently kissed my left cheek, the only place on me that didn't hurt.

He asked, "I have only one question for you, babe."

"What's that?"

With an enigmatic smile, he asked, "Were you serious when you said you'd be willing to start over?"

"Of course."

"Well then, you'd better hurry and get well soon, because as of tomorrow morning, I'll be out of a job." Seeing my look of confusion, he added, "Yup, I'm quitting as of nine A.M. tomorrow. The authorities are examining the evidence that will prove the firm funded the illegal sale of weapons to unfriendly nations.

"I'm not included in the indictment, because my position is so new, but the other two will probably be out of circulation for quite some time. In fact, I'm wondering if the firm will survive the scandal this will create. Old money clients are bound to run from even the slightest hint of a scandal."

My eyes were closing again as he kissed my hand. "You sleep now, babe. I've got to go get started, rebuilding our life together, but I'll be back in the morning. All right?"

I nodded as I drifted off.

Three very long days later, I was finally disengaged from the contraption that held my leg. A youthful physical therapist, by the name of Sam Barber, began to work with me, encouraging, coaxing and finally, forcing me to work my muscles. Over the next few days, he had me upright, and not long afterward, walking slowly but surely, with the aid of crutches.

Over the next couple of days, Chrissy and several of the teachers from the school visited and brought chocolates, which I passed around to the nurses, and a basketful of flowers and handmade get well cards, from the budding geniuses in the second grade.

By day number nine, I finally bid a not so fond farewell to the hospital and let Brian ferry me home, where I could only dream of a speedy recovery.

My husband, I learned quickly, was a changed man. He was gentle and solicitous—supportive, encouraging me at every turn. I knew, although he hadn't explained, that he had had an epiphany when the accident nearly took my life.

One day, Chrissy called after lunch, and Brian, who sat beside the phone, picked up. I could hear him trying, not to defend, but to explain his recent reprehensible behavior. As he brought the phone to me, I could hear her screeching at him in her lilting Irish brogue. The brogue only surfaced in the heat of anger.

"You think you're too good for the likes of the Irish? Well, here's what the Irish think of you." With that, she slammed the phone in his ear and left him blinking in shock.

Looking at me, he murmured, "She hung up on me."

"I heard. Listen, let me call her back and apologize. Maybe if things work out, she'll even agree to forgive your temporary lapse in judgment."

"Yeah? Well, I won't hold my breath."

"Just put it on speaker, why don't you?"

He pushed the speaker button as I dialed. When she answered, I said, "Hey there, Chrissy. Just wanted you to know that if you'd given him half a chance, Brian was planning to apologize. So what do you think?"

"I'm not holding my breath."

I laughed and immediately regretted my reckless impulse. Holding my breath, I waited for the pain, in my midsection, to subside.

"What is so all fired funny?"

"Brian said the same thing about you not a minute ago."

"Okay, so where's this apology you mentioned? I'm not hearing anything. Tell the man to get on with it, will you?"

I handed him the phone, but he waved it away, and just spoke up so she could hear.

"Listen, Chrissy, I want you to know I feel terrible about everything, but especially about speaking prejudicially against the Irish people. Forgive me, will you?"

She hedged. "Oh, I suppose. Just don't do it

again. I mean, you must've lost your everlovin' mind to go and do all those things to hurt poor Jolie—threatening to dump her exquisite furniture…."

"I know," he said, aiming a tender smile at me. "I'm just blessed she's not holding that stuff against me."

"You got that right, Mister Big Shot Lawyer."

"Now listen," said Brian, looking slightly piqued, "let's not be saying things we're going to regret, all right?"

"Hey, put the little woman on, will you? I want to chew her ear for a while." I could tell she was in a rare mood.

Laughing, he handed the phone to me. "She's all yours, babe."

Smiling, I said to her, "Sorry I missed our garage sale date last week. Did you go without me?"

"Of course, and I found you a little present."

"What's that?"

"Can't tell you. It's a surprise, and I'm bringing it over tomorrow, all right?"

"I can't wait."

Chapter Twenty-two

It was dusk when I woke to hear Brian fiddling around in the kitchen, a place nearly akin to foreign soil where he was concerned, except for the occasional packaged mix.

He appeared at the kitchen door and noticed I was awake. "Honey, where do you keep the big soup pot? You know—that tall one you use for chili?"

"Under the blender counter, next to the fridge. What are you making?"

"I got a new soup recipe that I think you're going to love."

"What?"

"You heard me. Soup…"

"Brian, what's come over you? You've always hated anything to do with kitchens or real cooking."

"A guy can change, can't he?"

Sounding doubtful, I said, "Boy, I'm not sure."

He laughed. "Give a guy a break, will you, babe? I spent hours sifting through your old magazines for recipes that sounded both good and easy."

"Are you sure you want to do this?"

"Of course. Haven't you heard? I'm a new man, turning over a brand new leaf."

I laughed, splinting my ribs with my arms.

When I could speak again, I said, "This I gotta see."

When Brian finally exited the kitchen, I tilted my head. "I forgot to ask, are we going to lose the house?"

"No, but neither will we be moving up in this lifetime. In fact, with the bonus that went with the partnership—I paid off the mortgage."

"Really? Well, that takes a load off my mind, if you want to know the truth. As far as moving up goes, I have no desire for anything fancier than this, and besides, I love our neighborhood."

His head tilted thoughtfully. "Well, I'm glad you like it here, because we're going to be here a really long time—maybe forever, and I've been thinking of converting part of the main floor into offices if it's all right with you."

I gave him a strained smile. "Hey, what a great idea!"

Studying my face, he said, "I'll bet you wouldn't be opposed to a pain pill right about now. Am I right?"

I nodded, feeling tiny beads of sweat break out on my upper lip.

"Sit tight, honey. I'm on it."

While the pills he handed me did their crackerjack job of pain relief, they also had me nodding off in mere minutes.

"You going to feel like eating some soup in a little while?"

I gave a wide yawn. "I'm too tired to eat."

Brian laughed when he saw my head bobbing. He patted my shoulder before gently pushing me to rest against the pillow. "Okay. You sleep now, babe. You'll feel better tomorrow."

I was wakened to a dazzling sunny day by the sound of hammering outdoors, and I slowly pulled myself to my feet, hurting like crazy, and headed toward the kitchen on crutches. After swallowing another pain pill, I looked out the window and saw stacks of lumber, and Brian, dressed in cutoff jeans shorts and a sleeveless tee, setting giant upright posts in the ground. His face shimmered with sweat, pink from the effort. What on earth was going on? And why was he doing it at the crack of dawn?

I frowned as a glance at my watch told me it was well past ten. *Oh well.* I could only blame my skewed perception on the pain pills. *Nothing like setting up housekeeping in Lala Land.*

Balancing precariously on crutches, I struggled to pour and then carry a cup of coffee to the table. Shaky on my feet, I spilled the hot liquid down the leg of my soft cotton shorts.

I cringed, perturbed, blotting the stain with a dishtowel.

After a couple of sips of coffee, my curiosity got the best of me, and I made my way out to the deck, where I plopped into a chair and hoisted my splinted leg onto a cushion-covered bench.

A wide grin spread over Brian's face when he saw me. "Hey, what you doing out here, kiddo?"

"Trying to imagine what all the racket is about."

Wiping his dripping forehead with the back of his arm, he sprinted toward me until he was looking up from just below my perch. "Don't you remember? I'm building you a tree house."

"A what?"

"A tree house."

Seeing my confusion, he ascended the four deck stairs and sank into a green and white striped canvas chair under the patio umbrella. Suddenly he got up and gently kissed my lips. He lifted his chin and sniffed.

"Ooh, coffee sounds great," he said, heading for the door. He was back in a minute, sipping as he walked.

"Mmm—good."

"I should think you would want something cold, as overheated as you are."

"Nope. Not in the morning." He slurped another sip and looked up grinning. "So how goes it, chief?"

"Oh, you know...."

"Listen, it will get better everyday if you can be just a little patient."

Still confused, I tilted my head, staring at the pile of lumber and the upright posts, now drying in their subterranean cement overshoes.

"What's the matter, honey?"

"I don't get it. What did you say you're building?"

"A tree house—for you."

"But tree houses are for kids, and ours are grown, in case you haven't noticed."

Turning to face him, I added, "You haven't heard from the boys lately, have you?"

"Actually, they've been in touch every couple of days, demanding the latest status reports. They've been worried about you, sweetheart."

"So how are they?"

"Oh, fine, from the sound of things. They both asked if my parents had been here for their annual visit, and I had to admit, I had no idea."

"Well, that was the plan, but with all that happened, I forgot to pick them up at the airport. When your mother called, she was steamed, royally steamed."

"So what happened?"

"I just told them they would have to book hotel rooms, because you didn't live here anymore."

"You're kidding. I'll bet I'll have some mighty tall explaining to do the next time I hear from Mother."

"I'm sorry, Bry. I didn't know what else to say."

He patted my thigh. "It's okay, honey. Life dictates the moves. We simply go along for the ride."

I smiled. "You're certainly waxing philosophical for so early in the morning."

"Listen, I need to get back to work. So are we all straight on the tree house?"

I frowned. "Honey, please. I don't want you to go to all this work for such a silly notion."

"I want to. And besides, it will be for grownups. Probably the best investment in our mental health I could ever make."

"Whatever you want, I guess," I said, shrugging, then cringing in pain.

He laughed. "You might want to stifle the body language for a while. Yours isn't much thrilled by the subtleties of non-verbal communication just yet."

"Tell me about it," I said with a sigh.

"Want some coffee before I go back to work?"

"Yes, please, I spilled most of mine on my shorts."

"Listen, go easy, will you, girl, or you'll have me gray before my time worrying about you."

I grinned. "Too late. You're already gray."

"My point exactly," he said with a raised brow, as he tweaked my nose.

He had just set my newly filled cup down when I heard a shout at the gate.

He frowned. "Who can that be?"

A moment later, he admitted a crotchety Chrissy Dailey.

"Hey, you two. I told you I was coming by today. Some welcome, and with me bearing gifts, too."

I smiled. "You're crazy, do you know that, Irish?"

She raised her brows and made a face. "Should I be insulted by that remark?"

"I hope not, because it's the basis of a long and abiding friendship."

"Oh, well, good then. Just thought I'd better ask."

"So what's in the bag?" I asked, gesturing to the large brown paper sack in her arms. Whatever it was, it looked heavy.

"Here," she said, holding it out to me. "Open it and find out."

She set it in my lap, and I smiled as a wet black doggie nose appeared through the top. "Oh, Chrissy, he's darling."

With my awkward left arm, I gently scooped out a tiny cream, buff and black canine, obviously a mutt, but clearly at least a distant relative to Cupcake, with that funny bristly hair and the most beautiful dark eyes I had ever seen.

"Oh, he's darling. How old is he?"

"*She* is twelve weeks. I've been working on housebreaking this last week, so she's good to go. I know how Brian feels about animals in the house."

He waved a hand in the air. "Well, I appreciate it. I mean, I'm loosening up about animals, but I still don't much cotton to the idea of puddles underfoot."

"Never mind," said Chrissy, waving away his concerns. "This little girl has lovely manners. In fact, she's practically perfect."

I looked up to meet Chrissy's astute gaze. "What's her name?"

"That's your job. She has no name yet."

"I think I'll name her Baby. What do you think?"

Brian smiled. "Whatever you think, honey."

He put out his hand and stroked her soft head. "She is kind of cute, isn't she?"

Chrissy nodded. "I thought so. She's exactly the kind of dog Jolie needs."

Just then, Baby pressed her nose against the palm of my hand and licked it.

"She's waiting for you to pet her. That's the signal. She fusses with your hand until you give her just what she wants. Her mother didn't raise any dummies."

I stifled a laugh. "The things you say... What would I ever do without you?"

"I don't know, but let's hope you never find out. Now, I need to know—at what point do you think you'll be up to garage saling again?"

"I don't know. Can I get back to you on that?"

"Sure, I'll keep in touch. Okay, well, I've got places to go and things to do, so I'd better hit the road." To Brian she said brightly, "Nice to be back on speaking terms with one of my favorite people."

He grinned. "That goes double for me, Irish. Keep your nose clean, will ya?"

"Got it," she called as she headed for the gate.

⁓⁓⁓

"Well, girls," said Brian, with a winning smile, "I'd better get back to work. Will you be okay?"

"We're fine."

Feeling sleepy, I laid my head against the chair back, and let the sun warm me as Baby continued to lick my hand.

Some time later, Brian shook my shoulder, waking me. "Listen, honey, you need to get out of the sun. At least sit under the umbrella. You don't need a sunburn, on top of everything else." He took Baby in his arms, helped me stand, and supported me to a nearby chair in the shade. "That's better." After a brief hesitation while he frowned at me, he said, "You sure you don't want to go inside and lie down?"

"I guess I should, huh?"

"Okay, let me get your crutches." Moments later, he settled me on the sofa and then set a glass of ice water on the coffee table beside me. "Listen, I'll be in and out, babe, so you sleep, okay?"

Baby curled up beside me, nestled her head under my hand, and we both fell asleep.

At some point, I roused to noise from the kitchen and got up to use the facilities. As I exited the bathroom, Brian came toward me. "Hey, how about some of my yummy vegetable soup? I mean, you probably had no breakfast, and it's past one. Join me, huh?"

I nodded, intent on keeping my balance. Baby, at that moment, followed us to the kitchen and settled under my chair, out of the way of my crutches. Definitely a clever move on her part.

Chapter Twenty-three

Brian covered my hand with his and asked the blessing before looking up to meet my gaze. "When we're finished eating, I want to take you out to see the progress on the tree house."

"But Brian, you don't have time to build a tree house."

"I have all the time in the world now that I've quit the firm."

"But that's just it—we need to convert the house and get ready to open your new office—before we run out of money. Tree houses should be the last thing on your list right now, as far as I can see."

He gave me a wry smile. "Aw, honey, now you're doing a Brian imitation. Cut it out, will you?"

"What?"

"All our lives, I've done nothing but push, rushing after the next *thing*, and just look where it got me. No. Listen, I think this tree house is doing something miraculous inside me, restoring my dreams—you know, the child in me." After a slight hesitation while he gathered his thoughts, he added, "Does that make any sense at all? Are you getting what I'm saying here?"

"I am. I guess it's just that when I look ahead and see so much work to do at our ages and—well, it's a bit overwhelming."

He patted my hand. "You're absolutely right, so here's what we're going to do. We're going to finish the tree house first, trusting the Lord to be our provider. He promises to do that, you know."

"I know."

"Well, then, let's test that promise."

When I made a face, he said, "Oh, I know I've made a one eighty that's not to be believed. Here's what you're thinking. You think that at any minute, the old Brian will reappear like a genie out of a bottle and start cracking the whip again, but believe me, that's not going to happen. I know it's hard to imagine me changing so radically, but I've got to tell you, when I saw you in that hospital bed, at death's door, and realized you nearly died because someone wanted *me* dead, well, brother, that was enough to sink my ship. I thought I'd die if I lost you, babe. I really did. I mean, money, status, all the things I was reaching for—it all paled in significance to life and breath and health and happiness. Know what I mean?"

"I think so."

The sun broke through for me when he flashed me his million-dollar smile. "Well, okay then. We're building a tree house—to kick back, to get into our kid mode often and joyfully, before facing life and its challenges. I think that's a reasonable way to deal with what comes next, don't you?"

I smiled. Now *this* was the man I had fallen for, hook, line and sinker, and at that moment, I understood why. The man had dreams I could latch onto, dreams big enough to carry us forever, as long as we held tightly to God. At that moment, I felt my spirit smile, as though someone had just lifted a thousand-pound weight off my back.

His brows danced upward in question. "What?"

"I was just thinking how much I love you."

He rolled his eyes. "Oh, boy. You'd better cool that kind of talk toot de suite, or I'll have to resort to cold showers, woman." His eyes twinkled merrily as he fanned his neck with his hand.

I couldn't stifle a giggle. "Sorry."

He lifted a doubtful eyebrow. "Yeah, I'll just bet you are."

With a glance down at our food, he said, "You know, we've messed around so long that this soup is stone cold. Want me to reheat it?"

"Sure, thanks."

"Listen, as soon as you're on your feet, we've got some serious necking to do. I mean, I haven't exactly been the most loving husband lately—but I guess I'm just saying—don't tempt me until you're up for it, okay?"

Playfully, I retorted, "That's going to be a tall order. You realize that, don't you?"

He shook his head and glared at me, feigning upset. "Now you've gone and done it. Say, how much pain are you in anyway?"

I laughed. "Well, I doubt if I'm ready for that yet, so give me a day or two, all right?"

"Well, then, stop looking at me like that."

I made a face. "Like what?"

"Like that. With those googoo eyes of yours. They've always made my heart turn over—you know that."

I grinned, shaking my head. "I know nothing of the kind."

"Well, you do now, so I'm giving you fair warning."

"Just heat my soup, will you? I'm starved."

His merry, ringing laugh filled the air, and I

felt unexpected tears swell in my throat.

Giving me a look of affection, he asked, "What's the matter, babe?"

"I've missed that wonderful laugh of yours, Bry. I've always loved your laugh, you know."

He kissed my cheek and smiled. "Well, from now on, you'll be hearing it until you think you want to throw a pot at me. All right?"

"I can live with that."

"Good. Now let's eat."

Setting my fragrant, steaming soup in front of me, Brian said, "Need anything else?"

I blinked, unused to his solicitude. "A pain pill would be more than welcome right about now."

After setting the tiny brown bottle in front of me, he said, "I can't wait till you're off those things. You take them and they effectively put out your lights for hours at a time. All you do is sleep."

He saw my look of consternation.

"Oh, I'm not complaining. I want you to be comfortable, but now that we're having such a good time together, I miss you something awful."

I couldn't stop a silly smile. "Why, Brian, I think that's just about the nicest thing you've ever said to me."

"Yeah, pathetic, isn't it? Now quit smiling and eat, will you?"

I laughed. "I'm eating. I'm eating."

He pouted. "That's not all you're doing, girl. I meant what I said about the cold shower. So just hush and eat."

After he had tidied the kitchen, he steered me out to the deck, where I opened my eyes wide.

"Wow. You must have untapped talent for building things. It's great."

"Think so?" His eyes looked hopeful.

"I do. It's amazing."

"Thanks. Sad, isn't it, to think that maybe I've always had a knack for working with my hands? I just never realized how satisfying it would be until now. Wasn't all that crazy about it in junior high shop class, but then, nobody ever let me build a dream tree house either."

Together we admired it, and he went into great detail, explaining what would happen next. He had already affixed the three-quarter inch pine flooring to the tops of the four posts. He had set four primitive wood posts at the top of the stairway opening in the center and started framing the corners of the openwork walls with upright eight by eight rough hewn logs.

"So it's going to be more like a covered patio than an actual tree house, right?"

"Yes, I don't want to obscure the view. Know what I mean?"

"I think so."

"It will even have wide overhangs, so we can sit out in rainstorms if we want to, without getting wet."

"I think that sounds kind of nice. Romantic."

"Well, listen, I think we'd better get you inside before the mosquitoes begin their feeding frenzy and you're the main dish."

I laughed. "Where have you been hiding that crazy sense of humor all this time?"

"Beats me, but it's here to stay now. I promise."

I kissed then caressed his cheek. "Glad to hear it. Welcome home."

"Okay, that's it. You're treading on thin ice here. I need to go put away my tools and then run a *nice cold shower*, thanks to you."

"Sorry, Bry."

He waved away my apology. "I know, I know. I've heard it all before. Oh, before I go outside, I need to say one more thing."

"What's that?"

With a mischievous glimmer in his pleading eyes, he whispered into my ear, "Please, get well soon."

Brian had just headed for the shower when a huge thunderbolt shook the house and sent my heart leaping into my throat. Baby instantly jumped into my lap and hid her face under my arm.

"Oh, it's okay, sweetie. It's okay," I said, softly stroking her head.

Suddenly the sky opened, letting loose a deluge, deafening as it hit the skylights overhead, as if Jack In The Beanstalk's giant had just overturned his bucket.

Brian appeared at the top of the stairs, wrapped in a towel, and I could see his lips move, but the sound of rain completely obliterated his words.

"What?" I yelled.

As he descended the stairs and began to walk toward me, he answered loudly, "I said maybe I'd better wait until after this storm. I mean, we certainly need the rain, but this is a little much."

"Will it hurt the cement footings?"

"No, they were pretty well set before I ever started on the floor and framing."

He motioned me to move over, cuddled close to me on the sofa and put his arm around me.

"Listen, big guy, maybe you should get dressed. No one knows how long this storm will last. You might freeze to death."

"Well then," he said, brightening hopefully. "It will be your job to keep me warm, right?"

"I'm an invalid, remember?"

"You might be surprised what you can do if you put your mind to it."

I grimaced. "My mind has nothing to do with it, Mister."

He laughed and turned my chin up to gently kiss my lips.

He pulled me snugly into the curve of his arm and pushed my head to rest on his shoulder, brushing a stray lock of hair from my eyes. "Say, I should've started a fire, shouldn't I?"

Just then the lights flickered for an instant, went back on and then off, leaving us once again in thick darkness, broken only by brilliant lightning flashes overhead.

"Excellent idea, Sherlock," I said, deadpan.

"Hey, you. You're a wiseacre tonight, aren't you? What is that?"

"Just feeling playful, I guess."

"Better watch that. Well, if you'll give me a shove off this thing, I'll go find some kindling."

"There's still some in the wood box, I think."

"Oh, yeah?"

"Yup. I checked it out not long ago."

"Well, good. I would rather not go out to gather twigs, while wrapped in a towel."

I grinned. "Not excited about giving the neighbors a show, huh?"

"Not particularly—no."

I gave him a gentle shove, and he grabbed

the towel just before it fell to the floor.

"Oh-oh," I said, laughing and shaking my head.

A few minutes later, the fire lit the room with its soft ambience, comforting me with gentle crackling sounds.

"Okay," he said, making his way back to the sofa. "Make room for the man, will ya?"

"Think so?" I teased.

"You—are in for it now. Giving me a hard time."

I laughed. "I didn't say a word. Not a single word."

The storm's fury knew no bounds, and I felt grateful not to be alone.

We sat quietly, snuggled together, listening to the storm and watching the flames dance and snap. After a time, the room had warmed, making me feel languid and sleepy.

Finally, he said, "I think the storm is dying out. Ready to go upstairs?"

I nodded.

"Okay, let me secure the fireplace and turn off lights, otherwise we'll wake up to a light show in the morning."

Brian helped me to my feet, tucked the

crutches under my arms and called Baby, offering to let her out one last time.

Making my way to the staircase a few minutes later, I saw a last flicker of lightning through the skylight at the top of the stairs. Were my eyes deceiving me, or was Brian standing on the upstairs landing?

In near total darkness now, I could see nothing and suddenly, I felt shaky and frightened.

"Brian, is that you?"

Silence.

I stood rooted to the spot, but grew weary of leaning against the crutches that chafed my armpits. Just getting from point A to point B was like running a marathon these days. Sweat broke out on my forehead, upper lip and palms as I anxiously strained to hear—what?

Thunder crashed in the distance, but only faint lightning lit up the space at the top of the stairs, which was now empty.

"Nuts to this. I'm going to bed. Now I'm hallucinating on top of everything else."

I struggled to ascend the stairs on crutches in the thick blackness, gingerly feeling my way, testing my footing, one step at a time.

Chapter Twenty-four

A couple of days later, we had just finished breakfast, when Bryan said, "Okay, now. Are you ready to see my masterpiece?"

"What?"

"The tree house. It's finished, and not too shabby if I do say so myself."

"Of course. Lead the way."

Leaning against the deck rail while standing on crutches, I gave him a wide smile.

"Oh, Brian, it's fabulous. Really." My vantage point was only a few feet below the floor of his masterpiece, so I had a good view.

"Like it, honey?" he asked, sounding hopeful.

"Oh, yes. I can't wait until I can get up there and enjoy it myself."

Craning my neck, I studied his design and building efforts. The deck part appeared to be

about twelve feet wide by fifteen feet long, suspended ten feet above the ground, with a huge,
slightly pitched green-shingled roof that overhung
the perimeter by several feet on every side. He
had enclosed the deck floor with a rail, made of
willow branches, arranged in continuous primitive
inverted V-design all the way around, reminiscent
of work from the Arts and Crafts period.

The deck held a new glass top table and two
padded wrought iron chairs, as well as two reclin-
ing padded deck chairs with a small table between
them. A tiny refrigerator and a small closed shelv-
ing unit sat near the top of the steep stairs that
ran up through a hole in the floor. Tiny lights
flickered from the top of the railing and the edge
of the deck floor, making it look like a fairy's cottage. Swedish ivy and jasmine vines, anchored in
fancy terra cotta pots, climbed the posts that held
up the roof. More lights twinkled out from behind the vines.

"Oh, Brian," I said again. "It's exquisite.
Really. I love it. Can't wait to feel strong enough
to enjoy it."

"Well, that will be a while," he said dryly.
"But no one goes up there until you do, okay?"

"That's silly. At least you could enjoy it."

"No. I built it for you, sweetheart, and I
won't go up there without you. So, as I said before, please, get well soon."

"I will now, for sure." After that, I made a point to navigate the first floor several times a day in an effort to build my strength.

Two weeks later, the doctor X-rayed my shoulder and leg and pronounced the hairline crack in my left fibula completely healed. After examining my leg for swelling and my shoulder for range of motion, Dr. Peterson, a tall, gangly-limbed orthopedist who reminded me of pictures of Ichabod Crane, commented, "You should be good to go, since you've already been up and around, but go slowly at first, okay, Jolie?"

By the time I had walked from the car to our living room, I was worn out by the excursion. I shook my head, again feeling discouraged at my lack of stamina.

Brian leaned down to kiss my cheek.

"Don't worry, babe. It won't be long now before you have the world by the tail. You're coming right along. You are. You just can't see it like I can."

"Keep telling me, will you, Bry?"

"Of course. Now, what shall I fix for lunch?"

I thought about it for a time. "Got any hot dogs?"

He made a face. "Hot dogs? No, I don't

think so. But let me check the freezer, all right?" I knew he had always regarded frankfurters the way he would Dog Chow.

Not long after, he returned, holding aloft a package of Armour Jumbo dogs.

"Bingo. One package, buried deep in the nether regions."

"Hey, all right," I said, smiling. "That really sounds good."

"Regressing, are we, love?" he said, tickling my cheek with the edge of the frozen plastic.

"Never," I argued with a feigned pout.

"Coming right up. In fact, you know, a hot dog sounds kind of good, even to me, garnished with diced onion, sweet pickle relish and mustard. Mmm…makes me hungry just thinking about it."

"Then why are you just standing there?"

"I'm not. I'm on it," he said, awkwardly laughing as he bounded toward the kitchen.

When he returned a while later, he carried two plates, filled with perfectly prepared dogs in buns, alongside baby carrots, tomato slices, olives, dill pickle spears and white seedless grapes. He turned, left again and came back carrying iced tea glasses topped with lemon slices and mint sprigs.

"Oh, honey, this is great. You've really out-done yourself. Thanks," I said as he set the plate on a tray he had placed on my lap. Baby, wide-eyed, sat at my feet until I tossed her a tiny bite of hot dog, which she deftly caught in midair.

After we were situated, he said, "So, how does it feel to be free of that splint and those crutches?"

"Good. A little odd, I guess, but I suppose progress always feels strange, huh?"

He took a huge bite of his frankfurter and closed his eyes. "Mmm—I don't think I've had anything this good in—well, ever, maybe."

"Regressing?" I asked, in a teasing tone before biting into my own.

After a long drink of tea, he smiled. "I guess so. Not so bad, though, is it? This regressing thing, I mean."

I swallowed a bite of hot dog and licked a glob of mustard from my lips. "Mmm. Yummy."

After lunch, Brian looked surprised when I rose, picked up dishes and began cleaning up the kitchen.

"Feeling better, huh?"

"Well, I don't know if I'd go that far, but I can't just lie around forever, now, can I?" I was now able to manage with over-the-counter pain meds taken twice a day for stiffness.

He nuzzled my neck as I rinsed dishes to put in the dishwasher.

"Brian, that tickles."

"I know. That's what I was going for."

"Here, put these in the dishwasher, will you? I'm running out of steam."

"Listen, leave them, why don't you? I'll do dishes later."

"I guess I will."

He led me into the library, where he laid out a thick, soft quilt over the carpet in front of the hearth and helped me onto it.

With a twinkle in his eyes, he said, "I'm building a fire, and we're going to snuggle on the floor. Then I'm bringing the wine and the affection, and all you have to do is show up. Okay?"

I made a face. "What is this?"

"I'm courting you."

"Honey, last time I looked, we were already married. Or have I missed something?"

"Oh, no. I just did such a lousy job of romancing you over the past few years that I've decided to get it right this time. So what do you think?"

I felt a warm flush crawl up my neck. "Wow. I don't know what to say."

Chapter Twenty-five

He helped me pull fat, cushy pillows from the sofa to the floor, and I watched while he started a fire. Then he lit candles that shortly scented the space with my favorite jasmine fragrance. Not long after, he put on my treasured classical harpsichord music and disappeared down the hall. When he reappeared, he held two glasses of sweet wine, one of which he handed to me.

I laughed, "I can't believe any of this."

"Well, believe it, okay, Babyface?"

"Babyface?"

"Yup, *Babyface*. Now have a sip of your wine and then kiss me, will you?"

I laughed as he sank down beside me on the floor.

He shook his head. "No laughing. This courting is supposed to be serious business. Don't you know that?"

I stifled a smile. "Nope, never been courted be-

fore, so you'll have to show me the ropes."

"Show you the ropes? Gladly." He gently pulled me into his arms and began kissing me as I'd never been kissed before.

When I could finally catch my breath, he grinned. "Impressed?"

I laughed at his silly grin. "I'll say. Listen, could we try that again?"

With a wide smirk, he pushed me onto the pillows and settled over me, nibbling my ear, getting a little too close to my ticklish neck.

As we lay holding each other in the steamy, scented room, I was surprised at sudden tears that made my chin quiver before cascading down my cheeks to drip on Brian's bare shoulder.

He turned my face to meet his gaze. "What's wrong?"

"I never dreamed I'd feel this way again. So much in love, I mean."

"Aw, babe, it's okay. I feel like we've recaptured a secret we lost, don't you?"

I nodded, unable to speak.

By the time the music ended, the fire was dying out, and only tiny embers flickered as I watched through the partially filled wineglass, my eyes closing in sleep.

Brian whispered sleepily, "Come on, babe, we'd better get you upstairs while you can still navigate. Here, give me your hand."

The next morning, after my shower, Brian led me outside and handed me a cup of coffee. "So, think you'd like to tour your new love nest?"

After sipping my drink, I tilted my head and smiled. "How could I possibly say no to that?"

He took my coffee cup and followed me down the deck stairs. "Easy does it, now."

I felt my excitement mounting as I made my way across the yard.

Pointing, he said, "Hold onto the handrail. That's it."

At the top of the stairs, I made my way to the railing where I could look over the tree-filled slope behind our home.

"Oh, Brian, it's like a dream. It really is."

He gave me the grand tour and said, "So what do you think? Think we can be happy in our little love nest?"

I rolled my eyes. "Need you even ask?"

"Okay. Now that that's taken care of, I think we need to get busy on remodeling the house into our new offices. What do you think? Ready to knuckle down and help me plan the next phase of Operation Revamp?"

I hugged him around the waist. "I think I'm up for that. When do we start?"

"Well, I've been drawing up some ideas, getting them on paper. Oh, by the way, Jeanette called a few days ago, and I told her I'd have you call when you were back on your feet."

"Oh dear. I was supposed to go with her the day after the accident, to pick out a nursing home for Ruth. I'll bet she thought I'd dropped off the face of the earth."

"Actually, she phoned while you were in the hospital, and after I explained what had happened, she was very understanding. She said she would have Steven accompany them to the various nursing homes on their list. I imagine they've probably already made a decision."

"Well, I'd better call her back right away. I feel like I've been out of the loop for way too long."

He downed the rest of the now cold coffee and followed me back into the house, where I settled at the kitchen table and picked up the phone. As her phone rang, Brian set my newly filled cup in front of me and caressed my cheek, smiling.

"Thanks, honey," I whispered, returning his smile.

On the fourth ring, Jeanette answered.

I said, "I heard you phoned. I'm sorry I couldn't help with the nursing home search."

"Listen, when Steven heard about your mishap, he decided to pitch in and lend a hand with the search. We all went a couple of days after your accident. Ruth is now safely ensconced at the Glendon Hills Retirement Center. I like the name—not as depersonalizing as the phrase, 'nursing home'. Don't you agree?"

"I do. So how does she like it?"

"Well, of course, she isn't thrilled with being dependent, but as nursing homes go, it's quite classy, and I'm convinced, from what I've seen so far, that she'll get excellent care there."

"Oh, I'm so glad. I do still want to meet her."

"I appreciate that. So tell me, how are you feeling?"

"I'm bouncing back, not as fast as I had hoped, but everyday I feel just a little stronger, and I was really gratified to finally get rid of the splint and the crutches."

"Well, that's good news, isn't it?"

After a pregnant pause, she said, "Well, I would like to take you out to lunch when you feel up to it. And maybe I can stop by Ruth's new place and introduce the two of you. What do you think?"

"I'd like that very much."

"All right. I'll give you a buzz early next

week. Take care of yourself, my dear."

I couldn't stifle a smile. She had called me her 'dear'. That was the closest thing to an endearment I had heard, and more than I ever expected.

Brian, now doing dishes, tilted his head. "What are you so happy about?"

"Jeanette called me her 'dear'."

"Wow. Things, they are a changing, huh?"

Not long afterward, Brian led me into the office and said, "Sit down and I'll show you my ideas for the remodel."

Handing me a set of plans finely detailed on graph paper, he said, "These are to scale. I think the best thing will be to use the back entrance into the library, if you don't mind me commandeering it for use as a reception room. The three downstairs bedrooms—" He pointed toward the plan, "I've numbered them there—will be used, one for my office, the second for storage of files and the third for doing research and housing all my law books."

"Hey, that will work."

"We'll also have to start using the living room a lot more if we convert the library, so we'll have to make use of that chintz furniture you love so much. And maybe you'd like to paint, or add a few more pieces to warm up the room. I guess that will be up to you, with your wonderful flair for decorating."

My eyes widened at the compliment. "I didn't know you appreciated my decorating skills."

"Honey, there are a lot of things I appreciate about you that I've never mentioned, but from now on, that's all going to change."

I made a face, flushing in embarrassment at his warm tone. I looked away as he came and sat beside me, wrapped me in a warm embrace and pressed a kiss to my cheek and neck.

"I mean that, babe. I've come to realize that you're the most important person in my life, and I vow never to do anything to jeopardize our relationship again." He lifted my chin, turning my face toward his.

"Thank you."

He smiled. "So what do you think of the plans?"

"They're perfect. So when do we start, and what do we do first?"

"We need to have a sign made, install a business phone line, and purchase an ad in the Yellow Pages. I want to move the furniture out of the bedrooms. I know it sounds like a huge undertaking, but we'll just take it one step at a time, okay? And I can hire help for the heavy lifting."

"Just tell me what I can do to help, all right?"

"For right now, you can stay right there and compose an ad for the Yellow Pages and the Sentinel. All right?"

"I can do that, I guess."

Brian and I spent the next four days, finishing up the plans and shopping for oak cabinets in which to store files and law books. I helped him compose letters to his client list, most of whom he felt would be eager to use his services.

He hired a crew of four starving college kids, who constructed a frame and, under his supervision, installed a door in the hallway, separating our living area from the office space. They also put together the floor to ceiling cabinets and did the heavy lifting, moving and rearranging furniture under Brian's direction. They finished by adding the final touch, a fancy scrollwork sign, suspended from a sturdy wrought iron post in our yard, in essence hanging out his shingle, announcing that we were open for business.

The kids evidently had a good time, at least if the laughter that drifted down the hall was any indication. At lunchtime, I set out a huge tray of ham and cheese hoagies, along with potato salad, cole slaw, chips and dipping veggies and chocolate fudge cake for dessert.

While they ate, I cleaned up dishes and listened to them talk about school, cars, girls, football and dorm living. It sounded like they had moved in, for the summer, with a friend who owned a small house. I wrinkled my nose, imagining how crowded and smelly the place might be, housing five messy, young males.

By the time I finished the dishes, they had polished off every last morsel of food and were all properly grateful afterward.

After the crew left, I did the final cleaning and added a few finishing touches to the new spaces, including a couple of huge back-lit plants and classic framed hunt prints that accented his office and the new waiting room.

I found a burgundy and navy welcome mat on a shelf in the storeroom and set it outside the French door that led into his reception room from outside. The effect was perfect, except that the small covered patio seemed a little bare.

Once again scrounging in the storeroom, I found a three-foot tall artificial rubber plant and a stunning, but long-forgotten silk flower wreath, in burgundy and navy. After dusting them off, I hung the wreath on the wall beside the door and the plant along the opposite wall. Standing back to survey it, I was pleased. They were the perfect finishing touches.

I had just poured myself a cup of coffee and stood in the hallway, admiring his new office, when Brian rounded the corner after paying his departing help. Following my gaze, he gave a low whistle.

"Wow. This is a knockout. I couldn't have

done better had I hired the best decorator money could buy."

"Think so?"

"It's dynamite. Really."

"Well, thanks. Want to see it from the outside?"

"Sure," he said, following me through the french door. We stood in the yard as he eyed the new entrance.

"It's perfect. Looks like an established business. Classy and welcoming. I love it."

"I'm glad you like it," I murmured. "But I'd be glad to entertain any other suggestions you might have."

"I think you've covered it perfectly. So how about me taking my new business partner out to dinner after I shower?"

"Sounds like a plan to me."

He gave me a mischievous grin before kissing me hard on the lips. "Good. I'll be back down in a few minutes. Don't forget me, will you?"

"Not likely, big guy," I said with a laugh.

We hadn't been out to eat since the fancy restaurant where we'd met during our separation, and I wondered where he would choose to go, now that his tastes had settled within more reasonable limits.

I looked up when Brian came down the stairs, dressed in tan chinos and a white, blue and tan golf shirt. He smiled then frowned before asking, "What's wrong?"

"I wasn't sure what to expect—you know, as far as restaurants are concerned."

He made a face. "Oh, man. I'm sick of fancy food. Some of it isn't even that good."

"Do I need to change? I mean, I have no idea where we're going."

"The Black Angus Steakhouse. And you look just fine, honey."

He opened the car door for me and stood aside to let me slide in, before he continued, "Anyway, as I was saying, this one night, I went out with the partners to some fancy French restaurant, and you know what?"

"What?"

"I learned I'm not fond of French cuisine. I mean, talk about your rich sauces."

He pulled out of the driveway and headed west, as he said, "Feel like a steak tonight, honey?"

"I don't know. I don't have much of an appetite these days."

"I've noticed. Well, never fear, we'll find something to tempt your taste buds if I have to rope it myself."

I laughed. "You're crazy, do you know that?"

"I seem to remember you mentioning that a time or two."

Chapter Twenty-six

The restaurant, decorated like many western style steakhouses, displayed a plethora of cowboy regalia and steer horns lining the walls. By the time the dark-haired thirtyish waiter took our order, the entryway was overflowing with other hungry patrons.

Over our meal, Brian asked, "So what do we still need to do to get this business up and running? Got any ideas?"

After finishing the last of my yummy French onion soup, I pulled a plate of batter-dipped shrimp toward me. "I think we're pretty well set. Oh, you did call the ad into the Sentinel, didn't you?"

He chewed a bite of T-bone steak and nodded, swallowing before he said, "I most certainly did. Yesterday. It should be out in Friday's paper."

"Then we're good to go. I guess now, we just wait to hear from those you notified by letter."

He smiled. "I'm excited about this, honey. I really am. I mean, I guess I'm surprised that I'm feeling like a kid at Christmas. This is so much more exciting than being a partner. Like we're on our own private adventure."

"Well, that's because we are."

"But you didn't say how you feel about it. Are you anxious about the money?"

"No. I know you'll do fine. I was only anxious when I couldn't see any income. Only outgo. Know what I mean?"

"You know I've put money away for years, don't you?"

"I guess I assumed as much, though you never really said it in so many words."

"I guess I haven't done you any favors, just handling things my own way. I'll fill you in on our finances when we get home, all right? That way, you'll have no reason to worry. What do you think?"

"That's a good idea."

Brian's eyes opened wide just then, and I turned to follow his gaze. James Lester III, one of the partners we thought was incarcerated, stood stiffly at Brian's elbow, glaring at him. The distinguished looking man, with every silver-white hair in place, seemed to have shrunken since I had seen him last. He wore a gray three-piece suit and a pale blue dress shirt and tie. His eyes were ringed by shadows of sleepless nights gone by, or possibly worry.

Brian stammered, "Hi, James…." He seemed to be struggling for words.

I picked up the ball and ran with it. "Won't you sit down? Have you eaten yet?"

He said stiffly, "No, thank you. We just ordered."

I smiled, trying not to look as nervous as I felt. "You guys out on the town tonight?"

"Yes, a last fling before I have to turn myself in to the authorities."

"I see," I said, feeling increasingly uncomfortable.

Fortunately at that moment, our waiter stopped and refilled our drinks, shattering the tension. Meeting the partner's angry gaze, Brian said, "Listen, James. I hope there are no hard feelings."

Instantly, James turned on his heel and stalked away.

In response to the strained look on Brian's face, I said, "I thought that went well, didn't you?" Of course, I was being facetious, but it had the desired effect.

He stifled a belly laugh, put his hand on my shoulder and said, "Oh, honey, you're a pip. You really are."

We left a short time later, with no further sightings of The Third.

The ride home had been quiet, until Brian took hold of my hand and kissed it.

"You know, honey" he said softly, "I don't know what I'd do without you. Know that? I mean, your well-timed humor is like a life pre-server to me."

"Really?"

"Yup. I just realized it tonight. I mean, with all you've been through this past several weeks? I guess I'm surprised your sense of humor survived intact."

When I said nothing, he said, "Tired?"

"A little."

He squeezed my hand. "Listen, thanks for jumping in when The Third tried to intimidate me."

I laughed. "Is that how you referred to him at work? The Third?"

"Of course, only not to his face. But you've got to admit the name fits. He looks and acts ex-actly like *The Third.*" He'd said it in his deepest bass voice and added, "the stuffed shirt."

"That he is," I said, snuggling against his shoulder as he stopped at a traffic light.

I felt sleepy and languid after our late meal, but as promised, I stayed awake to learn about our finances. When Brian had finished his explanation, he smiled. "Feel better now, knowing our ship isn't about to sink?"

"Much, thanks."

"Good." In a teasing tone, he added, "Now don't go spend it all in one place, okay?"

"I promise. Let's go to bed, Bry. I'm bushed."

"Me, too."

The next morning, Brian slept on when I woke and dressed. Downstairs, I put coffee on and retrieved the newspaper from the front porch, stopping to admire Brian's office from the hallway.

I had just turned to go when I heard a knock on the new office door. Feeling self-conscious, I glanced at my watch. Who would be knocking on his office door at eight ten in the morning?

I had not bothered to put on makeup or do my hair, and I knew I must look a mess, but I smoothed my shorts, heading toward the entrance.

At the door stood an unfamiliar woman, in her sixties, dressed in a lavender crop pants and matching oversized tunic with white ballet slippers. Her platinum blonde hair and makeup were perfect.

"Hello," she said, somewhat nervously. "Is Brian here?"

"I'm sorry. The office isn't open for business yet. Not until tomorrow."

"Oh, I'm not here as a client, but I do need to talk to him. Is he here?"

"Listen, come in and have a seat, and I'll go get him. It will be a few minutes. Hope that's all right."

She sighed. "I've got nothing but time."

Brian stirred as I strode into the room.

"Honey, there's a woman sitting in your waiting room. She says she needs to talk to you. Sounds worried, if you ask me."

"She didn't give you her name?"

"No. Oh, dear. I'm sorry. I didn't think to ask."

"Well, you did tell her I'd be a few minutes, didn't you? I'm not even dressed yet."

"I told her you'd be a few minutes."

"Okay. I'm on it. Say, did you make coffee?"

"Yes. I'll get you a cup."

"Thanks. Maybe it will help get my sluggish brain into gear."

"Be right back with it."

Downstairs again, I slipped back to where the woman sat, planning to offer her coffee, but the waiting room was empty. I stood there, puzzled, until it occurred to me to check Brian's office. The woman, who didn't see me, was hurriedly digging through Brian's file cabinets, most of which were still empty.

"What are you doing?"

"Oh, uh—nothing." Startled, she turned and fled past me just as Brian came around the corner.

"Mavis, what are you doing here?" he demanded.

The woman glared at him, flinching out of his sudden grasp as she ran out the door, leaving it ajar.

I frowned. "Who was that?"

"Mavis Lester. The Third is her husband."

"Well, I caught her digging through your file cabinets."

"You're kidding. Did she find anything?"

"She took nothing with her when she left, so I doubt it. She was rifling through the empty drawers as fast as she could."

He shrugged. "Not that I have anything to hide. I wonder what possessed her to come here?"

"What could she have hoped to gain?"

"Beats me. Where's that coffee you offered me, babe? I really need it now."

Brian wore a glum look when I rejoined him at the office door and handed him coffee.

"You okay?" I asked.

"I suppose. It just threw me to have that woman in here, digging around when I know she feels nothing but hatred for me."

"See, that's the thing I don't get. Why would she even think to come here and poke around?"

He shrugged. "The reason escapes me, but it bothers me no end that she did it at all. That just isn't the kind of thing partners' wives do."

"I thought it seemed a little out of character."

He frowned. "Do you suppose she's got something up her sleeve? Some kind of retribution?"

"Honey, you're asking the wrong person. I had no idea even who she was."

"Right," he said, absently and turned toward the kitchen.

As I set his breakfast in front of him a short time later, Brian suddenly perked up and said, "Okay, enough moping. Let's take our breakfast up to our love nest. What do you say?"

"Really?"

"Yes. Let's put our food on a tray, and I'll carry it up. This should be fun, especially since it's so nice and cool up there, this time of the morning."

Huge trees hovered over the love nest, except to the north, where it had a magnificent view of the surrounding valleys and adjacent rolling hills, covered with oaks and pines and the occasional farm in the far distance. The shade was cool as we sat enjoying each other's company.

Brian swallowed a bite of bacon and sipped his coffee.

"You know," he commented lightly, "this place is almost like an enchanted cottage—much nicer than Orlando."

I laughed. "I think so, but what made you think of that?"

"Oh. Well, when I golfed down there—at least on the two holes I managed to play, we were surrounded by trees, but somehow this feels much more carefree, doesn't it? I guess even Mickey and Donald have nothing on our love nest."

I patted his hand. "Listen, honey, I'm really sorry your vacation didn't turn out the way you planned."

"You know," he said, with a tilt of his head, "I think maybe the Lord was trying to get my attention on that little trip. I mean, if you think about it, the whole thing was a fiasco—the flight, the weather—everything. If you recall, we did nothing but argue from the time we left home until the time we returned."

I smiled. "I may be a bit biased, but I'm also excited with the way your office turned out."

"Me, too."

We were descending the stairs when Brian said, "You know, I didn't call this our love nest for nothing."

"What do you mean?"

"I want us to come out here late at night and make love."

I felt a flush of heat warm my cheeks. "Honey, keep your voice down. You're embarrassing me. What if the neighbors overhear?"

"What on earth is so embarrassing about that? Married couples make love all the time."

"Well, it's just that it's so—out in the open—with no walls to keep other people from looking on."

"Honey, it's densely treed all the way around. Nobody could see a thing if I decided to make love to you up there."

"I'll think about it."

He stopped on the deck, set the tray on the patio table and turned me around to face him. "Don't think about it too long, love, 'cause I'm thinking about tonight."

I rolled my eyes and made a face.

He laughed. "So…."

"Don't ask. I said I'd think about it."

The phone rang just then, and Brian ran to answer it as I picked up the tray to follow him inside.

A wide smile crossed his face as he said, "Oh, of course, George. I'd be happy to handle your business affairs. You just let me know when you need something, all right?"

Turning to me as he hung up the phone, he smiled. "That was George DeWitt. He owns a chain of nursing homes across the state and wants to retain my services. So what do think of them apples?"

"Oh, honey. That's wonderful."

"And not only that, but he says he's talked to a half dozen friends, who were also clients of our firm, and they are planning to call as well."

He pulled me into his arms and buried his head in the curve of my neck, which made me hunch my shoulders in defense.

"Relax, babe, and enjoy the moment, can't you?"

"Not when you do that."

"Okay, okay, I can take a hint." He sat down and pulled me onto his lap, smiling mischievously. "You're beautiful, do you know that, Mrs. S?

"Yeah? And you're crazy."

Chapter Twenty-seven

He was kissing me when the phone rang again. He picked up and handed the phone to me. "It's Jeanette." In a whisper, he said, "Don't forget where we left off, okay, pretty woman?"

I shook my head and waved him away before saying, "Jeanette. Hi. Is everything all right?"

"Everything is fine. I just wondered if you would be up to having lunch today. Then after lunch, I thought I could introduce you to Ruth."

"Oh, that's a great idea. Hold on a second, while I check my calendar." I placed my hand over the receiver.

Brian raised his brows. "What does she want?"

"She wants me to go out to lunch and then meet her sister, Ruth."

"Today? I was hoping to have you all to myself."

I grimaced, making him laugh. Then he said, "Just so you're not gone all afternoon, okay? I still need help with the final prep of the office."

I knew it was just an excuse, since the office was as ready as it would ever be, but I nodded and said to Jeanette, "That would be fine. When shall I pick you up?"

"How about one? I know it takes you a while to get here."

"That works for me. See you then."

Upstairs, I jumped into the shower, did my hair and makeup and, at the last minute, remembered my handbag. Brian laughed and caught me in his arms. "You forgot something, honey."

"Not now, Brian. I'm going to be late."

He pointed to my feet. Flushing in embarrassment, I said, "Oh, man. I forgot my shoes."

"I noticed," he said, letting me go. He was grinning widely as I slipped into my sandals.

"What?" I asked, feigning irritation.

"You must be really nervous about this meeting if you can't even remember your shoes."

"Goodbye, Brian."

"Bye, honey. Have fun," he said, waving me off.

The drive to Jeanette's, for some reason, seemed interminable. It was as if my radar had picked up something in her voice that piqued my curiosity.

After parking in front of her home, I locked my purse in the car and headed for the door.

I felt confused when I saw her wearing at-home lounging clothes, a lavender silk pajama set with very wide legs and batwing arms.

After letting me in, she said, "I hope you'll forgive me. I was on the phone with Ruth from the time I spoke with you until just a minute ago. She's very unhappy with one of the nursing home staff."

"Oh, well, maybe you'd rather do lunch another day."

Her hands lifted apologetically. "Actually, I'm not much in the mood to socialize, and I'm not sure Ruth is in the mood to meet a stranger."

"Okay," I said, feeling strangely displaced. "Well, why don't you give me a call when you're ready to try it again."

"I'll do that," she said, showing me to the door.

In my car, I felt foolish when tears bubbled up in my throat. I quickly drove off, in case she was watching. Couldn't have her knowing she had hurt me.

I arrived home by two thirty, surprising Brian when I walked in the door.

"Honey," he said, frowning. "What are you

doing home so early? I mean, you couldn't possibly have had time for lunch."

"You're right. She called it off."

"What? What are you talking about?"

"She was upset because Ruth was having a bad day. Anyway, to make a long story short, she didn't feel like doing lunch today."

A frown creased his mouth into a grim line. "How rude is that, when you had just driven ninety miles? To say nothing of the ninety miles home afterward...."

Apathetically, I said, "Never mind. I'm going to go change."

He followed me upstairs and into the closet, where I began pulling off my outfit. Wrapping his arms around me, he said softly, "I'm sorry, honey."

"Oh, I'm okay. Just learning not to expect much from her these days. I figure if I don't get my hopes up, I can't be disappointed. Right?"

"Honey, look at me."

I couldn't meet his gaze for fear that I would fall apart.

"Jolie..."

I sank against him, suddenly unable to stop the sobs that issued from deep inside me.

He held me for a long time as I wept, disappointed down to my toes at her reception. Especially when I had thought we were breaking through toward a real relationship.

Brian pulled me toward our bed, where we snuggled and he whispered that he loved me.

He said, "Honey, I know it isn't much consolation, but that woman isn't a Christian, and she has hurts from which she's never recovered."

"I know," I said, shuddering as the last sobs died away.

"It's still disappointing, though, isn't it?"

"I guess I thought we might have something special, even if it wasn't a normal mother/daughter relationship."

"I thought so too, from the way things were going. Did she say why she didn't just call and cancel instead of letting you drive ninety miles for nothing?"

"She said she was on the phone with Ruth from the minute we spoke until just before I arrived. I don't think I gave her my cell number, either."

"I did, honey. The first day we visited. I handed her one of my cards."

I bit my lip. "Oh, well. I guess this crisis with Ruth is consuming all her attention. And I'd better get used to taking a back seat in her life, because it sure seems like the way this is headed."

"Oh, honey, I wish I could do something to help."

"Thanks, Bry, for being so sweet. I really struggle with this stuff."

"I know. But let me say that if she doesn't choose to get close to you, it's she who will be missing out. You are a wonderful friend and companion. I can attest to that."

I kissed him hard on the lips, feeling very emotional. When he deepened the kiss, I could feel myself being drawn to him.

Curled up together later, I could feel his warm breath on the back of my neck, just before I slept.

I woke some time later to hear him singing in the shower, his exquisite baritone rendition of, "You Light Up My Life." I smiled, just hearing it.

I laughed as I joined him in the shower.

"Oh, hi, babe. Sorry if I woke you. I was just overflowing with unspent passion."

I giggled. "Oh, Bry, you are something else. Do you know that?"

"So are you, honey. So are you." He kissed me and one thing led to another until I said, "Brian, I didn't mean to start anything. Maybe I should just leave?"

"What? Are you crazy? Kiss me, woman."

A half hour later, I exited the shower, shaking my head. From now on, I'd go cook if I knew what was good for me.

Brian stuck his head out the shower door. "Is

that the phone, honey?"

I hadn't heard it until he spoke, but I ran toward the bedroom phone and picked up to hear a strange man's voice.

"You folks looking for trouble?"

"Excuse me?" I asked, puzzling over his words.

"You're going to get it," he said succinctly before slamming down the phone.

"So who was it?" asked Brian, towel drying his hair and wearing a second towel tied around his waist.

My voice shook when I answered. "A threat. Why would someone be threatening us?"

He came to stand beside me. "Honey, what on earth are you talking about? What kind of threat?"

"Some guy just said we were asking for it."

"Who was it? Any idea?"

"I've never heard the voice before that I can recall."

"Well, come on. Let's get dressed and check the caller ID."

The caller ID displayed a phone number but no name. Brian went into his office and opened the giant crisscross directory, looking up the number, which turned out to belong to James Lester IV.

"I should've known," said Brian, pointing to the directory reference.

"What do you think he meant when he mentioned trouble?"

"I have no idea. I wonder if the whole family isn't slightly crazed, even vindictive because The Third is being tossed in the slammer. I mean, think about it. This is a clan who would do anything to protect the family name. As far as they're concerned, nothing is more important than their reputation. You know the type. They can live a lie, but let it be exposed, and it's the one who tore the lid off the lie who's looking at big trouble."

"Oh, honey, I hope not."

"Well, somebody sure tampered with your brakes."

I frowned. "You think they're responsible?"

"Probably not personally, but I would put money on their involvement one way or the other."

"It frightens me, just thinking about this. I mean, do we need to be worried about more sabotage?"

"I doubt it, but just be aware of your surroundings from now on, okay? Can't hurt to be cautious."

I nodded, my head reeling from this new knowledge. I find it tough, living in fear all the time. My nature is to trust people, and somehow I never know what to do when they betray that trust.

A short time later, I tried to work on my list of chores, simply to take my mind off my fear. Sorting a load of whites to wash, I started the washer and added Tide detergent before turning to straighten the house. There wasn't much to do since we'd both been too occupied with other things to make any messes.

Jeanette phoned and left a message while Brian and I were outside, with me watering the flowers, while he mowed.

Jeanette's voice sounded melancholy as it re-played. "Listen, I just realized you had driven over three hours round trip for our luncheon en-gagement, and I never even apologized to you. Forgive me, will you? I'll be in touch."

Brian filled a glass with ice water and drank it before he wiped his mouth on his sweatshirt sleeve and looked in my direction.

"What did she want?"

"Oh, just apologizing for my long drive. Nice of her, huh?"

His left brow did a little jig upward. "I sup-pose. A little late, though, isn't it?"

A short time later, Brian left for the nursery, planning to buy a few colorful potted plants to brighten up the new office entrance. While he was gone, I browned some ground round and cooked lasagna noodles, trying for a change of menu.

When my stomach began to growl a short time later, I realized I hadn't had lunch, and made myself some toast with peanut butter and a glass of milk. I had just sat down to eat when I got up to check the freezer for French bread and salad fixings. Coming up empty, I picked up the phone to dial Brian's cell number. The phone was dead. Tapping the button did nothing. What on earth?

After retrieving my cell phone, I dialed Brian's number, only to get his voicemail, asking me to leave a message. I did, on the outside chance that he might remember to check it. I set down the phone and turned on the kitchen television. Nothing happened. I opened the refrigerator and saw that the light was off.

It was approaching five-thirty when I shoved the lasagna pan in the fridge and checked my watch. Only the remaining daylight forestalled my fear, but as I looked out the window, the clouds were gathering quickly, as if thunderstorms were inevitable.

"Please, Lord, help Brian to get home soon. I don't want to be alone in the dark."

Only moments later, the sky turned black as night, and once again let loose with a storm, this time of hurricane proportions. Winds whipped the trees around the house and whistled an eerie tune down the fireplace flues in three rooms on the main floor.

Looking at my watch again, I saw that it was now six thirty. Where was Brian?

With a nervous glance out the window, my heart swooped into a staccato dance in my ears as I noticed that lights from my neighbors' homes flooded the neighborhood on every side.

"Baby, come on, we've got to go now," I said, trying to coax her out from under the kitchen table. Nothing terrified her more than an earsplitting lightning storm.

She wasn't cooperating, so I yanked her out and then, remembering Cupcake, I let her go. She would be safer left at home. Maybe.

Chapter Twenty-eight

Grabbing an umbrella and purse, I slid into my new-but used replacement Oldsmobile and backed out of the driveway.

With no idea where to go, I headed for the hardware store and then tested my brakes just to forestall a repeat performance of my last hair-raising adventure. Not five seconds later, I noticed a four by four behind me, tailing too close for comfort on my bumper. I sped up a little, but it kept the pace, refusing to allow me breathing room.

Even more anxious now, my palms began to sweat as I prayed, asking for wisdom. Scanning the area ahead of me, I saw the lights shining from inside our local police precinct, and hurriedly parked in the nearest stall, watching the four by four shinny on past. *Praise you, Lord!*

At the station, I slipped from my car and dashed through the deluge and into the building.

"Please," I said to the tall, middle-aged officer at the desk. "I need someone to check my house. Please."

"Okay, now slow down, ma'am."

He gestured me to sit, so I did, still breathing hard. I noticed then, that I was his only customer. There obviously wasn't a lot of crime in our upscale section of the city, particularly during lousy weather.

"Now what is all this? Let's start at the top, okay?"

I explained how my lights and phone had been out and how I'd been terrified with Brian gone.

The man, whose nametag read, S. McAfee, stood and pulled some papers from the top of a file cabinet before sliding back into his chair and picking up a pen, poised to write.

He looked to be in his mid-forties, stood about six feet four inches tall and wore the regulation brown uniform. He had shiny reddish brown hair with rugged features and wide set brown eyes that seemed to miss nothing. My first impression was that he was perfect for his job.

I had begun to shiver with cold, dripping, as I was, on his floor.

Nervously, I stammered, "'Scuse me. But a man was just following me in a four by four. I lost him when I pulled into your lot. Please, something is wrong."

"Ma'am, take a deep breath and calm yourself, will you?"

My teeth began to chatter as I let my shoulders sag and tried to relax.

He stood and said, "Stay put. I'll be right back."

When he returned a short time later, he unfolded a thick wool blanket and put it around my shoulders before resuming his seat.

"Thanks," I murmured, wishing I could take a long, hot shower.

"Okay, now. Let's start again. I need your name, please."

I felt anxiety rise inside my chest as he slowly and methodically asked his questions. When I dictated my address, he wrote it down and then looked up. "Haven't you had several EMT calls to your address lately?"

I nodded. "Well, this time, when the lights and phone went dead while the rest of my neighborhood lit up like a Christmas tree—well, that was just too much of a coincidence. I had to get out of there."

"Didn't they find that your brakes had sustained damage—as in tampering, after your accident?"

Again I nodded.

His dark eyes intently studied my face while absently tapping his pen against his palm. "So this isn't just idle speculation. Someone is after you. Why is that?"

"I'm not sure, but I think it may have something to do with my husband turning in his boss for the sale of illegal arms."

"Whoa, now you've lost me. Listen, wait just a minute, while I call in a couple of officers from the field."

I spent the next hour clearing up the man's confusion, before he finally said, "So where is your husband now?"

"I don't know. He left to go shopping for plants at a little after four and never returned. That's one of the reasons I ran—to go find Brian, but then the ATV took out after me, and I just pulled in here."

"Okay, tell me what kind of a car your husband drives."

I gave him the description of the car, which he sent out over the radio as an all points. Then he turned to me. "Where was your husband going to shop?"

"I don't know exactly."

"Okay. We'll see if we can get a line on him."

"Thank you."

"Listen, why don't I have someone drive you home and we can worry about your car later? That way one of my men can search your home."

"Oh, dear. No. I can't leave without my car. What if I need to leave?"

"Okay, then. We'll have someone follow you home."

"All right."

"Good. Let me go see about this, then."

A short time later, he introduced me to a pair of young male officers, probably younger than my sons, who, it seemed, were miffed to be called in off their break. I know, because, as I sat waiting for them, I overheard their derisive comments.

"Man, I hated to leave The Donut Stop," said the younger of the two, in a low tone. "I mean, why did he have to call just as Jeannie offered us danish—and lemon-filled? That's just about my favorite thing in the whole world."

"Mine is the Bavarian crème. I had my mouth all set for one, too. You know, they weren't even going to make us pay."

I felt discouraged, realizing they weren't thrilled about helping me.

When the two finally stood beside me, I smiled, nervously slid out of the blanket that still hugged my shoulders, and said softly, "Listen. Thanks for your help. Maybe I'll bring you some danish one of these days, just to show my gratitude."

Embarrassed, they turned and headed toward the door, and one of them murmured, "We'll follow you."

The rain had stopped and the house was still dark by the time I arrived and the police cruiser pulled into the driveway behind me.

Both officers motioned me to stay back while they searched and secured the area. I left the car running and left the heat on high, trying to warm my chilled core.

I pushed the garage door button and watched the officers disappear inside, then I sat in my car, nervously tapping my index finger on the steering wheel, waiting as their flashlights flitted past the windows. The moon emerged from behind a cloud for a few seconds, but its light was snuffed just as quickly by another bank of clouds moving in.

A few minutes later, the lights went on throughout the main floor.

The officers exited some twenty minutes later and strode to where I stood, by then leaning against my car.

"We found no evidence of anyone inside, ma'am, but your breaker was thrown, turning off the electricity at its source, in the basement. We turned it back on."

"But who would do that?"

"You tell me," said the older of the two, his expression slightly impatient, as if this whole incident were my fault.

"I don't know. I mean, not really. Any sign of my husband? Oh, his car isn't here." Glancing around as if I could magically make him appear by the strength of my will, I said to myself, "Where on God's green earth could he be? What time is it?"

The younger officer glanced at his watch and pushed a button to light the dial.

"It's nearly nine o'clock, ma'am."

"What should I do?" I asked, trying to keep my voice from shaking as I shivered.

"Well, that's certainly your choice, but I don't think I'd stay here alone if I were you."

"Well, okay. Thanks for everything."

"No problem, ma'am," said the older one again. After a last glance toward the house, they walked toward their unit and drove away.

"Well, even if I'm not staying, I can't leave Baby here alone," I said out loud, as I strode through the garage door. Baby was hunched beside the kitchen door as I walked in, making a kind of vibrating howling sound, as if on the edge of hysteria. I knelt on the floor beside her and stroked her head. "What's the matter, girl?"

She nudged her nose under my hand and then made a beeline for the back door.

"Oh, poor baby. Of course—you have to go out."

I opened the door and watched her zoom through it as if possessed. Frowning, I watched as she flew toward the far corner of the yard as though on a mission.

I was still shivering when I crawled into a hot shower a short time later. It took ten minutes for me to stop shaking. After drying off, I donned a heavy weight velour sweat suit, thick socks and Nikes.

Downstairs again, I stood on the porch, calling to Baby, but I couldn't see her anywhere, and for some reason, she refused to come. I was ready to close the door when I took another look. The security spot flooded the yard with light when it sensed my movement, but the far edges, near the dark stained wood fence, were too far away to be illuminated. After throwing my jacket over my shoulders and shoving my cell phone in my pocket, I stepped to the edge of the deck and called, "Baby, where are you?" I could vaguely see her, or what I thought was her, standing still, not moving. It seemed odd for her to stay put for such a long time if she had finished her business.

After being confined, she always makes a mad dash from one end of the yard to the other, as though let out of a cage. Brian and I always joked about it, saying, "Race track's open."

But Baby wasn't moving now, and the hair on the back of my neck prickled, making me wish the police had stayed just a bit longer.

My heart beat wildly in my neck, echoing in my head as I gingerly made my way to where she was. But as I got closer, I realized it wasn't Baby I was looking at, but Brian, lying in a heap not far inside the high wooden gate. For an instant, I felt puzzled, until I realized I had been looking at the shape of his head, mistaking it for my dog. Now, the gate stood open, and Baby was nowhere to be found.

"Brian! Brian!" I screamed as I knelt beside him and felt for a pulse. His eyes were closed in unconsciousness, when I felt a strong pulse and saw the rise and fall of his chest. I breathed a momentary sigh of relief. "Please, Lord, don't let anything happen to him."

After digging in my pocket for my phone, I dialed 911 and told them to send help.

"Don't worry, sweetheart," I said softly, caressing his brow. "Help is on the way, and I'll be right back."

His clothes were drenched, and he was shivering with cold when I dashed into the house and pulled several heavy quilts from the closet. I hated to think he had been out in such a terrible storm.

I bolted back out the door, feeling guilty for leaving him, then knelt beside him and wrapped layers of thick blankets as far under him as I could reach.

I wished I had grabbed a flashlight to examine him for bleeding, but couldn't make myself leave him again.

"Brian, please, honey, wake up."

After what seemed like hours, the sound of sirens pierced the air as a rescue unit pulled up to the house and screeched to a halt at the curb. Only seconds later, they hurled through the gate and got busy evaluating Brian's condition, then prepared him for transport.

I followed in my car, praying for Brian, as they ferried him toward the hospital.

In the waiting room of the closest hospital, I sat and drank three cups of bitter battery acid/coffee while I waited to hear about Brian's condition. Caffeine was the only thing holding me together by then.

When the massively built middle-aged doctor finally came out, he sat down without smiling and said gently, "I think your husband will be fine, once he awakens from his coma—that is, assuming he does waken. He sustained a blow to the head, of sufficient force to give him a concussion, but there don't seem to be any other apparent injuries."

The sandy-haired doctor looked ready to drop, his clothes rumpled, with dark circles shadowing his soft hazel eyes. Absently smoothing the wrinkles from his lab coat, he gave an audible sigh.

I smiled. "Well, that's good, isn't it? But what did you mean when you said, 'Assuming he does wake up?'"

"Well, in some cases, there is simply no explanation why a patient remains in a comatose state, but for whatever reason, he simply does not wake up. I'm sorry to have to be so blunt, but it's best that you go into this with your eyes open."

❦

I stopped by to see Brian, and kissed his forehead, before leaving to go pack a bag and return.

The house seemed eerily silent when I unlocked the door and walked in. I felt nervous as I turned on all the lights and even the stereo, for its noise value. I couldn't decide exactly why I needed it—to comfort me or scare away any intruders, but I packed in record time and flew out the door, glad to be away from the house. Baby, I noticed, was still nowhere to be found.

When I got back to the hospital, I made myself comfortable in a recliner beside his bed and after a restless few hours, finally slept.

Chapter Twenty-nine

By the time I woke, Brian's eyes were open and he was looking at me.

I scurried to his side and smiled. Kissing his hand, I asked, "Honey, are you all right?"

"I'm okay, I think, except for a whale of a headache."

"Listen, Brian, tell me what happened, can you? Where did you leave the car?"

"The last time I saw it was in the parking lot of the hardware store, after I picked up geraniums for the porch. I had stopped at the nursery, but their plants were too small and too expensive, so I bought some from Handyman. But after taking the package to the car, well—everything's just a big blank."

When the doctor came, he checked Brian

over and pronounced him sound, just told him to go easy.

"No touch football for a while, okay, my man?"

"What about other kinds of recreation?" Brian asked, with a twinkle in his eye.

"Brian," I said, in my most embarrassed tone.

The doctor laughed at what I knew was my pink face and said, "Listen, no rough contact sports. Other than that, the sky is the limit. Okay, big guy?"

"Sounds like a winner to me." Brian laughed and kissed my hand.

Not long after that, I took my husband home.

I breathed a sigh of relief when we pulled into the driveway and I saw Baby sleeping on the welcome mat by the front door. She was wet and muddy when I gingerly picked her up and hauled her out to the breezeway sink for a warm bath.

She seemed happy to be warm and dry after I finished blow-drying her fragrant prickly hair. Eagerly she leaped to the floor and headed for her food dish, where she gulped it down, then shortly curled up on the rug and slept.

We were snuggled on the living room sofa when Brian asked, "Honey, where did you find me? I mean, I'm so vague about everything that happened...."

"I found you in the backyard last night after the storm."

"Storm? We had a storm?"

"Yes, we did, Bry, and—hey, that means that you were already out of it by the time the storm started. Let's see, that would've been about six, I think."

"What would've been 'about six'?"

"The storm. I recall looking at my watch at 5:30, hoping you'd come home before the storm let loose."

"And what time did you find me?"

"I don't know. Let's see—maybe a little after ten. It's all such a blur. I was so frightened when I found you unconscious, soaked through and shivering."

"So the question is—where was I between five- thirty and ten?"

"Brian, was it dark when you left the hardware store?"

"No, but the sky was becoming cloudy as if it would get dark soon."

I nodded. "Okay, so that narrows the time to between five-thirty and six, when the storm began."

"But how does that help us?"

"Well, if it was still light out, perhaps someone in the parking lot saw what happened."

"Hey, good thinking, honey."

"Did you see any other people or cars around you—notice anything suspicious?"

"I don't think I paid much attention."

"Well, whoever it was had to be strong, to hit you with such force."

He rubbed the back of his head.

"Hurting, sweetie?" I asked.

He winced. "Boy, howdy, you can say that again. Do we have anything I can take for pain?"

"I'll get you something."

Brian looked thoughtful a minute later as I handed him his glass of water and pain reliever.

Suddenly remembering something, I said, "Brian, remember after the break-in, the detective said they had a good fingerprint?"

He nodded. "Hey, that's right. I should call and find out if they've identified its owner, shouldn't I?"

"What are you thinking, honey?"

"My question is this. If somebody wanted me dead, why am I still here to talk about it?"

"I've been wondering the same thing. Do you suppose something happened that stopped your attacker?"

"Can't think what it would be, can you?"

I resumed my place beside him and patted his hand. "Well, whatever the reason, I can only say one thing. From now on, I'm not letting you out of my sight until this thing is solved, one way or the other."

He smiled. "Sticking to me like glue, huh?"

"Something like that."

"Well," he said with a gleam in his eye, "how about a little practice session?"

"Brian, I can't believe this. You're barely upright. How can you even think of fooling around?"

"Beats me, but I am. So, how about it?"

"Cool your jets for a couple of days, will you? Give yourself a chance to heal first."

"Can't think of anything more healing than that, if you want to know the truth."

"Well, I can. Listen, I'll give you a backrub, if you like, or run a whirlpool for you. How about that?"

He shrugged. "You drive a hard bargain, girl. Sold to the knockout with the bedroom eyes."

I grimaced. "Brian Stevenson. What has gotten into you?"

"That's not a very smart question to ask under the circumstances."

I laughed and pulled him up off the sofa, supporting him as we trekked up the stairs toward the tub.

In spite of his best intentions, Brian was barely able to stay awake after the warm whirlpool bath. I managed to help him out of the tub, get him dried off and onto the bed, lying on his abdomen. I found some scented massage oil and began working on his back and neck, and except for a few faint moans of pleasure, I couldn't have guessed whether he was awake or not.

Finally, I kissed his cheek and turned away.

"Thanks, babe," he murmured softly.

Downstairs, I decided to check out the backyard, to see if I could find anything unusual that I missed in the dark.

Though I had reported the assault to the police, it looked as if a written report would be the extent of their investigation. They obviously weren't connecting the dots the way I had. Someone wanted to harm us, particularly Brian, for one reason or another, and chances were good that they wouldn't stop until he was dead.

In the backyard, I stepped over spongy ground, saturated with too much rain. The nice thing about saturated ground is that it squishes under your feet, leaving prints. I could see my prints and those of the paramedics from the night before. They wore crepe-soled shoes with not much in the way of traction.

Looking closer, though, I saw a large footprint, slightly obscured by tall grass. When I pushed away the grass, I smiled. A distinct running shoe print had etched its signature in the ground, not a foot from where I had found Brian's inert frame.

Back in the house, I picked up the phone before remembering it was still dead. Grabbing the cell phone from my jacket pocket, I dialed the police and asked to talk to the officer in charge.

"McAfee here."

I explained how I had found Brian unconscious in the backyard and was puzzled when there was a long pause before he spoke. Then it occurred to me that he would probably chew out his officers for failing to check the yard.

Finally he said, "Well, what can I do for you today?"

"I found a footprint unlike those of the paramedics, a running shoe print in a large size, deeply imprinted into the ground. I think it might belong to Brian's attacker."

"Okay, listen, I'll get some guys out there shortly. Will you be at home?"

"Yes, I'm not going anywhere with an injured husband."

I was annoyed after an hour passed and no law enforcement types had materialized. I had just picked up the phone to call again when my two favorite officers stood on the porch, looking distracted, as if they wished they were somewhere else.

"So," the younger one said, pulling out his notepad. "What's this I hear about a footprint?"

The man's name was P. DeLong and his partner's tiny gold nametag read, "D. Stillman".

Well, P and D, I thought, *let's get this show on the road, and put some oomph into it, why don't we?*

After leading them to the above-mentioned footprint, I stood aside, trying to look inconspicuous as they called in, asking for help from some footprint experts. If this was anything like the Matlock reruns I watched, they would pour some kind of casting liquid into the indentation and let it harden, eventually pulling up a useful print. I could only hope they knew what they were doing. So far I had seen little to engender confidence regarding their skills.

Two more officers, this time in plain clothes, joined them and I sat on the deck steps watching as they did their mix and pour routine, exactly as I had expected. And once again it occurred to me that Matlock was a pretty savvy guy.

An hour later, they wrapped it up, saying little to me, before they finally left.

I felt upset. It was like the officers were going through the motions simply to appease me, rather than intending to follow up with any kind of serious investigation.

Frowning, I did what any good second grade

teacher would do. I got out my plaster of Paris,
mixed it up and poured my own cast. Because of
the humid conditions, I found a fan, which I set
beside the print. I ran two heavy-duty extension
cords out to it and plugged it all in, blowing air at
the print, hoping it would dry quickly.

I checked on Brian just before lunchtime, but
he slept on, so I fixed myself a bowl of ramen
noodle soup and a salad, all the while making
notes, trying to piece all the facts together.

I checked the casting every hour or so, but it
was evidently going to be some time before it was
hard enough to pick up. I decided I must've
added too much water to the mix.

Checking the rest of the ground around the
print now, I frowned, remembering how the officers had not looked any further than their noses
for clues. I found nothing more.

To keep busy, I set up the ironing board and
pressed a half dozen of Brian's dress shirts, before going back out to check the mold. Even after
setting for two hours, it wasn't as dry as I wanted,
but I removed the fan, knowing Brian would have
a cow if he learned what I was doing.

As I toted the fan and dragged about seventy-
five feet of snaking cord back inside the house,
Brian stood watching me from the kitchen door.

He frowned. "What's going on in that cagey

little mind of yours, woman?"

I stammered, trying to look innocent. "Oh, uh, nothing. So how do you feel?"

"Jolie, what's going on here? And don't change the subject." He came to stand beside me, took the fan and the mass of tangled cords from my hands and glared at me.

"Why did you need this outside?"

In a high voice, I smiled and answered, "I wanted to keep away flies?"

He set the fan down hard and turned, tilting his head. "Want to stick to that story or try for something better?"

"Well." I wiggled out of his grasp and headed for the coffeepot, trying to think up a credible explanation, but my mind was a blank. I poured my coffee, playing for time.

"Well, what?"

I sank hard into a kitchen chair and set down my cup. My anxious words tumbled over one another.

"Well…the police came and took a cast of a footprint but they aren't taking this thing seriously so I decided I'd go ahead and make my own cast and I had to dry it so I used the fan." Because I had said this all in one breath, I gulped air just then, to keep from passing out.

He sat down beside me and stuck out his neck, essentially putting us nose to nose. "Say what? I didn't get a word of that. Want to start at the beginning and this time, make a little more sense?"

"Okay." I sighed and began again, explaining what I knew. Then I asked, "Know any competent police officers or private investigators who could help us?"

"Good grief. Who do you think you are? Nancy Drew?"

I grinned. "No, but it does sound sort of nice."

"Give me a break. You're liable to get in way over your head."

I shook my head in frustration. "I told you. They weren't giving me the time of day. When I reported it, all they did was take a report, and not very enthusiastically, at that."

"Jolie, why are you doing this?"

"They were annoyed that I took them away from their lemon danish, and I can see as plain as the nose on my face, that they have no intention of taking this investigation seriously. So I decided to take matters into my own hands. That's all."

"That's all, huh?"

"Yup."

Chapter Thirty

He frowned. "Well, I don't like this. Not one little bit. Whoever did this isn't going to like it that you're sticking your tiny nose where it doesn't belong. You might get it cut off if you aren't careful."

"Oh, Brian. Don't be silly. I'll be fine. Now tell me, do you know any really sharp cops or gumshoes?"

He shook his head and rolled his eyes. "You're not going to cooperate on this, are you?"

"It's not that. It's just that I can't stand seeing those guys do a sloppy job of investigating, or worse, no investigation at all. I just have to see what I can find out on my own. Okay, honey? Please. I need you behind me on this."

Shaking his head, he sighed. "Give me some time and I'll try to come up with a name for you.

In the meantime, do you think you might be able to scrounge something for an injured and starving man to eat?"

I laughed and hugged him. "Oh, honey, thank you. I promise to get to the bottom of this ASAP."

He made an effort to look perturbed, but I knew he was faking.

"Just feed the man, will you, hon?"

"I'm on it, okay? Just give me a minute."

I made him a thick hoagie, loaded with ham, cheese, tomato, pickles, green peppers, lettuce and onions, exactly the way he likes it.

After swallowing his first bite, he sighed. "Mmm...Honey, this is great. Thanks."

"Glad you like it. You never answered my question."

"What question was that?"

"How are you feeling?"

He was chewing another bite and stuck up his finger, gesturing for me to wait. "Not bad. Still have a doozey of a headache, but otherwise this concussion thing isn't as bad as I anticipated."

"Well," I said doubtfully, "I sure hope you're not planning a repeat performance."

"Nah, I've got better things to do with my time. Hey, did they ever find my car?"

"You know, I forgot to ask. They certainly didn't mention it if they did."

"Well, I need to get that car back before my flowers die."

I laughed. "Right. The car is missing. You almost died, and you're worried about the plants."

"Well, I hate to see good money for azaleas go right down the tube."

"Azaleas? I thought you bought geraniums."

"Azaleas—geraniums, who cares? They were colorful, so I bought them."

"Well, what do we do about the car?"

After swallowing another bite, he said, "As long as you're the chief investigator here, how about helping me try to get a fix on it?"

"Really?" I couldn't stifle a wide smile.

"I'll go get my shoes," I said, heading toward the stairs.

He called, "Oh, and honey, before we leave, I want you to show me that footprint you mentioned."

When I returned, he said thoughtfully, "You know, I used to know this guy, who worked for a divorce lawyer, by the name of Jinks, believe it or not. Anyway, I could call him."

"Honey, I'm totally confused. Why do we need a divorce lawyer?"

"We don't. We just need the guy who worked for him."

"Jinks?"

"No, Jinks is the gumshoe. I can't remember the name of the attorney."

"So the PI's name is Jinks? I'm not sure I'd trust somebody with a name like that."

He frowned. "He's really good, honey, that is if he's still in the business. I wonder if I can recall his first name. I mean, without that, I'd have no idea how to get a hold of him."

I took a final sip of my coffee before dumping out the rest. After setting my cup and saucer in the sink, I pulled the phonebook from the bottom drawer.

I glanced at Brian, who was wiping his lips with his napkin, with a blissful look on his face.

"Honey," I asked, "how do you spell Jinks?"

"Hmm…I think it's spelled J I N X."

"That's even worse than I imagined. Are you sure about this?"

"Don't be silly. Of course. He was top-notch. You'll see. And I think his name was Web or Webster—something like that. See what you can find, while I scrounge up my shoes, okay?"

I thumbed through the Js and found W. K. Jinx. How many W. Jinxes could there be in the Western Hemisphere, for heaven's sake?

I jotted the number on a pad, tore off the slip

and stuffed it in my pocket. Then I watched as Brian sank into a chair and slid into caramel loafers, complete with tassels.

He looked up and met my gaze. "So—did you find him? Jinx, I mean."

"Yup. I wrote down his number. Maybe you can call him from the car?"

"I'll do that. Maybe he can help us out."

Not long after, Brian slid behind the wheel of my Olds, against my better judgment, I might add. But he is one of those men, who, in spite of all his other stellar qualities, can't stand to be seen, driven around in the car by his wife. We've been at odds over the issue for years.

He took the same route to the Ben Harding Nurseries compound as he had the previous night. Its huge parking lot was nearly empty by this late in the afternoon, and for the life of me, I couldn't figure out why we were there anyway, since he said he had left there and gone on to the hardware store. I could only surmise that he wanted to retrace his steps. I kept still, waiting for him to speak.

"Okay," he finally said, as we pulled into the Handyman Hardware parking lot. "This is where I parked last night, when I went to buy flowers."

He put the car in park and sat looking around.

After a long minute, I asked, "Can you remember anything else, honey?"

"Hey, look over there."

I turned my gaze to where he pointed and saw what looked like trash near the curb about four feet from where we sat.

He got out and I followed. The two over-turned brown paper sacks each contained a large red azalea bush, and one held a receipt for twenty-one dollars and eighty cents.

"See? These are my bushes. Hey, looks like they might make it if I can plant them right away. Oh, shoot. The pots I hoped to plant them in were in the Lexus. Come on, let's go, drive around a bit and see if we see any sign of the car."

Brian generally drives either his four by four or our Lexus, depending on his mood. And his pride and joy, an old beater '59 Ford pickup truck, sits parked in the back of the yard, behind our storage shed. So although we had other means of transportation, I knew he felt it would be like striking a blow for justice to retrieve our sea foam green Lexus.

We were lost in our own thoughts riding home and had just passed the Hinky Dinky store. The huge chain grocery store had a parking lot that consumed the better part of a large city block. At the far end of the lot, under the only tree in sight, I sighted what looked like an aban-doned car. As we drove closer, it was immediately clear—it was our vehicle.

Brian grabbed a flashlight and jumped from the Olds, having barely shoved it into park, and ran toward the Lexus, inspecting it from every possible angle, running his hands over it as if it were a child he was checking for injury.

"Looks okay, babe. I guess we might as well just take it home, huh?"

"Are the keys still in it?"

"Yup. Looks like they got knocked to the floor in some kind of a struggle. You know, it's amazing no one stole it."

I stood beside him and saw a wide smile light his face. He loved that car.

I said, "Honey, don't you think we should report this to the police?"

"Why? What can they do? We've already found the car, and it doesn't seem to be damaged, so it's not like we're going to file an insurance claim or anything. I mean, what can the police possibly do that we haven't already done? I mean, even if we did report it, from what you said, they wouldn't pursue it."

I shrugged. "I guess you're right. But I did report both you and the car missing, so I should probably call and tell them it's been found, huh?"

"We'll do that. Listen, I'm getting tired, so I'll drive it home now while I've still got the steam. Meet you there, okay?"

I followed Brian, somehow feeling edgy, afraid to take my eyes off of him.

After we had parked both vehicles in the garage, Brian consulted his watch.

"Hey, I'm going to call that PI I mentioned. Where's that number you jotted down?"

I pulled the paper from my jeans pocket and handed it to him and a moment later, heard him speaking in low tones as I slipped out of my shoes in the next room. At that point, I could only hope he'd give us advice that would preclude the need to involve the local law enforcement contingent.

I could tell from the look on Brian's face that he had good news.

"So what did he say?"

"He's retired now, but he sounded bored, like maybe he hates the inactivity, and he jumped on the chance to help us."

"Oh, good. So what happens next?"

"He's coming over in a few minutes."

"You're kidding! Oh, man. The house is a mess." There were dishes in the sink and crumbs strewn over the table and floor.

Brian made a face. "He's not coming over to give you the Good Housekeeping Seal of Approval, you know. Men never even notice stuff like that."

Chapter Thirty-one

"Oh, yeah? Well, that's sad. I'll bet they live in hovels, too."

"Get a grip, love. He's only interested in the facts of the assault. Hey, don't let me forget to tell him about the tampering that caused your accident. Might as well give him the whole ball of wax, right?"

I was scurrying to load the dishwasher, after sweeping the floor and wiping the kitchen table. With a fleeting glance, I took in the living room. Shoes and socks sat beside Brian's chair. I frowned. When did those get there? And newspapers, six or seven, sat stacked ten ways from Sunday. I felt annoyed just before I remembered that Brian might've been killed and never made another mess—ever.

I whispered, "Help my attitude, Lord, and

make me grateful for the slob. Oh, sorry, Lord, I shouldn't have said that."

I turned to see Brian, scowling at me.

"I know, I'm just picking up a bit. I mean it has to be done anyway, right?"

"Like I said, it won't matter. Guys don't care about that stuff."

I wondered, at that moment, what had happened to the overachieving perfectionist law partner of a week earlier. Oh, well. I could only hope his cleanliness meter would head toward midrange sometime in the near future. The wild variations were driving me crazy.

I had just finished tidying the room when the doorbell rang, and Brian came in, leading a guest. Brian turned to me and said, "Honey, this is Web Jinx. Web, this is my wife, Jolie."

The man, who looked to be in his late sixties, nodded and smiled. He looked more like a Cedric Svelte than a Web Jinx. With beautifully styled salt and pepper hair, he was dressed unlike any television private eye I had ever seen. He wore perfectly creased tan tweed slacks with a robin's egg blue dress shirt, over which was an exquisite tan suede vest. The outfit was topped off by a camel corduroy jacket with suede patches and an updated, tan and brown version of the 1950's saddle shoe.

He had congenial blue eyes, framed by long

dark lashes, and was undoubtedly the most gorgeous senior citizen I had ever seen. Over tiny bifocals that sat perched at the end of his nose, he perused the room.

"I must say, your home is lovely." He didn't talk like Kojak either. He was obviously college educated.

I said, "Won't you sit down, Mr. Jinx? May I get you coffee or a soft drink?"

"Coffee would be nice if it's not too much trouble."

"Oh, the pot is always on around here."

When I returned later with his coffee, Brian turned to meet my gaze.

"Honey, do you suppose the footprint cast is set yet?"

"Oh, yes, I would imagine so. Want me to go see?"

"Never mind. I think I'll take Mr. Jinx out there for a gander. If it's dry, he can take it with him."

The two of them wandered out to the backyard, while I cleaned up the coffee grounds I had just spilled, trying to make a fresh pot.

About five minutes later, the two men returned and Brian was carrying the footprint cast in his hands. He turned to me. "I need to wrap this in a soft dishtowel. These things are somewhat fragile, you know."

"Oh, sure. Let me get you one."

I helped him wrap it in several towels and set it in a gallon sized zippered plastic bag.

Brian said, "Honey, Jinx wants to ask you some questions."

"Really?"

Until that moment, I wasn't sure how much of a part I would play in this little drama.

Over fresh cups of coffee, Jinx said, "I need you to tell me everything you can think of that's happened since—well, since your husband became a partner, I mean, as far as the mishaps are concerned."

"Okay. I can do that. Let's see…"

I began by telling him about Hittner's first visit, then backtracked to give him a bit of background. He took notes, nodding as I talked. He seemed particularly interested when I mentioned Mavis Lester's attempt to search Brian's files and the threatening phone call from her son.

When I had finished speaking, he set down his pad and pen and picked up his now tepid coffee.

"May I warm that for you?" I asked.

"Oh, no. If I had to warm my coffee every time I let it get cold, I'd never set foot out of the kitchen. This is just fine. Thanks."

A thought occurred to me.

"Listen, Mr. Jinx, you might check the police

reports. I think they took fingerprints from the door to the garage the night our house was vandalized."

"I'll do that. Thanks for the help."

At length, he drained his cup, set it down and stuck the pen and pad in his jacket pocket before turning to me. "I think I have all I need to begin checking things out. Let me say, though, that I'm impressed with your investigative skills. If you'd ever like to make a career of it, I could use a sleuth who doesn't mind getting her hands dirty—as in plaster of paris. Not many women would've thought to do that."

"Oh," I said, flushing in embarrassment. "That's just the second grade teacher coming out in me."

"Well, whatever it is, it should serve us well. And you were right. Your husband said you had commented about the officers mucking up the crime scene." He clucked his tongue before adding, "Bad job they made of it. I mean, what kind of law enforcement folk are these, who don't come out to check a crime scene in daylight."

Standing to his feet, he added, "Anyway, I'll see what I can do with the information you gave me, and I'll be getting back to you."

Brian saw him out and came to snuggle beside me on the sofa. "So what do you think of him? Kind of unique, isn't he?"

"That's an understatement, if I've ever heard one."

"Yeah, well, let's get some sleep. I'm beat with a big stick."

For the next four days, Brian took calls from old clients, wanting to retain his services. I could hear him whistling while he set up files under each new name.

The following morning dawned rainy and humid, with a thick fog hovering in the air for hours, until a slight breeze blew it away just before noon.

I had fixed chicken salad sandwiches, cole slaw and added white grapes and baby carrots to each plate and set them on the table.

Brian came in, caught me into his arms and said, "Listen, beautiful, why don't you and I have lunch up in our love nest? It's gorgeous out there today. And from the sound of it, we might want to make hay while the weather is cool, because it looks like we're in for a steamy summer."

"Okay. Sure." I followed him up the tree house stairs, carrying two glasses of iced raspberry tea with lemon wedges perched on top.

He set our plates on the table and smiled. "Oh, honey, this is like heaven. Good food, a lovely breeze and the most wonderful woman in the world for company. What more could a man want?"

He pulled out my chair and held it as I sat down, then sank into his own chair and folded his arms behind his head. "This is definitely the life."

I couldn't stifle a grin.

"What's funny?"

"Not funny. Just cute. I love it when you wax poetic."

"Oh, really? Well, you ain't seen nothin' yet. Let me see...."

After a brief hesitation, he said, "How does that verse go now? 'How much do I love thee? Let me count the ways?'"

I laughed. "That's sweet, honey, really, but let's not be starting anything we won't want to finish."

"Who won't want to finish it?" he said, looking up from the cluster of grapes in his hand.

"Never mind. Just eat."

After eating for a few minutes, basking in the cool shade of our nest, Brian said, "I wonder how Jinx is making out with our investigation?"

"Oh, dear. You're not going to keep bugging him about it, are you? I mean, he only started investigating a few days ago, for heaven's sake."

"Of course not. But if I haven't heard from him by tomorrow, maybe I'll give him a jingle."

"Honey, please, give the man at least a week before hounding him, will you?"

He frowned. "What do you mean 'hounding him'? I'm just an interested party, who wants to keep him on his toes."

"Listen," I said, shaking my head. "He's the last person you'd have to prod to get the job done."

"You're probably right. That's what I liked about him when we first met. For as old as he is, he seems to be on top of his game, doesn't he?"

"No question."

The rest of our lunch was spent in quiet contemplation and contented sighs coming from Brian's direction. I decided he was right. The tree house had been a wise investment in our future mental health.

A short time later, Jinx phoned, and Brian took the call, putting it on speaker so I could hear. Our new friend reported that he'd checked out the fingerprint and thought he had a line on its owner, but for some reason, he seemed hesitant to say more over the phone. Before hanging up, however, my trial attorney husband exacted the identity of our vandal. The fingerprint belonged to James Lester, The Fourth.

As I was cleaning up the lunch mess some time later, I heard the doorbell sound in Brian's offices. Seconds later, I heard Brian talking to someone inside the waiting room door. I couldn't hear what they said, but became alarmed when the soft murmur of voices rose to fever pitch and a yelling match ensued.

Hurrying toward the waiting room door with a full crystal glass of iced tea in my hand, I paused, speechless, seeing a man I knew must be James Lester IV. The man was the image of his father, down to the seething anger in his eyes.

Brian said to the man, "Put the weapon down, James. We can talk about this."

He held the revolver in midair, aiming it toward Brian's head, and didn't look like he was in any mood to negotiate. James, who was only about four feet from me, had not yet seen me. I heard the click as he cocked the gun.

Feeling desperate, I aimed, then hurled, my full tea glass at the man's head, hitting him with a loud crack, above the left ear and cheek. He instantly dropped the gun and toppled to the floor.

Brian turned to me and said, "Call 911, honey."

As I picked up the phone, I could feel myself begin to shake. I could hardly talk for the chattering of my teeth, when the dispatcher took my information and said she would send someone immediately.

Brian used a long nylon scarf to tie up The Fourth, who lay crumpled in a heap, with blood running from a cut just left of his eyebrow.

Watching the scene as if in slow motion, I slowly slid down the wall, feeling my breath coming in quick puffs. The room swam before my eyes as Brian turned to look in my direction.

A short time later, the police hauled The Fourth out in handcuffs as I watched from the doorway. Brian turned and smiled at me. "You know, he would've killed me if you hadn't been such a quick study with that glass of tea. I mean it, honey. I'm proud of you. Maybe you *should* think about a career as a private eye."

"Oh, yeah. I can see it all now. Get the situation well in hand and then fall on the floor in a dead faint. Now that's what I call a class act."

He laughed. "Hey, I hadn't thought of that. But you are fast on your feet in the clinches, and that's what counts."

I made a face. "You're too kind. But I don't think I'm cut out for this stuff. Makes me nuts."

"Did you hear what happened as The Fourth came to?"

"No. What?"

"He's evidently never been in trouble with the law before and found himself singing like a bird, about how he and his mother were planning to get revenge at me, for turning in The Third. It sounds like they were responsible for everything."

I shrugged. "Well, if that's the case, maybe Jinx can turn in his badge and go back to being a gentleman of leisure."

"I'll talk to him and see what he says, okay?"

"Sure."

The phone rang a short time later, and I answered to hear Jeanette's voice.

"Listen," she said softly, "I know you probably feel like giving up on me, but I hope you won't. I've missed you lately, and I still want to take you to lunch. And this time, we're going no matter what happens. Are you willing to try it again?"

"Of course," I said, feeling breathless with anticipation.

"Good. Would tomorrow work for you—at noon?"

I smiled. "That would be fine."

"Okay, I'll look forward to it."

Brian walked in just then and saw me smiling.

"So who was that?" He sank down on the sofa beside me.

"Jeanette. She wants to try it again."

"You up for that?"

"I think so. I'd really like to have a relationship with her, even if it's only as friends."

"Then you should do it."

"I am. I'm picking her up for lunch at noon tomorrow."

Brian took me in his arms. "I just spoke to Jinx."

"And what did he say when you told him we caught The Fourth?"

"He said, and I quote, 'Nuts. And just when things were getting exciting, too.' Sounds like he's hoping to come out of retirement, now that he's tasted the thrill of the hunt. He seemed tickled at the idea of getting back to work and credits us with pulling him out of a near coma state of retirement. Said he'd like to take us out to dinner to show his gratitude."

"Really? How sweet of him."

"I offered him a job."

My mouth dropped open. "Doing what?"

"Any investigations I'll need, now that I'm in private practice."

I laughed. "Well, this should be very interesting."

Pulling me deeper into his embrace, he nuzzled my ticklish neck. "So do you think you can live without the constant stimulation of excitement? I mean, it could be addictive, you know."

I kissed his cheek and rested my head on his shoulder. "Not for me. I'm looking forward to a little boredom. In fact, this whole thing feels like a really weird dream, and I can only praise God that it all turned out okay."

Wide-eyed, I shuddered and sighed, reviewing the past weeks, and realizing the awesome truth of the scripture verse in I Corinthians 2:9.

"Eye hath not seen, neither have entered into the heart of man, the things which God hath prepared for them that love Him."

Hugging Brian's arm, I smiled.

ABOUT THE AUTHOR

Nancy Arant Williams

Nancy Arant Williams is a multi-published author, whose works include articles, essays, award winning short stories and poems. She and her husband, John, are recent Missouri transplants, who have two children, and six grandchildren, still residing in their home state of Nebraska.

Nancy and her husband are the hosts of a Christian Bed and Breakfast, The Nestle Down Inn, in the heart of the beautiful Missouri Ozarks.

Her desire is to encourage believers, knowing that God is an ever present help in time of need, and delights to run to the aid of his beloved.

VISIT OUR WEBSITE
FOR THE FULL INVENTORY
OF QUALITY CHRISTIAN BOOKS:

http://www.capalliance.org

Quality trade paperbacks
Visit the website, then bookmark it.